RAISING OFFA

RAISING OFFA

The silent Prince of Angeln

ELIZABETH BELL

Dedication

Dedicated to the memory of Kathleen Herbert whose work ignited my passion for the Anglo-Saxon period and inspired me to write this novel.

Acknowledgements

Thank you to:
Jean Gordon and Pat Stephenson
Lorna Reynolds and Julia Newsome

And a special thank you to:
Mary Walsh
without whose unfaltering encouragement
and involvement this work would never have been completed.

And special thanks also, to:
Anglo-Saxon Books for their kindness and support.

Map

Showing that the Angeln tribe occupied a land called Engle.
The Myrging tribe occupied land below the River Eider.

People

Legendary:

King Waermund	King of Angeln.
Prince Offa	Waermund's son.
Earl Freawine	War Lord.
Eadgils	Prince, then King of Myrging
Wigheard	Son of Earl Freawine.
Cedd	Son of Earl Freawine.
Modpruth (Honey)	Daughter of Freawine.
Lord Hengest	Prince of Jutland.
Rowena	Hengest's daughter.
Lord Horsa	Hengest's brother.
Rhufon	Son of King Cunedda
King Witta	King of Swarbia.
Meaca	King of Myrging.
Mearcweard	Brother of Meaca.

Fictional:

Tanwen	Foster daughter of Thorndor.
Hunlaf	Companion of Tanwen.
Arild	Hunlaf's cousin.
Queen Aelfrun	Wife of King Waermund,
Mae	Slave to Queen Aelfrun.
Edyth	Slave to Queen Aelfrun.
Leofrun	Wet Nurse to Prince Offa.
Hilde	Nurse to Prince Offa.
Lady Hebeke	Wife of Freawine
Hafoc	Bodyguard.
Halfdane	Myrging Warrior.
Vodine and Cadoc	Christian pilgrims.
Wulfrun	A foundling.
Eawyn& Cwenhild	Daughters of Hilde.
Old Hren	Wood-smith.
Herjan	From Infected village.
Swuste	From Infected village.
Willow, Dan & Matti	Children from infected village.
Urith	Village leader.
Ursa	Geata's wife.
Gaeta	Ursa's mother.

Words and Places:

Anglo-Saxon words:

Churl	Peasant or farmer.
Clouts	Swaddling clothes.
Fyrd	Military service imposed on free men.
Haerfest	Harvest.
Mordants	Dye fixative.
ronanary	Child speak for honorary.
The Lady, Nethrus	Goddess - The Earth Mother.
Wergild	Compensation.
Winterfrith	Winter.
Woden	One of the chief Anglo-Saxon Gods and said to be the father of all kings.
Wyrd	Fate, Destiny.

Place names:

Aegelsthrop	Kent. England.
Britta	Angeln name for Britannia.
Bryniech	Land between the Firth of Forth and Newcastle. Britain.
Cantwarbyrig	Canterbury. England.
Dumnonia	Cornwall, England.
Eriu	Ireland.
Gwynedd	Dutchy of Gwynedd. North Wales.
Ynys Medcaut	Lindisfarne, Holy Island. England.
Ynys Weith	Isle of Wight, England.
Ypwinesfleot	Ebbsfleet. England.

Table of Contents

One

Angeln. AD 439

'This is useless, we're wasting our time.' Tanwen lowered her wooden sword and dragged the back of her hand across her brow.

Hunlaf groaned in exasperation. 'Now what?'

'You must have noticed.' She ran through the movements in her head. 'The whole thing feels stiff and awkward, but I can't understand why.' She stepped forward and swung her blade over her right shoulder. 'See. The strongest cuts come from this position, but if I step backwards, as you say I should, I'm unstable. I lose my balance and I - wobble. The footwork is all wrong.'

Arild snorted. 'There's nothing wrong with his footwork, it's you, you can't keep up.'

Hunlaf propped his lean frame against a nearby tree and emptied the contents of his water bag over his head. 'It's the move the Geat taught us yesterday.'

'No, it's not,' said Tanwen.

'How would you know, you weren't there?' Arild always sided with his cousin.

'Because it doesn't work,' she said slowly through clenched teeth. 'He's supposed to kill me, not dance with me.'

'It wasn't that bad; battles are always more difficult on wet grass.'

Trust Hunlaf to find an excuse. A fine warrior he was going to make, he hated confrontation,' but Tanwen was not prepared to lose this battle. 'Battles are fought on mud, shit and spilt guts, not dry grass. Your moves were clumsy and clumsy footwork leads to sloppy swordplay and early demise.' She paused, expecting an argument but none came. 'We have to get it right, go back to basics,' she continued. 'From tomorrow we'll drill every day before weapon practise.'

'That's not fair.' Arild protested.

'Since when has battle been fair?' his cousin asked.

'We've already had a full morning of warrior training with the Geat before she turns up. If she has her way, we'll be working all day.'

'I can't help being late. I have chores to do.'

'Only women's chores, so why don't you stay home and do your cooking and spinning and leave us men to do the hunting and fighting?'

Tanwen's jaw tightened. Approaching his twelfth winter, Arild had not even begun weapon training, yet he strutted around like an experienced warrior and thought he knew it all.

'What's the matter with you? Are you too young, or too witless, to appreciate how privileged you are to have daily weapon training with the Geat? I'd give anything for the opportunity to train with him, he's the best weapons master in the land. But I have to study word-craft and herb-lore and make do with second-hand battle training from a lumbering ox and an undisciplined little toad.'

Hunlaf rushed to Arild's defence. 'Leave him alone, Tanwen. He tries his best, we all do.'

'Then our best is not good enough.' she retorted and was immediately contrite. She must not risk falling out with Hunlaf and Arild, because they were the only youths in town willing to train with a girl.

'I'm sorry,' she said softening her voice, 'but there is no point in rushing through the rudiments. Footwork is the foundation of good swordsmanship; it can mean the difference between winning and losing a fight.'

Arild sneered. 'So, you're our teacher now, are you?'

'No. I just want to survive my first fight, don't you?'

They were fighting with wooden training swords known as singlesticks and Hunlaf wiped the blade of his with the same loving care a warrior would bestow on a real sword.

'Arild is right,' he said, 'we spend enough time weapon-training as it is, but if it will keep you happy, we'll ask the Geat's opinion. If he agrees that our footwork needs attention, we will drill with you, but only until he's satisfied with the improvement.'

Arild unhooked the rag-stuffed dummy they had suspended from a tree for fist fighting and archery practise and snatched his singlestick from Tanwen.

'Hunlaf doesn't need you anymore. Now that he has Princess Rowena in his life,' he said, with a smirk in Tanwen's direction.

Tanwen's icy glare brought an unexpected blush to Hunlaf's cheeks. 'Then don't let me keep you from your Frisian maidservant.' she said, spitefully.

'Rowena is not a servant, she's a princess.' Hunlaf had apparently recovered from his embarrassment.

'Princess. A fine princess she is, being hawked around all the kingdoms on earth to be sold to the highest bidder.'

'Lord Hengest has every right to seek the best possible husband for his daughter.'

'The best possible kingdom you mean. He won't settle for the youngest son of a lesser noble if that's what you're hoping.'

'My father is not a lesser noble. He is a cousin of the king. And if the king dies without an heir, my father could be king.

Anyway, how would you know what Lord Hengest has in mind?' Hunlaf said.

'Because I've overheard his conversations with Thorndor and King Waermund. Lord Hengest is landless, he needs somewhere to settle. He brought Rowena to Angeln hoping to marry her off to King Waermund, but Thorndor convinced the king that her cousin, Aelfrun, who really is a princess, would be a better choice.'

Hunlaf's eyes narrowed. 'You are only saying that because you're jealous. I don't believe you.'

'I've no reason to lie and why should I be jealous?'

Arild pulled a face and spoke in a silly voice. 'Because she is pretty and gentle and knows how to behave like a lady, which is more than can be said of our present company.'

'In that case, I wish you luck with her, you'll certainly need it.' Tanwen scooped up her belongings and stormed off.

***

People from all over Angeln and the lands beyond were pouring into Angeln to celebrate the wedding of King Waermund, to Aelfrun, a princess from Waernas.

Farmers, merchants, servants and slaves, jostled good-naturedly for a place where they would be sure of a fair share of the marriage feast. Tanwen smiled, knowing they need not worry. Thorndor told her that King Waermund had ordered two identical feasts, one to be served in the great feasting hall to the official guests and the other to be served outside on the grass, to his loyal subjects. No one would go hungry in Angeln today.

She strolled through the impromptu market that had sprung up in the main street; haggled over a clay pot she did not want and could not pay for, gaped in awe at a group of acrobats twisting themselves into extraordinary shapes, and laughed at a scop's ribald tale of a Geatish maiden and her many lovers.

She helped herself to an apple from a merchant's basket, polished it on her tunic and slipped it into her pouch. Moments later, she kicked up a turf and stuck out her tongue at a small boy who was peeking at her from behind his mother's tunic, but when his bottom lip quivered, she smiled an apology and tossed him her stolen apple.

Tanwen paused at the crossroads and allowed the crowd to bustle around her. She usually spent her afternoons in the learning chamber, studying rune law and word-craft under the demanding eye of her foster father, Thorndor, who had found her on the beach, clinging to a tree, after the incident. He was King Waermund's chief advisor and today, the king's wedding day, he was too busy fussing over the marriage arrangements to spend time with Tanwen.

It was a glorious day and the land shimmered in the late summer sunshine. She should go home to help with the chores but, as everyone would be too busy to notice she was missing, she might as well stay here and make the most of it. She would go to the well, splash her face then settle down on the hillside and imagine her life as a shield-maiden. From the day Thorndor found her Tanwen had dreamed of nothing but leading an army against her brothers who had left her to drown, and to that end, she trained with weapons at every opportunity.

'Tanwen. Tanwen.' Wynn was waving frantically to attract her attention. Tanwen returned the wave. Wynn was Thorndor's wife, and when he brought the bedraggled five-year-old to their home in Angeln, Wynn had taken her in, bathed her, gave her clean clothes and fed her, and there Tanwen had remained ever since.

Not that she was the only one. Tanwen groaned, suddenly remembering her promise to look after the beastlings while Wynn helped Thorndor with the wedding preparations. "The beastlings" was   Thorndor's   name for the assortment of foundlings, half-wits and cripples that no one wanted or cared about, except Wynn, who could never turn a child away. Her door was always open, and Thorndor did not seem to mind as long as his wife was content, and the children kept out of his way.

The truth was, no child would dare to get in the way of Thorndor, for fear of being turned into a lizard or a weasel. She chuckled. As far as she was aware Thorndor had never done such a thing and she doubted if he had the power to do so but the children, and many adults, believed he had the power, and that was enough to make them wary.

Wynn pushed and shoved her way through the crowd until she reached Tanwen's side. 'Thank goodness. I've searched everywhere for you. Where do you get to, child?' She was panting and tiny beads of sweat glistened on her brow. She was short and stout and not used to rushing about. It took her several heartbeats to get her breath back.

'Why aren't you with Waltrude and the children?'

'Waltrude said she could cope, so I went weapon-training for a while. I was delayed, but I'm on my way back now.'

'In this direction?' Wynn looked suspicious but shook her head and swept the matter away with a flutter of her plump fingers. She raised her eyes to the sky. 'Nethrus has indeed smiled upon us.' She clasped her hands and spoke in short sharp bursts. 'Now, let me see, can we?' She stepped back, tilted her head and looked Tanwen up and down. 'Yes, yes, I believe we can. You'll do, with the help of Nethrus - and a large piece of soap.' Her nose twitched. 'You must have a bath, immediately.'

'A bath?'

'Of course. You must look, and smell, your best for the wedding.'

'Wynn, you are going to the wedding, with Thorndor. I wasn't invited, remember?'

'Yes, we thought it safer that way. But her cousin has succumbed to the spotted fever and now we are stuck.'

'Whose cousin?'

'Princess Aelfrun's cousin, of course.'

'Lady Rowena?'

Wynn frowned. 'Yes, Lord Hengest's daughter, do you know her?' Tanwen shook her head and chewed her bottom lip to stop herself from smiling. The pain was worth it. Rowena with spots. What a delicious thought. She wondered what Hunlaf would think of his pretty little princess now.

'Poor dear,' Wynn continued, 'what a day to go sick. She will be so upset. Still, we are fortunate Waltrude can manage; she's such a capable girl. You can take her place in the ceremony.'

'Waltrude was taking part in the ceremony?'

'Don't be silly, Tanwen, Lady Rowena's place of course.'

'Rowena's?' She was about to protest, but Wynn was already scuttling away. Tanwen caught up with her.

'Why me?'

'Because everyone else has the spotted fever.'

'I can't do it. I'll mess it up. You know how I hate being watched. What if I trip and fall, or have a sneezing fit at the worst possible moment?'

'Tanwen, you are a woman now, please try to behave like one, if only this once.'

'But what will I wear?'

Wynn's abrupt stop caused Tanwen to stumble into her. She whipped the cord from around her waist, dangled it from Tanwen's neck and carefully tied a knot where it had touched her ankle. She examined the length of cord, tutted and sighed.

'Really, Tanwen. Are you never going to stop growing? Fortunately, Lady Rowena's dress will just about fit you.'

'Please let someone else do it.'

'If I had a choice I'd gladly oblige; however, as there is no one else available, I'm afraid it is up to you.'

'Oh please, Wynn. Waltrude could do it.'

'A foundling. At the king's wedding. Whatever next?'

'I was a foundling.'

'I am aware of that, but your wit is sharper than Waltrude's and I don't have time for lengthy explanations.'

They reached the homestead and Tanwen sprinted through the longhouse into the healing chamber at the rear, where a spearman blocked her entry. Wynn hurried up behind, red-faced and short of breath. 'He is right, Tanwen, we can't have you catching the fever, not today.'

Undeterred, Tanwen ducked under the spear into the healing chamber where twelve straw and linen-covered pallets were arranged in a circle on the rush-covered floor. She stood at the side of Rowena, a golden-haired girl, slightly older than herself, who thrashed about in a feverish frenzy as if fighting off the evil pustules that were already threatening to defile her lovely face. Tanwen's eyes filled with tears. There was something extraordinary about this beautiful girl. No wonder Hunlaf was besotted with her.

'Will she be scarred?'

'Don't be a goose, Tanwen. She has the fever, not the pox. Now, outside please.'

'Let me stay, please. I'd like to help her. I could make an infusion.'

'Thank you, dear, but I aim to prolong her life. I'll make any necessary infusions.'

Despite her sharp tongue, Wynn was the kindest woman in Angeln and was skilled with herbs and charms. The sick could not be in better hands.

'She's so …'

'Pretty? Yes, I know. But right now, she needs rest, and you need a bath. Off you go to the lady hall. Princess Aelfrun's slaves, Mae and Edyth, are waiting to help you and I'll be along soon.'

Reluctantly, Tanwen turned to do as she was bid.

'And don't forget that tangle of rats tails you call hair.' Wynn called after her.

***

Tanwen squeezed herself into a tiny tub and doubled up her long legs until her knees were resting on her chin. She wriggled uncomfortably in the lukewarm water.

Wynn burst in carrying a homespun sheet over her arm. She laid it on the table and gently smoothed out the wrinkles.

'Ouch.' Tanwen scraped her backside as she tried to reposition herself. 'Now I have a splinter in my ...'

Edyth sloshed lukewarm water over her. Tanwen yelped and swore at the girl who quickly distanced herself from the tub. Wynn tapped the side of the tub. 'Enough. I won't have you being unkind to people who can't retaliate. Apologise to Edyth at once.'

'She soaked me.'

'That was the idea. I'm waiting, Tanwen.' Wynn's narrowed eyes and tightly pursed lips forbade further dissent. Tanwen scowled and muttered 'sorry,' as quietly as she dared, to Edyth, who stood in the corner, smirking.

Wynn beamed, 'good girl, now out you come. We mustn't keep the princess waiting.'

Tanwen grumbled under her breath as she stepped out of the tub and allowed Edyth to wrap her in a warm towel.

'Now girls, gather round, what do you suppose I have here?' She carefully peeled back the sheet. 'Well, what do you think? Isn't it wonderful? The princess insisted on having it made from the same bolt of cloth as her own dress.'

Used to dull homespun cloth, Tanwen was speechless. Wynn was holding up a long, milky white under-tunic, made from cloth so fine Tanwen could almost see through it. And to wear over it, in the softest cloth she had ever seen, a deep blue dress that glistened like a lake in bright sunlight. She reached out to touch it. Surely the highest ladies in the land, with all their brightly coloured dresses, had never worn anything so delicate.

'Oh, Wynn it's wonderful, it feels like - like, butterfly wings, and the colour …'

Wynn nodded happily. 'King Waermund had it brought from the east especially for the princess. It was made by worms.'

Tanwen chuckled. 'Worms can't make cloth.'

'I agree. But Thorndor says it's possible and he's right about most things.'

Tanwen smoothed her hand over the dress and shrugged. 'Then they must have been charmed,' she said.

Mae tapped on the door and entered, 'Princess Aelfrun is almost ready.'

Wynn panicked. 'Quickly girls. No time to dither. Mae, take the comb and tease the knots out of Tanwen's hair please, and Tanwen, do take off that amulet, if only for today.'

Tanwen clutched the amulet, and glowered so fiercely, the girl backed off without a word. Her birth mother had slipped the amulet over her head in the moments before being captured by the Picts. 'Wear this always, my love,' she had said. 'It will help keep me in your memory and will identify you when your father's men come to rescue you.'

Oblivious of the gesture, Wynn prattled on, 'Edyth, find someone to help you clear away this mess. Tanwen, Mae will help you dress and take you to the princess.' She wagged a finger. 'And don't be rude to her.' She glanced at the slave, 'nor to Mae. Now, where was I? Oh yes. Time to change. I must be in the feasting hall before the king arrives. Dear oh dear, what a day.'

She lifted Tanwen's chin with her finger. 'And don't you worry, dear, you will look gorgeous in that dress. Just do as you're told, speak only when you're spoken to and everything will be fine. Thorndor and I will be nearby and I'm sure you will make us both proud.' She hugged her fosterling, gently stroked her hair then hastily departed.

'I think she was crying,' Mae whispered to Tanwen.

Two

At fourteen, Princess Aelfrun was a year older than Tanwen and in Tanwen's opinion too young to marry, let alone be queen, besides, she looked much too pale and delicate for such a demanding role.

The princess stared at her, curling and uncurling her fingers around the arm of her chair for some time before she tilted her head and spoke. 'It was kind of Wynn, and you, to assist at such short notice.'

'Yes, Lady Princess Aelfrun, that is, we were happy to help.'

'You are rather tall for a flower girl.'

'I'm sorry, lady princess, I was the only one available, everyone else is sick today.'

The princess thrust her chin into the air. 'No matter; I shall still be taller than my attendant.' As if to confirm it, she rose. She was taller and thinner than Tanwen and stood as straight as a spear. Her grey, expressionless eyes stared past Tanwen to the far end of the chamber. Tanwen resisted the urge to turn and see what was so interesting behind her.

'Have you seen my cousin today?'

'Yes, lady princess, she is resting in the healing chamber. Wynn will take good care of her.'

'Your hair is an unusual colour, are you a Goth or a Roman?'

'Neither lady princess, I am from Bryneich.'

The princess frowned. 'It must be an insignificant land; I've never heard of it, where is it?'

'It lies to the west, lady princess, over the great sea and beyond Ynys Medcaut. Our village …' Tanwen stopped; the princess had clearly lost interest.

'Does the dress please you?'

'Indeed, lady princess; it's beautiful.'

'What colour do they call it?'

'Blue, lady princess.'

'I was referring to your hair. It is very dark, neither brown nor red but a mixture of both. What colour do they call it?'

'No one calls it anything, lady princess, although my foster father likens it to the colour of a mouse's fart.' The princess giggled and the ice was broken.

Slaves fussed around the princess, combing her hair and smoothing her dress, ensuring it hung without a crease, but the princess showed no interest. A girl offered her a collar of gold; she waved away. Mae carried over a silver tray bearing two garlands of cornflowers and violets and a basket of flowers.

'Princess Aelfrun, King Waermund has arrived at the feasting hall and Lord Thorndor sends word that it is time for you to leave here.'

The princess did not reply but sat rigid and unresponsive while Mae secured a garland to each of their heads and gave Tanwen a few words of instruction.

'You will leave first, sprinkling flowers for Princess Aelfrun to walk upon. The princess will follow exactly seven steps behind you - and take care not to use all the flowers before you reach King Waermund.'

Tanwen nodded nervously and practised a few steps. She caught sight of herself in the polished copper mirror and smiled. She would never be beautiful like the princess, but she knew she would be the envy of every woman in Angeln today.

There was a flurry of activity as they prepared to leave the chamber. Tanwen glimpsed a glint of tears in the princess's eyes. The princess blushed and quickly turned away. Tanwen wondered what could have upset her. The slaves retreated and Mae, standing behind the princess, shrugged, indicating that she did not know what was going on.

'What is it, lady princess, are you ill?' The princess shook her head.

'What has happened?'

The princess accepted a drinking horn of ale, offered by Mae, but did not drink from it. 'Nothing has happened, not yet.'

Tanwen noticed the soft rise and fall of the princess's shoulders and when she lifted her hand to her face Tanwen knew that she had turned away to hide her tears, Tanwen had done the same herself on many occasions. She took a step forward then stopped, fearing a rebuke.

'Don't you like the garlands? It doesn't matter, we'll take them off.'

'No. It's not the garlands - not only the garlands. It's everything. The flowers, the dresses,' her trembling voice trailed away.

Bewildered, Tanwen glanced around the chamber seeking support, but the slaves were huddled, gaping wide-eyed at their mistress. 'Don't just stand there,' she snapped at Mae. 'Fetch the princess another dress. Quickly.'

The princess turned. Her face was ruddy with crying. 'No. No, I don't want another dress.' Tears were streaming down her face. 'You don't understand. Nobody understands. Nobody cares.' The words tumbled out. She flopped gracelessly into a chair, covered her face with her hands and sobbed.

Tanwen took a few tentative steps nearer and knelt at her feet. 'We do care, lady princess, but we don't know what to do. Shall I fetch Wynn?'

'I don't want anyone. Leave me. Get out. All of you. Go away.' The slaves fled, bumping into each other in their haste to escape and Tanwen reluctantly followed. She knew she should do something, but what? What would Wynn do? She hesitated at the door.

'Shall I send a message to the king?'

'No. No, please. The king must not hear of this.'

'But lady princess, how can it be kept from him? He's waiting for you in the feasting hall. If you don't arrive …'

The princess gave another sob, then, with her chin twitching, she delicately wiped the tears from her cheeks with a fine linen kerchief. 'You are right. I know you are. But I can't face him, not yet.' She sniffed inelegantly and dabbed her eyes. 'Please, Tanwen, will you stay?'

'Certainly, lady princess.'

The princess sat in silence, staring at her feet and twisting the kerchief around her fingers. There were no more tears and the sobs slowly subsided.

Tanwen pondered what to do next. The Princess was trembling. Her beautiful pale face was puffed and blotchy and her eyes and lips red and swollen. She could not possibly marry a king in this condition. She found a fox fur and draped it over the princess's shoulders.

'I won't do it, Tanwen. I won't marry him.' Tanwen was bewildered. *Won't marry the king. She must be a lack-wit, or under a spell.* 'But he's waiting for you, in the feasting hall, with the ambassadors and guests and, Thorndor.'

Tanwen froze imagining her foster father's face, purple with rage. What he would do to the princess - and Tanwen - if the wedding was called off was too dreadful to contemplate.

'Please, lady princess, you must. Everyone's expecting it, goodness knows what the king will do if you don't marry him, it could mean war.'

The princess snorted. 'He wouldn't dare. My father's war band would easily see off a flabby, smelly old man and his aged warriors.'

Tanwen bristled. 'King Waermund is neither flabby nor smelly. He's a great warrior, Woden-born.' She paused. 'He is old. Very old. But he's tall and proud and …

'Taller than I?' The princess interrupted.

'Why, yes, lady princess, much taller.'

'An unusual trait in English folk,' the princess mused. She leaned forward in a conspiratorial manner. 'Describe him to me, this king of the Angeln tribe.'

Was this some kind of riddle, or a trick? Was the princess playing a game? What if Tanwen gave the wrong answer? *Oh, why did Rowena fall sick today?*

'Tanwen?'

'Well, lady princess.' Tanwen hesitated, wondering what the princess wanted to hear. 'King Waermund has a sad face. Gnarled, but kindly. With deep-green eyes and a silver streak in his beard.'

'A sad face?'

'Yes, lady princess, ever since Queen Aelfreda and the atheling died of the fever.'

'The scops sang of three strong sons.'

'There were three. The first was killed in battle, the second while breaking a horse, and the third of the fever.'

'A most unfortunate king.' The princess ran a slender finger around the silver rim of the drinking horn. 'Tall you say, and kindly. And he's not fat and …' she paused for a single heartbeat before leaning forward and lowering her voice, 'tell me, Tanwen, is he clean?' She glanced around to make sure no one could hear, and whispered, 'does he bathe regularly?'

'I - I don't know lady princess. I'm not part of the king's household.' Curiosity dispelled Tanwen's fear. 'But surely you've judged these matters for yourself?'

'How could I judge your king? I've never met him.'

'Never met King Waermund? But you've been here for weeks.'

'I was brought to the lady hall on my arrival and haven't been allowed out since. I believe Waermund has been away most of that time.'

'That's terrible. Surely your father will object. Even a princess shouldn't have to marry someone she's never seen.'

'My father would have married me to a bloated boar if strengthened an alliance or secured his borders.' The princess stared into the distance. 'I am an exile. I've lost my home, my possessions and everyone who was dear to me. Now my cousin has fallen ill, and I have no one at all.'

Tanwen's eyes stung. She remembered a hall filled with the smell of fresh rushes and the laughter of children, and her beautiful mother clapping her hands, trying to bring order to the chaos that was the family home. And she remembered standing on the shore, a child, homeless and friendless in a strange land. Even Wynn, with all her charms and potions, could not ease her pain at losing her family. Eight summers had passed, yet still, her heart ached every time she thought of home. She blinked away the threatening tears.

'You may be an exile lady princess, but you are not alone. Listen, the people of Angeln are calling for you, waiting to take you to their hearts.'

The princess glanced at the arrow-slit, but her head drooped and she said nothing. Fear chilled Tanwen's heart. No one would care that the princess was being forced into marriage, that was the way of kings and princes. Both kings had agreed to the union and there would be ructions if the princess refused to comply.

What could she do? She needed help. But from whom? Not Thorndor, he had gone to so much trouble arranging the marriage he would be furious if it did not take place; and not Wynn, because she would always side with her husband. And the princess had already refused to see the king. Tanwen visualised the guests being turned away from the feasting hall because there was to be no wedding. Lords and ladies, envoys and - Hengest - Lords Hengest and Horsa. The princess's kinsfolk. They would be sure to help.

'Lady Princess, we must ask the guards to fetch Lord Hengest and Lord Horsa.'

'My uncles?'

'Yes, Princess, when they see how distressed you are, they will call off the wedding and take you home to your father.'

'Take me home,' the princess shrieked. 'Have you lost your wits? If I refuse Waermund, my father will have me roasted and fed to the dogs. I can't possibly go home.'

Is there no way out of this mess? Tanwen wondered.

The princess fingered a gold casket. She opened it, examined its contents, then tipped out an assortment of gold neck-rings, enamelled amulets and jewelled trinkets. She gazed at them for several moments, lovingly running her fingers through them, before holding up a collar of gold decorated with jewels.

'Do you like jewels, Tanwen?'

'Yes, lady princess, but I don't own any.'

The princess giggled unexpectedly. 'Neither did I until I came to Angeln.'

'Really? I thought princesses wore jewels every day.'

'Perhaps the daughters of important, wealthy kings do, but my father is a king of little consequence who used his gold-hoard to pay his war band. And mother's jewels were shared as bride-price between my four older sisters.' She paused. 'I have brought nothing to Waermund except my father's promise that I would supply an atheling for Angeln, yet he showers me with gifts of precious jewellery and fine cloth.'

She held the collar to her neck and admired her reflection in the mirror. 'See how it glows.' She offered it to Tanwen for a closer examination of the precious jewels.

'It is exquisite, lady princess.'

'I would like to send it to my lady mother as a gift.'

Tanwen mulled this over. If the princess really was poor, perhaps the king's wealth would tempt her to stay.

'King Waermund is the most generous of kings, lady princess. And they say that his gold-hoard is as high as a mountain.'

The princess's eyes sparkled. 'Even with the help of my mother and all of my extravagant sisters, I couldn't spend that much gold in a lifetime.'

'I'm sure you would make many new friends in Angeln who would be only too willing to introduce you to merchants and goldsmiths.'

Mae tapped on the door and slipped into the chamber. 'Lord Thorndor sends greetings to Princess Aelfrun and wishes to remind her that the guests are assembled in the feasting hall, patiently awaiting her arrival.'

Aelfrun gave Tanwen an impish grin. 'I fear your father grows impatient.'

'It is not my father we need fear, lady princess, but the king.'

The princess stared out of the arrow-slit. 'They do make a lot of noise, these people of Angeln.'

'They are excited, lady princess, and eager to meet their new queen.'

The princess groaned. 'It seems I have two options. Return to my father and risk being fed to his dogs, or marry the very old, but kindly and enormously rich King of Angeln, who may or may not bathe regularly. Tell me, flower girl, which would you choose?'

Tanwen grinned. 'A difficult choice, Princess Aelfrun, but I would feel safer with an elderly king in my bed than I would feel facing a starving dog.'

The princess beckoned a slave. 'Fetch me water to bathe my face, then run to Lord Thorndor and advise him that the bride is on her way.' Tanwen beamed. 'I'm so pleased you have decided to stay, lady princess. You will soon grow to love Angeln as I did.'

Aelfrun frowned, 'You, Tanwen? You also came to Angeln as a bride?'

'No, lady princess, I am a foundling.'

'A foundling. How exciting. Well, foundling, you have persuaded me that a princess could do a lot worse than start a new life in Angeln.'

As the guards prepared to open the doors, Princess Aelfrun called to Tanwen. 'One small request, Tanwen, in future, when addressing me, please use only my name. I am accustomed to the informality of a large family and find the constant use of titles rather irritating.'

'Next time we speak, Aelfrun, I shall address you as queen.'

***

The crowd roared when the huge wooden doors swung open and Tanwen stepped out into the sunshine. A gentle breeze brushed her underskirt against her legs, and she revelled in the unfamiliar luxury of silk against her skin.

When Aelfrun emerged, there was a moment's hush, followed by a cacophony of whistles, cheers and applause as she passed slowly and shyly through the throng. The people of Angeln welcomed her and no wonder for she was as lovely as the light elves and far lovelier than any other lady in Angeln.

Thorndor greeted them at the door of the feasting hall. He gave Tanwen a reassuring wink and inclined his head to the princess. The entrance chamber was crowded with lesser nobles and lower-ranking members of the king's war band, who had not been allocated places in the feasting hall. Thorndor pushed them aside and spread his arms wide, clearing a passageway for his foster daughter and the bride. His greying beard and shoulder-length hair were frizzier than ever but the small bones and rings that adorned them were gleaming. Tanwen wondered what charm Wynn had used to keep him still while she cleaned them. As always, he was dressed in a dull brown homespun robe under a wolf skin and carried a plain ash staff. Thorndor needed no adornment to emphasise his power.

The feasting hall buzzed with excitement. Thorndor tapped his staff and silence fell immediately. He glanced over the heads of the guests, bowed to the king then proudly led Tanwen into the hall.

She could hear nothing but the rapid pounding of her heart. Something was wrong. She desperately needed reassurance from Thorndor but did not dare look at him. Where was the princess? Seven steps behind. That was where she should be seven steps behind Tanwen.

Tanwen hesitated. How many steps had she taken? Five, six? She had lost count. Without moving her head, she glanced left and right. All eyes were on her, but still that eerie silence. *It must be more.* Eight, nine, she was running out of flowers, what was she to do? A harpist played. *Ten. Please Princess, please.*

A murmur rippled around the hall. Tanwen peeked over her shoulder. The princess stood, smiling and serene, in the doorway. There was a gasp of astonishment and burst of applause before a roar of approval erupted from the guests.

Elated, and with a spring in her step, Tanwen continued walking and spreading the few remaining flowers until Thorndor signalled that she was to stop.

King Waermund and Princess Aelfrun stood on either side of Thorndor. Lord Horsa, resplendent in blue and gold, stood behind the king holding a sword with its blade flat across his palms. He shot a questioning glance at Tanwen as she took her place behind Aelfrun and Tanwen realised he had expected to see his niece, Rowena.

Thorndor stepped back. King Waermund and Princess Aelfrun faced each other. The king offered a gold armband to his bride.

'Aelfrun, will you accept this band as a sign that you are willing to take me in wedlock?'

'Gladly, Lord King.' She solemnly accepted the band and slid it up her arm. Thorndor held their arms up high so the guests could see that the band had been accepted then took the sword and held it horizontally between the bridal couple. They placed their fingers on its gleaming blade. 'Do you, Waermund, swear to care for this woman in sickness and in health and to feed, clothe and protect all the children she bears you?' he asked.

'I do swear,' the king replied.

'Do you, Aelfrun, swear to be loyal to this man and to honour and obey him at all times?'

'I do swear.' She answered.

'And do you Waermund, and you, Aelfrun, swear to keep faith with each other as man and wife, for as long as you live?'

'I do swear,' they said, together.

Thorndor lowered the sword and addressed the assembly. 'Then let all present bear witness that Waermund and Aelfrun have sworn fidelity and shall be man and wife from this day forward.'

'So be it.' The guests replied in unison and a great cheer resounded around the hall.

Three harpists played as the king and queen took their places at the table and when all the guests were seated the wedding gifts were carried in for the royal couple's inspection.

The queen's pale eyes shone as the marvellous treasures were paraded before her: wine; fine horses, hunting dogs, rare furs, bolts of beautiful cloth and gold, many caskets of gold. Tanwen watched her reaction and knew she had been right to use the king's gold-hoard to entice Aelfrun to stay.

Tanwen was sitting with Wynn, opposite Lords Horsa and Hengest. She glanced in their direction and found Lord Horsa looking back at her with a smile that brought blood rushing to her cheeks. He winked at her before returning to his conversation with his brother. To settle the strange stirring in her stomach she helped herself to another jelly and ate it slowly, hoping he would look her way again, to no avail.

Prince Eadgils of the Myrging tribe perched himself on the bench beside Tanwen. He had been taken hostage by King Waermund during his first raid on Angeln. He was twenty now, and according to all the maidens in Angeln he was the tallest, fairest, bravest unbloodied warrior on earth. On his left temple, he had an angry-looking raised patch, which he swore caused him no discomfort.

'It's a mother-spot.' Wynn had explained when Tanwen asked about it. 'It's what happens to a baby in the womb if something unpleasant happens to its mother; or if she has a fright.'

'Or more likely a stray elf-shot,' Waltrude had added, nodding knowingly.

'What are you doing here?' Eadgils asked. 'I thought Rowena was going to attend the bride.'

'Rowena thought she was going to be the bride, but alas, Aelfrun beat her to it.'

Eadgils laughed. 'Do I detect a trace of bitchiness, Tanwen?'

'Why should I bitch about Rowena? I hardly know her.'

'Why indeed, when she's given you this golden opportunity?'

'Opportunity for what?'

'For finding a wealthy husband; can't you see them all eyeing you up?'

Tanwen glanced around the hall and grinned. 'They are all too drunk to eye up anything but the next cask of mead. And besides, I have no intention of marrying - ever.'

'Then let us hope the Wyrd sisters do not have different ideas. Eadgils offered her a cup of wine. 'It seems my fortunes have changed today.'

Tanwen looked up sharply.

'My father's envoy is here, and he is, at last, prepared to accept Waermund's demand for a piece of land in exchange for my safe return.'

'Eadgils, that's wonderful news, you'll be going home to your family at last.'

'I've been in Engel Land for five years. I'm more English than Myrging. When I return to my family, I'll be a stranger to them.'

'Don't say that, Eadgils. Please don't say that. I've been here for eight years and have the same fears. I have to force myself to believe that my family still remembers me. At least your father knows where you are and that you are well cared for.'

'True.' He squeezed Tanwen's hand. 'Goodbye sweet, Tanwen. I wish you success in your desire to become a shield-maiden, and I pray we never meet in battle. I may never see you again, but I'll always remember you, and I hope your father finds you soon.'

A nudge from Wynn reminded Tanwen to attend to her duties. Night was falling, the torches were being lit, and the queen was shivering.

'Queen Aelfrun, would you like me to fetch your cloak?'

Aelfrun preened. 'How grand it sounds, Queen Aelfrun - Aelfrun, Queen of Angeln, which title suits me best, Tanwen?'

Tanwen grinned. 'Both titles suit you perfectly, Queen Aelfrun, of Angeln.' They both giggled and Aelfrun beckoned Mae. 'Fetch our cloaks and we will retire to my chamber. Tanwen can tell me about her adventures as a foundling while you help me dress for bed, and tomorrow, after breaking fast we will ride out together.'

Tanwen blushed. 'I'm sorry, Aelfrun, I can't do that.'

'You can't ride?'

'No. That is, yes, I can ride, but I have lessons in the mornings, with Thorndor.'

'Then tell Thorndor he must excuse you.'

Tanwen's jaw dropped. 'I'm sorry, I couldn't possibly tell Thorndor.'

Thorndor was in deep conversation with Lord Hengest but must have sensed their eyes on him because he looked up and acknowledged them with a smile.

Aelfrun returned his smile and turned back to Tanwen. 'He's a dear old man, I'm sure he won't object.'

'And I am equally sure, that lord Thorndor will object to anything that interferes with learning.'

Aelfrun gave a haughty flick of her head, 'then we shall hear what my husband has to say about that.' She smiled demurely. 'My lord husband, I have invited Tanwen to move into the hall as my companion, but she is too timid to ask Lord Thorndor to excuse her from lessons.'

The king arched one eyebrow. 'Very wise, Tanwen,' he said, with a nod and the hint of a smile.

Aelfrun pouted. 'My lord, you must speak to him,' she cajoled. 'Tell him Tanwen is too old for his silly lessons and that from now on she is going to ride every morning with her queen.'

'My dear, no one tells Thorndor to do anything,' he replied.

Aelfrun looked peeved. 'But my lord, you are the king.'

'And he, my lady is Thorndor, and not to be crossed.' He gently patted her hand and turned back to his companions.

Tanwen's knees buckled with relief. Thank Nethrus she would not have to give up her lessons and anger Thorndor.

But the queen was determined. 'Mae, tell lord Thorndor I would like to speak with him,' she commanded.

Mae looked nervously at Tanwen before glancing over her shoulder to Thorndor. 'Tell Lord Thorndor, my lady?' She asked.

Aelfrun pursed her lips. 'Now, Mae, if you please.'

Thorndor strolled over at a leisurely pace. He gave a brief, almost imperceptible nod and waited for Queen Aelfrun to speak.

'My lord Thorndor,' she began. 'Tanwen and I have much in common.'

'I am delighted to hear it,' he replied, courteously.

'I miss the company of my sisters and it would be a great comfort to have Tanwen move into the queen's hall as my companion.' Aelfrun paused, waiting for a reply but Thorndor remained silent and Aelfrun continued. 'However, Tanwen is afraid it will anger you if she misses her lessons.' Still no response. 'She is rather old to be having lessons, don't you agree, Lord Thorndor?'

'One is never too old to learn, my lady.'

'But surely you wouldn't force her to attend, my lord?'

Thorndor feigned surprise. 'Force, my lady? I never use force; I find persuasion much more effective.'

Aelfrun frowned. 'Then will you persuade Tanwen to give up her silly lessons and move into my hall as my companion?'

'Would that please you, daughter?' Thorndor asked, and without allowing Tanwen time to reply, he continued, 'as I thought, my lady. Although my fosterling has some knowledge of word-craft and herb-lore, I fear she still has lots to learn, and I understand her warrior skills leave much to be desired. Perhaps she could move into the queen's hall as you suggest, but each day after the noon meal, while you are resting, she could attend her lessons and weapon-training?'

The queen clapped her hands in delight. 'Perfect, Thorndor, that is exactly what I had in mind.'

Thorndor bowed briefly and turned away, winking at Tanwen as he left.

'See how readily he agreed, Tanwen?' Aelfrun gloated, 'he accepted my authority without question, I believe I am going to enjoy being queen.'

***

That night, Tanwen shared a trestle bed with Edyth and Mae in the king's hall. She lay absolutely still absorbing the unfamiliar sounds of her new home. Dawn had not yet broken but the house churls were already about their daily chores. She wondered how they knew when to get up in the dark, and why they would need to. No one rose before the sun in Wynn's household.

Mae nudged her. 'Queen Aelfrun is awake. Go into the chamber to see if she needs help dressing.'

'I'm not going in there.'

'Shh. Just knock twice on the door. If you are needed the new queen will call you in. If she doesn't, try later,' Mae replied, sleepily.

'Why me?'

'Because you're the new favourite and she'll expect you, but don't forget to dress first.' Mae yawned and pulled the blanket over her head.

Tanwen cursed, got out of bed, and pulled on her tunic. She ran her fingers through her hair, rinsed her mouth with water from a jug and tapped twice on the royal sleeping chamber door. The queen answered, though her voice was so soft Tanwen could barely make out the words. She entered the chamber. Aelfrun was sitting on a chair at the side of the bed, with a fur around her shoulders.

'Shall I help you dress, Aelfrun?'

The queen glanced at her husband who was sprawled, naked, face down, across the bed. 'Yes, please, I'd like a breath of air before my husband wakes,' she replied.

The hall thane had been busy. The fire in the centre of the hall was blazing invitingly and an iron pot, filled with milk was warming at its side. He gave them each a wooden cup of warm milk and departed.

They sipped their milk in silence for some time before the queen spoke. 'You were right, Tanwen, the king may be very old; but he is clean, and not flabby, and he didn't snore, or fart, and for that I am thankful.'

Tanwen smiled, but the queen looked sad. 'Unfortunately, he does not love me,' she added unhappily.

'Then why did he marry you?'

'Because Thorndor insisted, I believe he would have preferred Rowena, or perhaps someone nearer his age. I fear I am a disappointment to him.'

'How can you tell so soon? It has only been one day.'

'And one night.' Aelfrun retorted. 'My lady mother spent countless days instructing me in what she called, "the delicate art of marital pleasure," but I had no opportunity to put any of it into practise.'

The thane returned. 'My lady may I …'

Aelfrun dismissed him. 'Soon,' she promised. 'Waermund didn't want me,' she continued when she could see the thane was out of earshot. 'Anyone would have done. He just - rode me like a horse. Then, when it was over, he said,' she paused, her bottom lip quivering and her eyes glistening with tears. "Forgive me my child. What I do, I do for Angeln." What an insult. Not that I care. But my mother would be furious if she found out, and father, well, I can't imagine what father would say.'

She sipped her milk and threw the remainder into the fire. It hissed. 'It was cold,' she said. 'And to add further offence, he told me that as soon as I deliver an atheling, he will allow me to return to my family, in Waernas. Can you imagine the disgrace?'

Tanwen wondered if the queen was hurt or angry or both. 'Surely that proves he wants you to be happy. He knows you miss your sisters, perhaps it's his way of caring for you,' she suggested.

'Do you think so?' Aelfrun asked, with a broad smile, and Tanwen marvelled at how quickly her mood changed.

'Has he not been very generous and shown you every kindness since your arrival?'

Aelfrun nodded. 'Yes, and it wasn't too terrible. I closed my eyes and dreamed a handsome young warrior, like Prince Eadgils, lay in his place, and I didn't mind too much.' She sprang to her feet. 'You must excuse me, Tanwen. My husband may have need of me.'

Tanwen marvelled at how quickly the queen could change her mind and watched her hurry back to the sleeping chamber. 'Who would be queen?' she mused. 'Thank Nethrus Thorndor never forces any of his fosterlings into marriage.'

Three

The spotted fever rampaged through the town. When Wynn was not treating those fortunate enough to find a bed in the healing chamber, she was busy rushing from house to house with herbs, instruction, and kind words for those caring for the sick in their own homes.

Thorndor excused Tanwen lessons to help Wynn fight the illness and, despite Wynn's objections, Aelfrun insisted on joining them. Together, they bathed fevered bodies, changed soiled sheets and emptied stinking bile buckets, from dawn to dusk. Tanwen and Wynn were amazed at Aelfrun's compassion for the sick. She worked tirelessly without complaint and never shirked a task no matter how unpleasant. However, on the sixth day she fainted from exhaustion and Wynn insisted she return to the queen's hall for rest.

Two spearmen guarded the door to the healing chamber, and no one was allowed to enter except Wynn and Tanwen but two days after Aelfrun left, while Wynn was out, lord Horsa demanded to see his kinswoman, Lady Rowena and forced his way past the guards.

Startled by the unfamiliar masculine voice Tanwen turned too quickly and for a moment the chamber swirled around her. She swayed, and Horsa was immediately at her side with his powerful arms holding her close to his body. She tried to escape, but his grip was firm, and she found herself captivated by a pair of deep blue eyes set in a wind-burned face.

'I'm sorry, I was afraid you would faint,' he said.

Flushed with embarrassment, Tanwen pulled herself free. 'I never faint. You startled me, that's all. What are you doing here, anyway? Visitors are forbidden.'

'I am here to satisfy myself that my kinswoman, the Lady Rowena, is receiving the care due to her rank.'

'In Angeln the sick receive the best possible care regardless of their rank.' Tanwen retorted.

'I didn't mean to offend you, but we are foreigners here, how am I to know she is being treated fairly without seeing for myself?' He took Rowena's hand in his. 'Except for Hengest, Rowena is all I have. She is precious to me and I feared for her life. Does she respond to your herbs? Will she live?'

'We killed the fever with viper's bugloss, and cold compresses then piled on hot blankets to sweat out the mist-wraith,' she said. 'The crisis is now past, and she sleeps peacefully. Today she sipped honey in warm water. Tomorrow she will take thin broth, the following day bread in milk and soon she will be back to normal.'

Horsa kissed Rowena's brow and took his leave. 'Thank you for your kindness, Lady Tanwen. It will not be forgotten.' With his eyes on hers, he drew up her hand and kissed it, sending an unexpected quiver of excitement through her body.

***

Wynn believed the spotted fever was spread by the mist-waifs who lived in the dyke at the rear of the queen's hall, and she gave Thorndor and King Waermund no peace. 'It's unfit for habitation,' she complained bitterly. 'Even cattle would be reluctant to enter, we can't possibly allow Aelfrun and the ladies to return to it.' Eventually, the king agreed, the hall was abandoned and in winterfrith, the queen and her ladies moved into a new hall.

Built between the orchard and the herb plot, away from the water meadow and mist wraiths, and set some distance from the feasting hall so that she would not be disturbed by the rowdy activities of warriors, cooking smells and byres. It was large enough to accommodate the queen, all of the children she expected to have, Tanwen, Rowena, servants, scops and musicians. Inside, the walls were hung with embroidered cloth from the east and furnished in the luxurious Roman style. A new bower was erected close by, surrounded by a tall fence to provide the queen and her ladies privacy and protection.

Rowena's health slowly improved and a few weeks later, accompanied by Tanwen, she was well enough to join them. Aelfrun was overjoyed at their return and eagerly showed them the fine silver mare that had been her morning gift from the king. 'I wanted pearls. They say pearls give you wisdom, and their creaminess would be perfect on my new red silk dress,' she said, wistfully. 'But Starlight is very pretty and was a great comfort while you were both away.'

She chatted happily about how she had filled her days while they had been gone. Her mornings had been spent riding Starlight or hawking with Hengest and Horsa and her afternoon's being bathed and pampered with precious oils, by Mae, who had learned the skill of massage from a Roman slave in Waernas and practised the art to perfection. Her evenings were spent in the great hall, serving mead and ale to her husband and his companions, while watching the antics of the young nobles of the hearth-troop at weapon play or listening to the stories of a visiting scop.

'One of the young warriors asked after the health of you both every day. He wanted to visit the healing chamber, but Wynn wouldn't hear of it,' she told them.

'Hunlaf?' Tanwen asked.

'Yes, Waermund's kinsman and your sword companion, I believe.'

'Then it was not me he wanted to see.' Tanwen replied, sourly.

Rowena blushed, Aelfrun noticed and clapped her hands in delight. 'How exciting. Do you love him, Rowena?'

'I barely know him, Aelfrun.' Rowena was obviously embarrassed.

'That means nothing. I had never even met Waermund before our wedding day, yet I love him dearly already.'

Every day, while Aelfrun and Rowena were at rest, Tanwen studied "The Old Ways" of the English in the learning chamber with Thorndor, before rushing to Anna's field to meet Hunlaf and Arild for weapon-practise.

The boys' footwork had improved, and their moves were less awkward, but Tanwen was still dissatisfied. Hunlaf lacked concentration and was making errors. She had missed training for four weeks, perhaps her poor performance was affecting him.

'It's my fault, I've been away too long. I'll drill alone in the evenings, until I improve,' she said, hoping to make amends. 'It shouldn't be too difficult to sneak out.'

Hunlaf looked uneasy. 'I may not be around much longer. I'll be going with the king next time he patrols the borders. You'll have to train with Arild while I'm away.'

Tanwen was horrified. 'Arild. Never. I'd rather wrestle a viper,' she said and walked away.

***

Rowena rarely spoke to anyone and treated Tanwen with cool indifference. Tanwen believed it was because Rowena considered her a servant, but Aelfrun called her a silly duckling and said she worried too much. It only seemed that way because

Rowena had been so sick. Aelfrun was enjoying her position as queen and too busy visiting merchants to concern herself with domestic trivialities.

Two weeks later Rowena began pestering Wynn to teach her herb-lore. 'My mother taught me how to grow herbs for the kitchen, but how much more rewarding and useful it would have been to teach me how to use them to cure the sick,' she said.

Hating to be left out of anything, Aelfrun agreed. 'We should all learn herb-lore then no one would ever die, except on the battlefield where warriors don't have time to pick herbs or tend wounds.'

Wynn shook her head. 'If only healing were that simple, Aelfrun, but sadly herbs cannot be counted upon to prevent death. A healer's skill lies in recognising the signs and symptoms presented to her, and in knowing the appropriate herbs to use to fight fevers and infections and to ease pain and discomfort. When she is successful, the patient believes she has cured him.'

'You cured Rowena.'

'I didn't cure Rowena. My herbs merely killed the fever, making it easier for Rowena's body to heal itself.'

'If you hadn't used herbs to kill the fever surely Rowena would have died.'

Wynn shrugged. 'Maybe, maybe not. It is for Wyrd to decide.'

'If you won't teach us, we will learn by trial and error. We will concoct potions and test them on the slaves.'

Tanwen and Rowena giggled but Wynn was aghast. 'You will do no such thing. Herbs can be dangerous in the wrong hands and learning how to use them properly takes time and commitment.'

Aelfrun pouted. 'We have little else to fill our time, and how can we show our commitment if you don't give us the opportunity?'

Tanwen doubted Aelfrun's commitment but not Rowena's sincerity. 'It's time to select the herbs for storing, if Aelfrun and Rowena help they will quickly learn to identify some of them,' she suggested.

Eventually, Wynn relented and took them outside for their first lesson. They picked an assortment of herbs and spread them on a table for closer examination. As Tanwen expected, Aelfrun soon became bored and wandered off with a basket to pick beans for the kitchen.

Wynn was never happier than when gathering in the herbs, tying them into neat bundles, labelling them with a rune stick and hanging them to dry for winterfrith use. 'Herbs smell so much sweeter than people,' she said, year after year.

Tanwen did not share her foster mother's enthusiasm for herbs and healing. However, Wynn was convinced she had a "special gift" and insisted she help gather and dry the herbs at haerfest. Although Tanwen was never sure what the gift was, and would rather have been weapon-training, she much preferred herb drying to looking after the beastlings, so she didn't protest. This year she would be very happy to leave the work to Aelfrun and Rowena.

She stretched out on the grass to soak up the feeble rays of the sun while listening to Wynn describing each plant in detail and painstakingly explaining its uses to Rowena.

'This is the primrose root, used to relax muscles. We also grind it and make a tea to ease moon-blood cramps. And what is our weapon against fever, Tanwen?' Wynn asked.

Tanwen started at the unexpected question. 'Tea made from willow bark?'

'Correct. And how do we treat ringworm?'

Tanwen grimaced and delved deep into her memory. The gut-wrenching stench of rotten eggs came to her and she pictured Wynn holding a feather over a small child whose backside was covered in rings of red scaly sores. 'Sulphur. Pounded together with - the juice of the mint plant and - vinegar and applied with a feather.'

Wynn smiled appreciatively. 'Well done, Tanwen. It's a special gift my daughter has,' she told Rowena. 'Now, my dear, you carry on labelling these bunches while I find work for Tanwen's idle hands.'

Rowena was crestfallen. 'I'm sorry, Wynn, I can't.'

'Can't?'

'I never learned how to read runes.'

'Never learned to read the runes?' Wynn was clearly shocked. 'You poor child. Your education has been sorely neglected.' She tutted and shook her head as if Rowena's lack of learning would cause the earth to crumble, but within a couple of heartbeats, her voice returned to its normal cheery tone. 'However, it is to be expected, after all, few households have a great teacher like Thorndor to guide them.'

She lifted Rowena's chin with a finger. 'Besides, if you are destined to marry a king the only things you need to learn are how to look pretty and how to spend your husband's gold hoard. The first you have already mastered and the second you will learn quickly enough, with a teacher like – Aelfrun!' She screeched the name as she hurried across the herb plot.

Tanwen looked up to see the queen with Wynn's arm around her waist for support. She rushed over to help. 'What is it? What's happened?'

Aelfrun, looking deathly pale, was standing by a pool of vomit. 'It's nothing Tanwen, truly.'

'Nothing? It must be something, Aelfrun. I'm not deaf, you threw up earlier, I heard you.'

'And yesterday,' Rowena added, coming up from behind.

Tanwen's heart plummeted. 'Oh Wynn, it's not the mist-wraiths again?'

The colour was returning to Aelfrun's cheeks and although she still looked frail, there was a glint in her eyes as she exchanged an impish smile with Wynn. 'I am told most ladies suffer sickness only in the mornings,' she said. 'However, it seems I'm to be cursed with it lasting all day long.'

'Oh, Aelfrun, that's the most wonderful news.'

'I'm so happy. I can't believe it. I will soon be the mother of the atheling of Angeln. Waermund was so pleased when I told him - I'll swear there was a tear in his eye.'

The queen prattled on, barely pausing for breath. 'And married only three months. Can you imagine what gifts he'll bestow upon me now? Furs for winter and gold amulets and pearls. Oh, he must. Surely now Waermund will give me pearls? I will make a shrine to Nethrus, where I can offer sacrifices and pray every day that my son will be as great and good a king as his father, and that I will be the best of mothers.'

'And the proud owner of a collar of pearls.' Rowena muttered under her breath.

'We will all pray with you.' Wynn said. Tanwen agreed, hoping Aelfrun had not noticed the frost in Rowena's comment.

As expected, the king was overjoyed and presented Aelfrun with a beautiful collar of perfectly matched pearls. She was ecstatic. 'It will make all the pain of childbirth worthwhile. I intend to bear Waermund a son every year,' she giggled.

'It's truly beautiful, Aelfrun. And it must be especially precious to you, having waited a whole three months for it; but what if it's a girl child?'

Tanwen wanted to snap off Rowena's head for blurting it out like that, but she knew someone was bound to say it sooner or later.

Aelfrun's eyes narrowed, and her jaw tightened. 'Don't say that. Don't you dare say that.' She put her hand on her stomach. 'I am carrying a boy child, the atheling of Angeln. Daughters of the King of Waernas do not carry girl children. I will never have a girl child.'

Tanwen was mortified. 'Oh, Aelfrun, I'm sure Rowena meant no harm.' Rowena walked away without a word.

***

Merchants, jewel smiths and dressmakers flocked to the hall and Aelfrun spent freely. She enjoyed giving gifts as much as receiving them and was almost as generous with Mae and Edyth as she was with Tanwen and Rowena. Afraid that some harm might come to the unborn child, the king confined her to the hall and bower for the term of her pregnancy, and to Tanwen's surprise, she obeyed without question.

The queen and the ladies spent the long days of winterfrith in the bower, spinning, sewing and doing fine embroidery, but Tanwen had never learned to use a spindle and hated sewing. Instead, she made salves of honey and almond oil perfumed with pounded lavender or briar rose petals to soften Aelfrun's skin, and an emulsion of ewe's milk, clary and balm mint to ease the discomfort in her growing stomach.

Aelfrun was barely able to hide her excitement when, six weeks later, she presented Tanwen with a leather tunic and riding breeches.

'Oh, Aelfrun, they are so beautifully soft and fit perfectly. I'll treasure them forever. How can I ever thank you?' She had never dreamed of owning such a wonderful outfit and doubted if she would ever have need of it.

'There is something I need you to do for me in return.'

'Aelfrun, you do not need to buy me expensive gifts to ask a favour.'

'I knew you would say that. But I'm asking for a special favour, and special favours deserve special rewards.' She led Tanwen outside where a groom was waiting with Starlight.

Tanwen was dismayed. 'Oh, Aelfrun, you're not going to ride? You mustn't, the king has forbidden it.'

Aelfrun laughed. 'No, silly duckling, I'm not going to ride her, but she does need to be cared for and exercised every day, and the grooms are much too heavy-handed to ride such a pretty filly. Horsa has agreed to borrow Thorndor's horse and ride with you until you gain confidence if you are willing? Will you do it for me Tanwen, until the prince is born, please?'

'Oh, Aelfrun, you know I will. Thank you, thank you, thank you. I swear I won't walk another step. I'll ride Starlight everywhere and she'll be in perfect condition for you to ride her through the town to show the baby atheling to his people.'

Since leaving Bryneich, Tanwen had had very little contact with horses until Aelfrun introduced her to Starlight. The English had such a deep-rooted mistrust of the animals that few used them regularly and even fewer used them solely for pleasure.

Thorndor's old stallion had a temper as black as its coat and it kicked or bit anyone but Thorndor who came within an arm's length of it. He claimed it had been raised by a dragon and was discovered in its lair after the dragon had been slain. Its mad eyes, steamy breath and flaring nostrils bore this out; but the rumour spread that the stallion was an unfortunate child who had defied Thorndor and suffered the terrible transformation as a consequence. Tanwen thought both stories unlikely, but whoever or whatever it was, the beast adored Thorndor and always carried him proudly into battle and safely out of it, and for that she was thankful, although she wondered how Horsa would cope with it.

To Tanwen's surprise, Horsa was a skilled horseman, and the stallion took food from his hand, nuzzled his neck and whickered when he stroked it.

The first time he helped her onto Starlight's back, a vivid memory of riding in front of her father, on his stallion, came to mind and she remembered his own body smell mingled with leather and horse sweat. An overwhelming feeling of comfort enveloped her as she realised, for the first time, that she would recognise her father by his own distinctive odour, no matter how many years she had to wait to see him again.

***

Tanwen wondered if Aelfrun noticed Rowena was distancing herself from her. More and more of her time was spent with Wynn, or in whispered conversation with Mae. Although frequently invited to ride with Tanwen and Horsa, she always declined. Every day she went out alone, sometimes riding but usually walking. She never said where she had been and the queen never asked, but as she usually brought back hazelnuts or mushrooms Tanwen and Aelfrun believed she had been to the bluebell wood, which lay on the hilltop just beyond the pastureland. Whenever Aelfrun teased her about a grass stain on her tunic or a leaf clinging to her hair, Rowena smiled and brushed them away without explanation.

When Tanwen heard that Arild had sprained his ankle and was unable to come to sword practise, she was elated. At last, she and Hunlaf could get down to some serious training without constant nagging from his cousin. How wrong could she be?

Rowena had been picking sloe-thorn berries for wool dying. She said that she was on her way back to the bower when she spotted Tanwen and Hunlaf and decided to sit on the grass to watch them, but her presence appeared to affect Hunlaf's focus, and her constant questions drove Tanwen to distraction.

She wanted to know the name of every move and why they had made it, and why they did it this way and not that, and would it not be easier if …?'

'Rowena.' Tanwen threw down her singlestick in exasperation. 'How are we supposed to concentrate on the fight with you constantly gibbering in the background?'

'I'm sorry. I was only trying to help.'

'You were not. You were …'

'Leave her alone Tanwen. You're always picking on somebody,' Hunlaf said.

'I'm not picking on her, I just want her to be quiet for a while. Is that too much to ask?'

'Oh no.' Rowena yelled. 'Here comes my uncle, he'll tell father. Come, Hunlaf, we have to go, quickly.' She grabbed Hunlaf's hand, and leaving their belongings scattered across the ground they ran for the cover of the woods.

Tanwen stuffed everything into Hunlaf's bag and put it on top of the basket of sloe-thorn berries. She remained on her knees, pretending not to have noticed Horsa striding up the hill.

'Lady Tanwen,' he said, offering a hand to help her to her feet. 'I have not forgotten my debt to you.'

'Your debt, Lord Horsa?'

'For saving Rowena's life.'

'Wynn did the saving, my lord. I merely carried out her instructions - with the queen's help.'

'Rowena tells a different tale. She says it was you who bathed her brow, emptied her soil bucket and sat with her night after night, and it was certainly only you, I saw on my visits to the healing chamber.'

Tanwen grinned. 'The mist-wraiths play tricks on fevered minds.' She wondered why he had chosen this moment to speak of Rowena's illness. There had been ample opportunities to do so on their daily rides.

Horsa cast a quizzical glance at the singlesticks protruding from Hunlaf's bag and Tanwen blushed.

'We use wooden weapons for training,' she explained, 'and Hunlaf left in such a hurry he forgot to take them.'

'It must have been a matter of importance for a warrior to leave his weapons behind.' He picked up the basket and walked with her to the bower.

'I see little of my niece these days, would the queen allow me to call upon her?'

Rowena might not have returned to the bower yet. Tanwen made a hurried excuse. 'It's not a good time. The queen will be at rest. If you come later, before the evening meal, I'm sure Aelfrun will receive you.'

But Rowena did not return and by early evening the queen was frantic. She questioned Tanwen over and over again. 'What were you thinking of to let her go running off like that? Is this Hunlaf to be trusted? What is her lord father going to say? What is the king going to say?' She swore Mae and Edyth to secrecy and sent them out to search the wood, while Tanwen combed the town, but the runaways were nowhere to be found.

By the time Horsa arrived, Aelfrun was almost out of her mind. 'You deal with it, Tanwen. It's your fault, you should have stopped her.' Without argument, Tanwen turned to leave, but Aelfrun called her back.

'Tanwen - Rowena is my responsibility and I allowed her too much freedom. I have failed in my duty of care to those around me. I will face her uncle and the wrath of my lord king.

Tanwen had never seen Aelfrun more regal than when she stood erect and grim-faced to greet her kinsman.

Horsa was about to speak when she held up her hand to silence him. 'You are welcome, cousin Horsa, but we have no

time for pleasant conversation. I'm afraid Rowena is missing.'
Tanwen winced; she had expected Aelfrun to be a little more diplomatic.

'Missing?' Horsa looked bewildered.

'She did not return from her afternoon walk. We believe she is with Hunlaf.'

'Hunlaf?' He glanced at Tanwen then back to Aelfrun. 'How could this have happened? Could you be mistaken? Perhaps she is simply misplaced.'

Aelfrun shot him a withering look, she hated being contradicted and was clearly not in the mood for humour.

'May I explain, Aelfrun?' The queen beckoned Tanwen forward.

'She was on the hill, watching Hunlaf and me at weapon-training when she suddenly cried out that you were approaching and was afraid you would tell her father. They dropped their belongings and ran.'

'Why didn't you tell me? We could have followed them.'

'Because I assumed Hunlaf would bring her straight back here, I didn't realise there was anything between them.'

'I sincerely hope there is nothing between them and that this is simply a childish prank, or my brother will not be pleased,' Horsa said in a grim voice. He turned to Aelfrun. 'With your leave, my lady, it will be dark soon and I ...'

'Indeed, you must go at once. Shall I inform Hengest?'

Horsa was already at the door. 'Not yet,' he said and was gone.

Once again Tanwen was touched by the Frisian's feelings for Rowena. No accusations, no harsh words, just a genuine concern for her wellbeing. She turned pleading eyes to Aelfrun.

'Yes, Tanwen. You may join him,' the queen said.

***

They rode through the town at a trot to avoid drawing attention to themselves, but as soon as they were clear of the stockade they leaned into the wind, dug in their heels and hurtled across the wasteland at full gallop. Tanwen's heart was pounding, and she gasped for breath.

It was the first time she had ridden Starlight at this pace, and she was terrified by the speed of objects rushing towards her, but the fear soon turned to exhilaration and she yelled at the filly to go faster.

They reached the forest and Horsa glanced over his shoulder before disappearing into the darkness. Tanwen followed at a slower pace, ducking to avoid low branches, but the further they ventured into the forest the darker it became and the more difficult it was to see the low hanging boughs that stung as they slapped against her face, bringing tears to her eyes. She continued crashing through the trees for what seemed an eternity until, at last, she heard Horsa shout that they were almost there, and she saw daylight again as they approached the clearing.

They galloped on until they reached a small village perched on a ridge overlooking the sea. For fear of spreading alarm, they reined in their horses and entered the enclosure on foot. The village was no more than half a dozen hovels with a handful of geese to sound a warning of strangers, and a few cattle grazing on nearby wasteland.

Curiosity brought the whole village out to meet them. Their leader was a slight, young man in coarse homespun garments. An old woman stood behind him.

'I am Horsa, of Frisia, and this is Lady Tanwen, daughter of Thorndor. We are looking for a young warrior named Hunlaf who may have lost his way.'

'Thorndor the wizard?' The leader moved closer to examine Tanwen's face.

'Yes,' she replied, somehow managing to hold her nerve under his intense stare.

'Nah. Not one of our kind,' the old woman said, snorting disapproval, 'not with that hair.'

The leader did not offer his name. 'Not much of a warrior, this Hunlaf, if he can't find his way home. Where was he headed?'

'To join the king; he is one of King Waermund's warband.'

'Travelling alone, is he?' Tanwen wondered if this man always spoke in questions.

'He may be escorting a kinswoman,' Horsa replied.

'May he indeed? And this kinswoman, what would her name be?'

Horsa was growing impatient. 'It is getting dark, and we have a lot of ground to cover. Just tell me if Hunlaf passed here today and we'll be on our way.'

The old woman spoke. 'We had a healer come by, pretty she was, didn't give her name. Knew what she was about, though.'

'Enough, Gaeta,' the leader warned.

'Saved my girl's life she did. None of this lot could.' The old woman jerked her head in the direction of the other villagers.

'Enough, I said.'

'What is your name?' Horsa asked the old woman, ignoring the command.

'Urith,' the leader said. 'And this is my wife's mother, Gaeta.'

Horsa undid the gold brooch from his cloak and offered it to Gaeta. 'Tell me about the healer and this is yours.'

Urith swiped the brooch from Horsa's hand. 'Keep your brooch. Geata's words were true, the healer saved my wife's life, we will not betray her.'

In an instant Horsa unsheathed his sword and held it at Urith's throat. 'Why you cursed son of a she-wolf …'

'Stop, Lord Horsa. Your argument is with me, not Urith.' Hunlaf was standing in the doorway of one of the hovels. 'As you see, I am unarmed.'

Horsa lowered his sword. 'Where is Rowena?' He bellowed.

Hunlaf stood aside making room for Horsa and Tanwen to enter. The hovel consisted of one room with a central fire, which threw out little warmth and even less light. Soiled rushes covered the floor. There was one chair, a wooden box and an assortment of pots and other household necessities. Herbs hung from the beams and a haunch of mutton dangled from a hook over the fire.

Rowena was sitting at the bedside of a young woman who was propped up on cushions and sipping ale.

'It was a snakebite. I used waybread. They had no wine, so I dipped it in seawater, and gave her warm ale with honey to drink. Father says Frisian seafarers use sea water to cleanse their wounds. Her voice was strained and her face pale and drawn, all her usual strength and confidence had deserted her.

'You did well, Rowena. Wynn will be proud of you.' Tanwen said.

Urith pushed his way into the room, sat on the edge of the bed and took the young woman's hand. 'This is my Ursa. We thank the Earth Mother for sending Rowena to us. Without her, Ursa would have died. If Rowena does not want to return with you, she may remain here, as our guest, for as long as she wishes, her man is also invited to share our home.'

Rowena stood. 'I thank you, Urith, but Queen Aelfrun will be anxious. I must return.'

'Then will you all accept our hospitality for the night? The road is dangerous after dark.'

'Thank you Urith, but if we ride hard, we will be home by nightfall. Come, Rowena,' Horsa said.

Hunlaf was still standing in the doorway; he had not spoken a word. Rowena averted her eyes as she passed him. Tanwen squeezed his hand and her eyes filled with tears. *Poor Hunlaf, what will become of him in this desolate, poverty-ridden place?*

The brooch lay on the ground, demonstrating the honesty of the churls. Horsa picked it up and spoke to them.

'Waermund is a just but vengeful king who shows no mercy to his enemies. Do not doubt, that should word of this incident spread, he will have the informant's tongue and ears fed to his dogs and the village razed to the ground.' He paused just long enough to let his words sink in. 'However, Waermund is also a very generous king and always rewards loyalty.' He placed the brooch in Gaeta's hand and offered a small pouch of battle-won gold rings to Urith. Urith accepted the pouch and tipped its contents into his hand. The villagers gasped in astonishment.

Horsa paused again, allowing them time to murmur among themselves, before continuing. 'Each Winterfrith the purse will be refilled by a messenger from the king. Rest assured that as long as the village remains silent your people will never go hungry.'

'Is the king aware of this?' Tanwen whispered in his ear.

'He will be soon,' Horsa replied, with a grim smile.

The villagers, singing, dancing and cheering for the king, led them to the gate but stayed well clear of the horses. Horsa smiled at their fear as he lifted Rowena onto the stallion. As

Tanwen mounted Starlight, she noticed Horsa glance at Hunlaf who was watching them from a distance, but he quickly turned away and leapt onto his horse.

'Well, boy,' he called, over his shoulder, 'are you going to share Tanwen's mount or are you planning to walk home?'

***

The king spoke of it as a silly childhood escapade, scolded Rowena and confined her to the lady hall and bower. He warned Hunlaf that such behaviour would not be tolerated a second time, made him swear an oath of allegiance and moved him into the men's hall, where he could, "keep an eye on the scallywag." Finally, he rewarded Horsa with a gold arm ring for bringing the runaways home safely and discreetly and promised to honour the annual bribe to the village. Everyone agreed that King Waermund was the most lenient of kings.

It seemed to Tanwen that Aelfrun did not know how to handle the situation. One moment she was ranting about how much she hated Rowena for putting her through such an ordeal, and the next moment insisted that her dear cousin had done no wrong and was the victim of a terrible injustice.

As usual, Rowena was silent. Forbidden even to go into the herb patch, she spent her time gazing out of the arrow-slit or learning to read runes.

Hengest was furious and decided that the only way to prevent further trouble would be to take his wayward daughter home, so the Frisians loaded their vessel and a week later Tanwen stood on the quayside and watched the men of the sea launch their ship.

Horsa lew a kiss and shouted, 'we'll meet again,' as they sailed away. Tanwen thought it unlikely, her father had said something similar the day she escaped from Bryneich with her brothers, and she had never seen him again. But she nodded, wiped away a tear and waved until the ship was out of view.

Four

Tanwen, Hunlaf and Arild had been out since dawn practising with their bows. Between them, they had brought down seven ducks and two brace of hare and they were well pleased with their archery skills.

They rode at an easy pace, laughing and chatting, with their catch dangling from their saddles and the hounds happily trotting alongside. Tanwen's dog unexpectedly gave tongue, scaring a hind from its cover almost under the nose of Starlight. It leapt into the air and shot off across the clearing with the hound at its heels. Tanwen whooped for joy and chased after them. In less than a heartbeat, the boys hurtled off in wild pursuit.

Tanwen galloped ahead, determined to be the first to reach the quarry. Faster and faster, she rode, racing far out over the wasteland and into the wood. The hound was snapping at the hind's heels but then, with a sudden burst of speed, the hind outstripped the hound until, at last, the hind collapsed and Tanwen closed in. Starlight, startled by a bird flapping as it rose from the undergrowth, whinnied and reared and Tanwen fell. Her disorientated dog ran round and round in circles, the hind seized the moment, leapt to its feet and disappeared into the distance. Tanwen was laughing and brushing herself down when the boys came to her aid.

'Are you all right?' Hunlaf asked, laughing with her.

'Yes, yes, I'm fine,' she said, whispering in Starlight's ear, to calm her.

'Thanks to you the hind has gone,' Arild complained.

'It wasn't my fault. You saw what happened, the bird scared her.'

'I'm fed up with you showing off. You're a pain in the arse, always holding us up and spoiling our sport.'

'What are you gibbering about? When have I ever held you up? I never lose my hawks and I can keep up with the riders as well as any man.'

'Only because we rein back to stay with you, it's the same with your swordplay. Hunlaf always lets you win in case you burst into tears. You women are all alike. If you dropped an earring, you'd stop the hunt in full cry to make everybody look for it.'

'I never burst into tears and I don't wear earrings.'

'You're being unfair, Arild,' Hunlaf said, 'the only time Tanwen ever dropped out of a hunt was to help you when you fell off your horse.'

'The horse caught his leg in a tangle of tree roots, and I fell with him. It was just bad luck; it could happen to anyone.'

Tanwen grinned. 'Shall I give you a lesson on how to handle a horse, little boy?'

Arild nearly choked with indignation. 'It's you who needs a lesson. You need to learn how to behave like a maiden and not a camp follower. A woman should know how to keep her place and not meddle in men's affairs.'

'Men's affairs? I don't see any men around here, and what do you know about camp followers, or women, for that matter?'

'Ignore him, Tanwen. That fall from his horse addled his wits. He hasn't been the same since.' Hunlaf slipped the reins into Tanwen's hands. 'Come on, I'll race you back.'

Arild sneered. 'Huh. And what do you think your father would say if he knew you were spending your days riding around with a woman?'

'I'm fifteen, and a warrior, I'll ride with Tanwen anytime I want.'

'That's not what you said yesterday.'

'Shut up, Arild.' Hunlaf snapped.

Arild turned to Tanwen. 'Yesterday he said it was wrong for you to ride and swordplay with us now that you are a woman.'

Tanwen glared at Hunlaf. 'Is this true?'

'Not exactly.'

'Then what, exactly, did you say?'

'I only said that - well it's true, Tanwen. I enjoy being with you but it's time you stopped trying to behave like a man.' He coloured and stroked Starlight's ears to hide his embarrassment.

'He said he doesn't want to fight with you anymore, it makes him feel funny.' Arild thumbed his puffed-out chest, so from now on, I'm going to be his sword-companion.'

'You? You pathetic bag of pig shit. You haven't got the wit to wipe your backside, let alone use a sword.'

'Stop it, Tanwen. Arild is right. When we were children swordplay was fun. But now things have changed, you've changed.'

'I have not. And I don't try to behave like a man. Why should I? I don't want to be a man. I want to be a shield-maiden, to lead men into battle. And to do that I need to be able to use a sword as well as any man. That's why I practise at every opportunity.'

'You have changed. Look in a mirror. And you'll never be a shield-maiden. Thorndor will marry you off soon and that will put an end to all your shield-maiden nonsense.'

'Don't you dare tell me what I can and can't do. I'll never marry. I'll be no man's chattel. Marriage and babies may suit English women, but I'm from Bryneich, and I will be a shield-maiden and take orders from no man.'

'Give it up, Tanwen. You are an orphan and if you had been found by anyone but Thorndor, you would be a slave.'

'I am not an orphan. My parents still live, my brothers ...'

'Didn't want you, they kicked you out of the boat and left you to drown,' Arild said spitefully.

'They did not. They put me ashore for my own safety.'

'Oh, yes,' he replied, with a smirk.

Hunlaf shifted uncomfortably from one foot to the other. 'What does it matter Tanwen? You are here and one of us now, come on, let's not quarrel, we can still be friends and ride together.'

'Friends? With you? A rabid wolf would make a better companion than you.'

She jumped onto Starlight and galloped off, fuming all the way to town. She loathed menfolk, all of them. Except for her father of course, and Thorndor and Hunlaf was tolerable if his insufferable cousin was not around, and Horsa. But Horsa wasn't like other men, Horsa was - Horsa.

She dismounted and plonked herself down by the stream to try and make sense of her life. A year ago, everything was so uncomplicated, she knew exactly where she was going. She planned to train every day until she was as strong and skilled as a champion and when she was fifteen, the age when most boys were considered old enough to go into battle, she would leave Angeln, and travel around Engle Land to raise an army and track down her evil brothers in Bryneich.

But this was her thirteenth year, time was racing by and she was no nearer raising a war-band than she had been a year ago.

It was all Rowena's fault, she muttered to herself. If she had not been sick, I would never have become involved with the queen and ...hog's breath. The queen. She had forgotten all about her stupid promise to take Aelfrun to watch the icon of the Earth Mother leaving its hiding place. She had better get back in time or there would be an awful fuss.

She tried to sneak past Thorndor's homestead without being spotted by Wynn, who was busily scraping honey from a comb, but Starlight whinnied and she was caught in the act.

'How is she today?' Wynn called, pulling off her gauntlets.

'She's fine.' Tanwen knew instinctively that Wynn was referring to Aelfrun but did not have time to get involved in a long conversation.

'Good, tell her I'll be over later; I've picked this lovely lavender for her.'

'Err, no, better not,' She did not want Wynn to come to the queen's hall and find them both missing. 'Aelfrun is a bit grumpy. Merchants have been visiting all day and she is overtired. I've persuaded her to rest before the king returns.'

'Wise girl. Her size is bound to make her uncomfortable, I wouldn't be at all surprised if there were two or even three in there. And do try to stop her going to the mead hall, Tanwen. Waermund won't expect her to serve ale to his companions in her condition. Here, you take the lavender, I won't bother her unless she asks for me, and don't worry about her moodiness; it's perfectly natural as her time approaches.'

***

Aelfrun was frowning at her reflection in a mirror when Tanwen entered the hall. 'Wynn thought this lavender might help you sleep more comfortably.'

Apparently uninterested in the gift, Aelfrun turned sideways, stretched her arms around her bulge and groaned. 'Oh, Tanwen, look at me. There must be more than one prince in here. If I get much bigger my arms won't reach all the way around.'

'If you get much bigger, Aelfrun, you won't fit into the birthing chair, and then where will we be?'

Aelfrun shrugged. 'Being pregnant is so unflattering.' She faced the mirror to examine the folds of her green dress then looked down and grimaced. 'It's no use. I can't see over the prince. How am I to know if the hem touches the top of my shoes?'

Tanwen placed the lavender on a nearby table and approached the queen; she stopped abruptly. 'Aelfrun. What ails you?'

'Nothing ails me.' Aelfrun twirled inelegantly to inspect the dress in the mirror. 'You are imagining things.'

'I'm not. See for yourself how pale you look.'

Aelfrun peered closely at her reflection, moving her head up and down and from side to side. She moistened her fingertips, smoothed her pale eyebrows into shape and patted her hair. 'There, does that satisfy you? I'm perfectly well, a little flushed perhaps, but that is because you weren't here when I needed you.'

'I'm sorry Aelfrun, but I worry about you. I wish you would take more rest.'

'Wynn makes sure I get all the rest I need, as you would know if you spent more time in the bower with me, and less time playing war games with your companions.'

'How pretty your new dress looks,' Tanwen said, quickly changing the subject. Aelfrun was easily distracted.

'Does it need a little something to set it off? An amber collar perhaps?'

'It is perfect just as it is.'

She smoothed the folds again. 'Well, Tanwen sourpuss, what of the hem?'

'As always, Aelfrun, your hem is perfectly placed.'

Aelfrun scowled. 'But are you to be trusted? If only Rowena was here. You have such little interest in important matters.'

'Then I'll call Mae. Let her reassure you.'

'No, no, don't. I can't bear her fussing about. I'll take your word for it.'

Tanwen struggled to hide her irritation. She was not in the mood for all this nonsense. Wynn had warned her that the queen would be anxious and moody as the birth approached but today, she was being just plain difficult.

Aelfrun buckled, placing a hand on her stomach.

'What is it, Aelfrun? Are you unwell?'

'Certainly not. A cramp, that's all.' She glanced in the mirror and tucked a stray strand of hair behind her ear. 'Send for our cloaks, please. I'll wear the green one with the ermine trim. It matches my dress perfectly and no one will recognise me beneath the hood.'

Tanwen rolled her eyes and silently asked Nethrus to restore her dear friend's wits. 'Aelfrun, you are the queen. Everybody will recognise you, especially in that sumptuous cloak.'

'Nonsense. They will be too busy with preparations for the festival to notice me.'

'I wish I had your confidence, Aelfrun.'

'A queen must always be confident. Waermund says I must appear confident at all times or the people will think we are weak, and that would never do. Now, our cloaks please, Tanwen. You know we have to be back before my husband returns from his hunting trip.'

'Please reconsider, Aelfrun, it's not too late to change your mind.'

'You promised you wouldn't nag if I allowed you to come along.' Aelfrun snapped, clearly losing patience, but Tanwen persisted, 'you will never find it without me. Please, Aelfrun, you don't understand these people. Anything could happen. What if they capture you?'

'Why would they do that?'

'To sacrifice you to the Earth Mother.'

'Have you lost your wits? I carry the atheling of Angeln, no man would dare hurt me.'

'These are not normal men. They are the Wardens of the Old Ways and they don't live by our rules.'

Aelfrun drew a determined breath. 'They are servants Tanwen, servants of a goddess maybe, but servants nevertheless.'

'Yes, and they drown anyone who discovers the hiding place of the Earth Mother's icon. Even the slaves who clean the wagon are drowned at the end of the festival.'

'Enough, Tanwen. You are trying to frighten me, and I won't have it. I've made up my mind. I don't care where they hide the wretched thing, I just want to be the first to see it. Besides, Waermund would never allow them to hurt me. Now, are you going to show me the way or am I to find it for myself?'

Tanwen muttered a curse.

'What was that? Aelfrun asked.

'Nothing, Aelfrun, just clearing my throat.' She should have known better than to tell Aelfrun she had discovered the hiding place of the sacred icon. Next time she would keep her mouth shut.

Their cloaks were in a chamber at the far end of the queen's hall. Tanwen decided it would be easier to collect them herself than to find a servant with enough wit to fetch the right ones, it was an opportunity to get a breath of air.

Outside, preparations were underway for the arrival of the ceremonial wagon. Bonfires had been lit and torches set along the streets ready to light its way. A sacrificed ox and boar were roasting over huge fires ready for the feast that would follow, and a timber hut had been erected to lock away all the iron objects in the town. No one would kill, hunt, take up arms or go to war while the Earth Mother was among them.

As Tanwen approached Thorndor's homestead, a feeling of homesickness washed over her. It was no longer her home, but they were always delighted to see her, and Tanwen knew Wynn would be hurt if she let the festival pass without visiting.

The hall was dimly lit by four burning torches and heated by a fire in the centre of the room. Clean rushes had been laid on the floor and Leofwine, an erstwhile beastling was heaping logs onto the fire, sending a slender stream of smoke to the high soot-blackened roof, while his wife set the table with wooden drinking vessels and pitchers of ale. Two giggling girls entered, one with tiny scissors to trim the wicks of the candles spread around the room, and the other with a small torch, to light them. The scissors would be locked in the hut before nightfall.

Thorndor was studying bones at a small table under the only arrow-slit in the room. His rune sticks were neatly stacked to his right. Tanwen hesitated. She had hoped to speak to Wynn. Could she confide in Thorndor? Aelfrun would be furious if she found out. But if something went wrong, Tanwen would have to face the king's wrath. Would Thorndor understand, or would he think her irrational, and berate her as a witless child? She deliberated for several heartbeats.

'Don't gawp, child. If you have something to say, out with it. Otherwise, be on your way and let an old man work in peace.'

Unperturbed by his grumpiness, Tanwen put her arms around her foster father's neck and greeted him with an affectionate peck on the cheek. 'You will never be old, Thorndor.'

He gave a wry smile. 'What brings you here today, daughter?'

She loved the way he called her daughter. She had never heard him say it to any of the other fosterlings. 'I came to see Wynn.'

'She's birthing the tanner's wife. You'll find them in the healing chamber.'

'I'm on an errand, to fetch cloaks. Aelfrun fancies a stroll.'

Thorndor pushed the bones aside and spread out the rune sticks. 'Slaves and servants run errands, Tanwen. You are neither.'

She ignored the reproach. 'What do the runes say, Thorndor? Are they favourable?'

'Favourable for whom?'

'Aelfrun.'

'Why shouldn't they be?' Thorndor's voice was sharp.

'She is near her time, I am concerned.' Tanwen hoped to sound nonchalant.

'See for yourself.' He indicated a chair. Tanwen sat and gazed at the sticks. 'Get on with it, girl. You haven't forgotten how, have you?'

'Not exactly, but …'

'Daughter, how are you going to pass on the Old Ways if you can't read the runes? You must make an effort to retain knowledge in that pretty little head of yours.'

Tanwen deliberately avoided the runes.

'They won't bite, child.'

'I'm sorry, I can't look.'

Thorndor stood. 'Why is that?'

'I'm afraid, Thorndor. She appears so …'

He examined his fingernails for several heartbeats, apparently uninterested in what she had to say. 'Well, speak up girl. How does she appear?'

Tears stung Tanwen's eyes. 'I don't know. Pale and wan and so delicate. Thorndor, sometimes, when I look at the queen, I fear she is ill. But no one else seems to notice and Aelfrun denies feeling unwell; accusing me of being spiteful and trying to spoil her pleasure.'

Thorndor walked to the fire. He warmed his hands and backside, paced around the hearth with his hands folded behind his back and returned to the table. 'How long has this been going on?'

'I'm not sure, three weeks - maybe four.'

'Can't you be more precise?'

She shook her head.

'Have you mentioned it to anyone?'

'Only to Aelfrun, and now you.'

'Wynn?'

'No. Wynn says she's as strong as an ox. But you must have heard the rumours about her size. The townsfolk say she is carrying a monster.'

'Bah. Foolish gossip. Ignore it.' He stared at her in silence for several moments. 'You worry too much, Tanwen, I'm sure the birth will go smoothly and Aelfrun will produce a normal, healthy, child.'

'And that's another thing, Aelfrun insists she is carrying a prince. She won't even consider the possibility of it being a princess. If she has a girl child, Thorndor, I don't know what she will do.'

'Don't fret yourself over things beyond your control. Like all mothers, she'll love her baby regardless of its sex and Waermund is a fair man, he'll give her another chance to produce a prince. Now, say no more of this to anyone, especially Aelfrun, she mustn't be disturbed so near her birthing time.'

'I've never mentioned my fears, only that she looks tired.'

'You are a good girl, Tanwen. Remember, I will always be near if you need me. Now, be on your way and enjoy your stroll with Aelfrun. I must prepare to greet the Earth Mother's entourage.'

***

'At last, Tanwen. I was beginning to think you'd been abducted by your wardens of the Old Ways.'

Aelfrun snatched her cloak and threw it around her shoulders. Tanwen fastened it in place with a jewelled brooch and eased the hood onto Aelfrun's head, being careful not to disturb her hair. As she did so her fingers accidentally brushed against Aelfrun's temple. Instinctively she withdrew them. Blood. She touched them. No, they were dry, it was her imagination. She began to sway, and the world was black. Her head and ears were buzzing with the effort of staying conscious. She must not pass out. *Please Nethrus ...*

'There, see, a perfect match.'

'Yes, Aelfrun, as usual, you are right.' Her voice sounded strangely distant and Aelfrun seemed to notice.

'What's the matter? Tanwen - Tanwen, are you ill?' Aelfrun's scared squawk jolted her back to reality.

'I'm fine. Sorry, just the excitement I expect.'

'Dear Tanwen, I work you too hard. Here, sit down until you feel better. I'll have Mae fetch some food.'

'No. I'll be all right. I'm sorry, I don't know what came over me. Let's leave, or we'll be too late.'

'Are you sure? I would hate you to faint while we are out, I'm in no condition to carry you home.'

Tanwen smiled. 'Yes, I'm certain. Thank you Aelfrun.'

Aelfrun gave Tanwen a quick hug. 'You silly duckling, what a fright, you gave me. You must take more care of yourself; how would I manage without you?'

The shortest route to the shore was over the stream, through the woods and across Anna's field, but Aelfrun's condition made this impossible. Instead, they bustled their way through the crowded streets. Aelfrun was right. The townsfolk were much too busy preparing for the coming of the icon to notice them. The smell of food filled the air. Women were hastily chopping, hacking and slicing at the roasted meat so that the job would be done, and the knives and axes locked away before the icon arrived. A group of maidens with flowers in their hair and wearing their best clothes were rehearsing their chant of welcome, and young warriors, deprived of their weapons, occupied themselves making torches to light the woods.

Tanwen and Aelfrun skirted the wood and walked along the edge of Anna's field. Aelfrun was pale and out of breath but refused to turn back, in her determination to watch the icon emerge from the island.

A hundred paces along the beach, over the first swell of the dunes, the small densely wooded island came into view. They settled themselves on the sand, behind the gorse and prepared for a long wait.

The sun was sinking and the water slowly retreating. A chill breeze was blowing in from the sea. Tanwen strained her eyes but could see no sign of life on the island.

'Perhaps I was wrong. Perhaps it's not tonight after all. Perhaps we should leave and return another day,' She suggested.

Aelfrun did not reply. She was becoming restless, shuffling about trying to make herself comfortable, but she did not complain.

'Let's go home, Aelfrun. If we wait much longer, we'll be walking back in the dark.'

'Don't fuss, Tanwen. There will be torches everywhere, to light our way.'

'But if we are not back before the king …'

A raft of shelduck took to the air. Something had disturbed them. Tanwen peered into the distance. 'Oh, look, they're coming.' She could see tiny figures rushing around. Four oxen emerged from the wood, dragging an enormous wagon behind them. The figures were goading, pulling, shoving and shouting at the animals, which stubbornly refused to cross the beach to the causeway.

'Oh!' Aelfrun cried out.

'Shush, Aelfrun. They mustn't know we're here.'

Aelfrun wriggled uneasily. 'Oh, Tanwen, I've got cramp. I've got to get up.'

Tanwen pursed her lips in exasperation. 'Aelfrun, please …'

But Aelfrun was on her feet. 'We must go, Tanwen. Oh, quickly, the prince is on his way.'

Not now. Surely not now. 'How do you know it's not just another cramp?'

'Because we expectant mothers know these things and because, ohh!' Aelfrun doubled up gripping her stomach. 'Please Tanwen …'

Tanwen glanced at the island. The wagon was on the causeway. They would be here soon. How was she going to get Aelfrun off the beach without being seen?

'If you're sure …'

'What else could it be? Ohhh.'

'You'll have to stay here while I fetch help.'

'I'm not staying here.' Aelfrun shrieked.

'You must. You can't make it back. I won't take long. I'll bring a horse and stretcher.'

'I am not staying here, and I will not be dragged home on a stretcher.'

Aelfrun began making her way along the beach. Tanwen heaved a sigh and reluctantly followed. Aelfrun was almost running. Every few paces she stopped, screwed up her face in pain and clutched her bulge, but she made no noise and was soon on her way again.

The wagon reached the shore as Tanwen and Aelfrun left the beach. Aelfrun stumbled and Tanwen rushed to her aid. 'That's it. You can't go any further. Stay here and I promise I'll be back with Wynn and the king before the pains get too bad.'

'Tanwen, I'm the Queen of Angeln. I will not give birth on the beach like, like …a common fishwife.'

Shocked by the sharpness of Aelfrun's tone, Tanwen helped her to her feet without argument. Aelfrun's face was purple with exertion. Stifling a scream, she clenched her teeth and squeezed Tanwen's hand until her nails pierced the flesh. Tanwen could not bear to see her in such pain. She tried to help by putting her arm around Aelfrun's waist, but Aelfrun shrugged her away.

They were about two hundred paces along the edge of the field when Aelfrun slipped, missed her footing and fell, banging her temple on a rock. She lay deathly still. Tanwen, transfixed, watched blood trickle from the open wound until a low moan startled her back to reality.

'Aelfrun. Aelfrun.' she cried, shaking the queen's shoulders, but there was no response. Blood dripped onto her fingers. She shuddered and wiped it on her tunic. What should she do? The wagon was making slow progress along the beach. Would the wardens help, or sacrifice them both to the Earth Mother?

'Aelfrun. Aelfrun. Please wake up.' Still no response. What could she do? The gods were testing her, and she did not know how to respond. If only Wynn were here.

'Aelfrun, can you hear me? I'm going to get you into the undergrowth, you'll be safe there while I go for help.'

She put her arms under Aelfrun's shoulders and tugged, but the queen barely budged. 'Please help me Aelfrun. Aelfrun, wake up. I can't do it if you don't help me.' Again, and again she pulled until her shoulders burned with the effort. The wagon was approaching. She searched Aelfrun's body for signs of life, but there was no movement, no sound, no breath. She crumpled into a heap and bit her lip until it bled. She had no choice, she must leave Aelfrun and go for help. *But what if the Wardens found the queen before she returned?*

A movement caught the corner of her eye. She dropped to her haunches and waited, motionless, holding her breath for several heartbeats to satisfy herself that there was no one lurking behind the bushes, but all was still. Cursing her imagination and trying to ignore a sudden urge to pee she glanced back at the wagon. It was almost here. Aelfrun groaned. Tanwen was sweating profusely. Aelfrun was alive, now she would have to get her into the bushes. Once more she put her arms under Aelfrun's shoulders and tugged.

She bumped into something. Not something, someone. She turned. He was tall and broad with dark eyes and long brown hair hanging loosely over his shoulders in the old way.

He prodded Tanwen with his spear. 'Move,' he said.

'I can't leave my friend.'

'Move - now.' But Tanwen stood firm. He pushed her with his spear, indicating that she was to climb aboard. Aelfrun moaned.

A rivulet of tears streamed down Tanwen's cheeks. 'Leave her alone, can't you see, my companion is with child, she needs help.'

'Did crying ever solve a problem, child?'

'Thorndor.' Tanwen threw her arms around her foster father. 'Oh Thorndor, I'm so glad you've come. I didn't know what to do. I didn't mean this to happen. It was an accident, she …'

Thorndor brushed her aside and sank to his knees over the lifeless body.

'Go,' he said, 'tell the king …'

But Tanwen was already running across the open field. She took the short cut through the wood. It was dark and she did not see the protruding root that turned her foot, threw her off balance and sent her tumbling into a nearby bush.

She tried to wriggle free, but her sleeve caught on an overhanging bramble and the more she struggled the more entangled it became. She tugged at it angrily then cried out in pain as the thorns pierced her flesh. Tears burned her eyes, but this was no time to cry. With a last determined effort, she blinked back her tears and braced herself for the pain as she wrenched her arm free.

She raced on: through the wood; sliding down the muddy slope and jumping the stream, grazing her knees as she scrambled, heart-pounding, up the steep bank on the other side. By the time she reached the top she was sweaty and panting, but she forced herself to carry on until, at last, she faced the guards at the open entrance chamber of the king's hall. She paused to catch her breath, squeezed her eyes shut to chase away the fear and darted between the guards into the hall.

The king and his hearth companions were drinking ale and recounting stories of the day's hunt. All eyes turned to Tanwen as she stumbled battered and bleeding into the room.

'The queen,' she gasped.

Waermund was on his feet in an instant. 'What's this?'

'Queen Aelfrun, my lord - she fell.' Tanwen's voice quivered.

'Where is she?' He demanded, striding to the door.

'In Anna's field, my lord, with Thorndor.'

'Fetch my horse,' he bellowed. 'And a stretcher.'

Outside the horse was already waiting. The king grabbed Tanwen's arm, swept her up behind him and galloped off, closely followed by a dozen warriors.

They had not gone far when they met Thorndor, walking in front of the ceremonial wagon. The icon was missing. In its place, surrounded by flowers, and guarded by six wardens of the Old Ways sat Aelfrun, deathly pale and still.

Townsfolk poured onto the street to watch their king lead the wagon bearing his queen to her hall. They muttered among themselves that it was an ill omen. The Earth Mother was displeased. The queen was ill and there would be no atheling for Angeln.

The king attempted to scoop Aelfrun into his arms, to carry her into the hall, but she resisted fiercely. 'Put me down, Waermund. I will not be carried like a weakling child.' She forced a smile, waved graciously to the crowd then quickly turned away to hide her grimace of pain. 'Our people must see their queen walk into the birthing chamber unaided, to deliver a lusty prince.'

Clinging to her husband's arm Aelfrun walked the few steps to the hall then turned and waved once again before entering.

Wynn was waiting inside, arms outstretched, to welcome the queen and prepare her for the birth, while the king, who was Wöden born and accustomed to the horrors of the battlefield, admitted that he was squeamish, relinquished his wife to the healer's care and beat a hasty retreat to the mead hall to avoid the gruesome mysteries of the birthing chamber.

The chamber was spotless. Fresh rushes covered the floor, the birthing chair had been scrubbed, the bed covered in clean white linen and at its side, a small, fur-lined basket was ready to take the baby. The customary fire was crackling in the centre of the chamber and Mae and Edyth were chatting while they steamed towels over a cauldron of boiling water.

'Pay attention,' Wynn barked at them. 'We won't have time to treat scalds.'

Tanwen had never been present at a birth and had no idea what was expected of her.

'Encourage her, talk to her and keep her comfortable,' Wynn advised.

Wondering how she could encourage Aelfrun to endure such pain, and if anyone could be comfortable under the circumstances, she found a bowl and cloth and stood by the birthing chair sponging blood from the queen's face. Aelfrun's contractions were almost back-to-back and with each one she strained so hard Tanwen was afraid her head would burst.

When Aelfrun stubbornly refused an infusion from Wyn, Tanwen stepped in and held the cup to her lips. 'Please drink it Aelfrun, it will soothe you and make the pain more bearable.'

But Aelfrun was adamant. 'I don't want your potion, take it away.' Her voice rose shrilly as another contraction arrived. 'I must be awake to greet the prince the moment he arrives.'

Tanwen said a silent prayer, *please Nethrus, let it be a boy child or the disappointment will kill her, and I couldn't bear it.*

'Then at least allow yourself to cry out, child,' Wynn said. 'I promise it will help ease the pain.'

For less than a heartbeat, Aelfrun's eyes flashed with anger instead of pain. 'The future King of Angeln will not enter the world to the sounds of pain and fear. Bring in the harpist and let her sweet music ease the pain.'

'Oh, Wynn, will this labour never end? How long can Aelfrun suffer such agony?' Tanwen whispered.

'Until the job is done.' Was the wise reply.

***

'A boy.' Wynn called out at last. 'It's done, it's all over. We have a fine atheling for Angeln.' She rubbed him vigorously with a warm towel and he screamed louder than a berserker.

'Did you ever see a finer prince?' Aelfrun asked, holding out her arms to take him. Tanwen's voice was tight with emotion. 'Never, Aelfrun.' She croaked. 'You have a fine son, thank Nethrus.'

Aelfrun held the baby for only a few heartbeats before fainting. Wynn immediately whisked him from his mother's arms and passed him to Mae. 'Wrap him in a towel and put him in the cradle. Tanwen, we need to get Aelfrun out of this chair. Are you ready?'

As they carefully lifted the unconscious queen, carried her across the chamber and gently lowered her onto the bed,

Tanwen marvelled at her foster mother's strength and confidence. She never fussed and nothing was beyond her capabilities. Perhaps there's more satisfaction in saving life than taking it, she thought, for the first time.

Aelfrun regained consciousness as Wynn was carrying the prince to the door. 'Where are you taking my son?' she shrieked.

'To his father,' Wynn replied.

'No. The king must come to him.' She held out her arms for the baby.

'No, Aelfrun, you're exhausted, you need rest.'

'Wynn, that is an order. The prince stays here, in my arms.'

Surprised at the unexpected authority in her tone, Wynn and Tanwen exchanged concerned glances.

'Mae, fetch the king. Edyth fetch refreshment for him, Tanwen, help me sit.' This was a new, confident Aelfrun, a true queen, and no one argued.

Tanwen propped Aelfrun into a sitting position with pillows, sponged her face and brushed her hair before Wynn passed the baby to his mother.

Aelfrun was smiling down at the prince cradled in her arms when the king blustered in. She unwrapped the towel and held the naked baby up to her husband. 'Behold your son, Prince Offa of Angeln; my bride-price, my lord husband,' she said.

The king took the baby and was visibly moved. 'No bride-price was ever asked for you, my love,' he replied.

'And for that I am truly grateful for, however small, it would have been beyond my father's reach and I would not be here, presenting the kindest, most generous of kings with an heir.'

The king's eyes glistened as he kissed Aelfrun's hand. 'He's a fine boy, my queen, a true prince, and I will be forever in your debt. And now, the people of Angeln are eager to meet their atheling.'

A few moments later, a cacophony of laughter, foot-stamping and shield banging emanated from the great hall. 'I think they are pleased,' Aelfrun whispered and then fainted.

***

Seven days later, Tanwen was at Aelfrun's bedside, holding her hand. The queen was so gravely ill she resembled a corpse. Her taut skin was a lifeless grey and her sunken eyes were circled with purple shadows. She lay flat against her pillow, struggling to draw breath and the effort seemed almost too much for her.

'See, doubting Tanwen, it was a prince after all.'

'Yes, Aelfrun, you were right as usual.'

'And I didn't cry out, not once.'

'You were very brave. I don't know how you did it. I am so proud of you.'

'I wanted to cry, I was so afraid, I thought I might die. I am cold. Why is it so cold in here?'

Tanwen rose to get another fur. 'Don't leave me Tanwen. Please don't leave me.'

'I'm not leaving you, silly puss. I'm just getting another fur to warm you.'

'I feel so weak and the pain is terrible, but I'm not afraid, Tanwen, it will be over soon.'

'Aelfrun, don't say such things.' Tanwen offered Aelfrun a pastinaca potion that Wynn had prepared earlier. Aelfrun sighed. 'Dearest Tanwen. My one true friend. I will drink it for you because I know that my doing so will bring you comfort. But first I want you to promise you will take care of my son.'

Tanwen smiled. 'You know I will. I'll be his favourite aunt.'

'Not an aunt, Tanwen - a mother.'

Tanwen frowned. 'Aelfrun?'

'More than any other child, the atheling will need a mother's love and guidance.'

Tanwen slowly realised what Aelfrun was saying.

'Promise me.'

'Oh, Aelfrun, you're not going to die. Wynn would never allow it. You're going to come through this.'

'Stop it, Tanwen. Don't lie to me. Wynn's spells and potions won't stop my lifeblood slipping away. Can't you see? I haven't much time left, and I must be sure that my son will be safe.'

'The king will not allow any harm to come to his son.'

Aelfrun smiled. 'Waermund is a good man. But what if he remarries and has more sons? Will a new wife stand idly by and allow another woman's child to become king? No, Tanwen, without a mother to protect his interests, the true atheling will be cast aside - usurped, possibly even murdered by his half-brothers.'

'Aelfrun, you're distraught. You've been through a terrible ordeal, but you are young and strong, you'll get over it in no time. You'll probably have another ten lusty sons.'

But Aelfrun was determined. 'My son is the rightful heir. Promise me you will see that he inherits the kingdom. Promise me, Tanwen.'

Tanwen was too exhausted to argue any further. 'Sweet Aelfrun, if it will make you feel better, I swear that if anything should happen to you, now or in the future, I will care for the prince as if he were my flesh and blood and that every day, I will remember his mother to him and teach him to love and be loved as she was.' She frowned, thoughtfully. 'Furthermore, I will do all I can to ensure he succeeds his father as the rightful

King of Angeln. Now, drink this and rest. I'll be right here by your side until you wake,' she added lightly.

Aelfrun drank the potion and lay back on her pillow. 'There's one more thing, Tanwen,' she said, fondling Tanwen's hand. 'When I die, I want Mae and Edyth to have their freedom. If it slips Waermund's memory, please remind him of his promise to provide them with an escort back to Waernas.'

Realising that there was little point in protesting, Tanwen smiled. 'Of course,' she said.

Wynn entered the room carrying the baby. 'What a boy. What lungs. Feel him kick. What strength.' She glanced at Aelfrun, thrust the baby into Tanwen's arms and put her hand to Aelfrun's brow. As Tanwen lowered the baby into the cradle, Aelfrun whispered. 'Let me hold my son.' Tanwen laid the precious, swaddled bundle, in her arms. Aelfrun smiled and stroked his face her eyes full of tears, then fell back exhausted.

'What did you give her?' Wynn asked Tanwen in a hushed voice.

'Only the pastinaca you prepared earlier.'

'How much blood is she losing?' Not waiting for a reply, Wynn lifted the cover to see for herself. 'That time is past, she needs confirma,' she whispered taking a tiny jar from her box. 'Fetch King Waermund.'

Tanwen shook her head. 'I promised not to leave her.'

'She's past knowing.'

'I'm staying.' Tanwen insisted.

Wynn tutted in exasperation but hurried out. Tanwen tenderly took the baby away from his mother and fell to her knees at Aelfrun's side, tears flooding her face.

She did not look up when Wynn returned with the king. She kissed Aelfrun's fingers.

'The queen is dead,' she said.

Five

Even at half a year old, Offa was a fractious sleeper, waking several times a night for a feed and tonight was no exception. He had cried for hours, refusing to be comforted.

Tanwen and his wet nurse, Leofrun, took it in turns to pace the floor with him. Rocking him, patting him and singing lullabies to no avail. Until at last, he could fight it no longer and fell into a restless, sobbing slumber. He was fast asleep now and no wonder, Tanwen mused; he must be exhausted.

She hated seeing him lying by his mother's empty bed surrounded by her belongings. The air seemed heavy with death, and memories of Aelfrun's pain endured here, but the king insisted upon it. Leofrun was sleeping on a trestle next to Offa's cradle. She was a gentle soul who had suffered the loss of her baby son the day before Aelfrun's death and was brought to the hall to feed and care for the prince.

Tanwen was absentmindedly finger-tracing the carved figures of the rune sticks, by candlelight. Dawn was breaking, and through the only arrow-slit in the chamber, she could see the stockade looming against the lightening sky. She wept, but the tears did not ease her sorrow. *I will keep Aelfrun's memory forever in my heart so that one day I can describe her to her son,* she vowed.

Mae, Edyth and Tanwen took the prince for a stroll to the harbour to watch the ships come in on the afternoon tide. The haven was bustling with shipwrights hammering, merchants chaffering and shouts from ships' masters to hurry stragglers aboard. There was always an air of anticipation on the shore as everyone waited to see what delights the merchants were unloading, but today the beach was buzzing with excitement and it seemed as if half the people of the town had turned out to watch one particular ship making its way into the bay.

It was Hengest and Horsa. Tanwen was ecstatic. She splashed into the water and at the same time Horsa leapt from the ship, scooped her up into his arms and swung her around laughing. They were soaked, waves sloshed around them and Mae and Edyth yelled at her to come back before she caught her death of cold, but she had never felt so warm and secure, and she wanted to stay in Horsa's arms forever.

The brothers had returned to offer Rowena in marriage to King Waermund for the second time. The prospect of a new queen to run the royal household and share the responsibility of caring for the prince was a happy one and Tanwen looked forward to seeing Rowena - she only hoped that this time they could become friends.

Horsa visited her every day and she never ceased to be amazed at his tenderness. He was fond of horses and lavished them with attention. He enjoyed the company of children and Tanwen had more than once found him relating stories of his adventures to a group of enraptured youngsters. And he loved Tanwen. He almost told her so one day in the herb patch.

She was with Offa, unwrapping his swaddling-clouts to let him kick freely when Horsa arrived. He was besotted with the baby. He waggled a grubby, calloused finger and the prince giggled, grabbed it and put it in his mouth to chew on.

Tanwen was immediately on her feet. 'I don't think Wynn would approve,' she said, removing the offending finger.

Horsa smiled and gently prodded Offa's ribs, 'I aim to have many of these.'

Tanwen laughed. 'You'll have to find a wife first.'

Horsa brushed her cheek with the back of his hand. She quickly turned away to hide her embarrassment and busied herself tidying Offa's clouts. Horsa took her hand and cradled it in both of his. 'Tanwen, please, there's something I've been longing to tell you.'

She felt the blood rush to her cheeks and cursed herself for behaving like a giddy girl.

'Since we last met, Hengest and I have been on an incredible voyage. We were sailing north across the narrow sea from Frisia when we came across a harbour where Frankish merchants were unloading their ships. They told us this place was called Britannia. A long road, as straight as a sword's edge, led us inland to a vast town. Instead of a stockade, it was surrounded by an impenetrable stone wall so high it must have been built by giants. They said it was built by the Romans in ancient times, but the Romans had left long ago, and the townsfolk named it Ypwinesfleot. Their king is a great warrior called Vortigern, who made us welcome and feasted us for three days in a great hall built of stone.'

Tanwen froze. *Vortigern.* The oddly familiar name sent an icy shiver down her spine. Her ears filled with the sound of rushing water until she feared her head would burst. His lips were moving, he was telling her something important, but she could not hear the words.

Her father's voice came to her. 'Get Gwynedd to Vortigern - get Gwynedd to Vortigern,' he repeated, over and over again. *Could this Britannia, and Ypwinesfleot be near Bryneich?*

Horsa was trembling with passion for this strange land. He paused, gazing into the distance as if he were seeing it in his mind's eye. 'It sounds like a wonderful place.' she said, hoping not to disturb the image.

He kissed her hand. 'It was the most beautiful place, Tanwen. I wish you could have seen it, so much space for everyone and the land green and fertile. I'll swear their sheep and cattle were twice the size of ours.'

Horsa's tales of other lands always brought excitement to Tanwen's unadventurous life. But this one was different and made her feel uncomfortable. 'Could this place be near Bryneich?' She asked.

Horsa shook his head. 'I've heard tell of no such place.' He took her into his arms. 'Come with me. Marry me, Tanwen. Be my wife and come and see Britannia for yourself. It's the perfect place to farm and raise a family. Once you've seen it you will never want to leave. We will have a good life there, sweet Tanwen, I know we will.'

Tanwen snatched her hands away and stared at him in astonishment. 'Marry you. Have you lost your wits?'

Noticeably taken aback by her reaction, Hengest's face dropped. 'I am sorry. I did not intend to offend you. I thought there was love between us - an understanding.'

'Oh, Hengest, I'm honoured, not offended. But I can't marry you and leave Prince Offa. I promised Aelfrun …'

'We will take Offa with us, Waermund will soon be looking for a foster home for him. I swear Ypwinesfleot must be the safest place on Earth to rear a prince.'

'The king would never allow us to take him on such a perilous journey. I'm sorry Horsa, but I must remain here in Angeln until the prince inherits his father's kingdom.'

They stood in silence for several moments then both spoke at once.

'Tanwen.'

'Horsa.'

They chuckled. Tanwen took Horsa's rough hands into her own and kissed them.

'Besides, dearest Horsa, you are a warrior and warriors do not settle down to raise families.'

'I will put that all behind me, Tanwen. I have had enough of killing and, with you at my side, I will never return to a warrior's ways. I have learned to love life and no longer want to destroy it.'

'And I wanted to be a shield-maiden, to raise an army against my brothers and spend some time with my blood father and mother before they make their journey to the otherworld, but now …'

'Now what Tanwen? What has changed?'

'Now there is Offa and I'm committed to his care until he is a man.'

'In fifteen years, when Offa is a man, you'll be too old to raise a sword, let alone an army.'

Tanwen's eyes flashed. 'King Waermund is much older now than I will be when I'm ready, and he's still the greatest warrior on earth.'

'King Waermund is a man.'

'And what's that to do with anything? I'm as good as any man and better than most with a sword.'

'Perhaps.'

'I know I am. But it's no use, Horsa. I will not break my promise to Aelfrun.'

'Then let us speak to Waermund, he can release you from your vow.'

'No, can't you see, if I leave Angeln Offa may never inherit the throne.'

'Nor can you guarantee his inheritance by staying here. It is for Wyrd to decide.'

'He will be king one day. I promised Aelfrun and I never break a promise.'

Horsa kissed her fingers and walked away.

She wanted him. She wanted to run after him put her arms around him and tell him how much she needed him, but she could not move, she could only stand and watch him leave. Her eyes filled with tears. Horsa was the kind of man that any woman would fall in love with, and he would make someone a fine husband. *But why did it have to be Britannia? If he truly loved her, he would marry her here, and raise a family in Angeln.*

She could not get Horsa out of her mind. She could still feel the pressure of his hand on hers and the warmth of his breath on her face. She called Leofrun to take care of the prince and went for a walk. At the harbour, the tang of sea spray, mingled with the odour of oiled leather and masculine sweat, reminded her of Horsa and she knew that just like her father's, Horsa's odour would be with her forever.

***

Some days later Tanwen was in the learning room with Thorndor when the king blustered his way in. Thorndor was teaching her how to unravel the mysteries of the weather and combine this knowledge with the lay of the land to decide whether conditions were favourable for the king to go into battle. Tanwen had little time for magic; to her mind, the only thing a king needed to know before going into battle, was whether he had enough warriors to defeat the enemy.

'To what do we owe this honour, Waermund?' Thorndor asked as he ushered the king into the main hall and called for ale. The door was left ajar, so Tanwen was able to see and hear them.

'These wretched matchmakers make my head spin. I'd sooner face a berserker than listen to their lies.' The king said.

Thorndor prodded the fire. 'Have they offered terms yet?'

'I'm not interested in terms. I won't re-marry. Offa is a big healthy boy, strong and likely to thrive. When I die there must not be any jealous half-brothers to be used against him by nobles greedy for power.' He paused for several heartbeats then sighed deeply. 'I am an old man, Thorndor, and I'm counting on you and Wynn to help me stay alive long enough to keep the land until Offa grows to manhood, can handle weapons and lead a war-band.'

Thorndor's voice was lighter. 'We are all old, Waermund, and getting older by the day, but if anyone can help you reach your goal, it's Wynn.'

Tanwen shivered. Rowena would not be coming back, Hengest and Horsa would return to Frisia and she would never see any of them again. She pulled her cloak around her and slipped out unseen.

Mae was crying when Tanwen returned to the queen's hall and neither sympathy nor harsh
words could console her.

Tanwen was not in the mood for this. 'Tell us what has upset you and we will try to help.' But the sobs grew louder.

Eventually, Tanwen lost patience. 'I can't stand any more of this noise. If you don't tell me what the problem is I can't help, so you may as well go to your chamber and sort it out for yourself.' But the wailing became so loud Tanwen feared her ears would pop.

'It's Lord Hengest,' Edyth volunteered. 'He has bought Mae.' There was an ear-piercing wail from Mae.

'Don't be ridiculous. Mae's no longer a slave to be bought or sold, she's a servant, free to do as she pleases.' Mae wailed again. 'Oh, do be quiet, Mae, or I'll lock you outside.'

The crying stopped almost immediately. 'It's true; I'm to go with Lord Hengest when he leaves for Frisia.'

Tanwen was baffled. 'Are you sure? No one has the right to sell you.'

Mae sniffed and wiped her eyes on her tunic sleeve. 'Lord Hengest asked the king if he could buy me as a gift for Lady Rowena.' She sniffed again and fixed her swollen eyes on Tanwen as if waiting for a reaction.

Tanwen rolled her eyes in exasperation. 'Presumably, Lady Rowena needs a maid servant, but who sold you to her father?

'No one sold me, when Lord Hengest asked the king, the king told him I was free and must make up my own mind.'

'And?'

'Then Lord Hengest told me that Lady Rowena had especially asked him to bring me back with him. She said I would be a constant reminder of her happy days here with Queen Aelfrun.'

'Did she?' Tanwen thought it unlikely. 'And you refused to go?'

'No, I told him I was honoured that the Lady Rowena remembered me, and I'd be pleased to serve her.'

Tanwen's heart dropped. How would she cope without Mae? 'Then why the tears?' She asked.

'Because I've heard such awful stories about Frisia. They say it's a land of marshes, where the earth is so low it is melting into the sea and people have to live on top of their middens to keep out of the mud. That's why Frisians spend all their time in ships, because they are drier than the land.'

'And all Frisians have webbed feet.' Edyth added with relish.

'That's nonsense, Edyth. You've both seen Rowena's feet, are they webbed?'

'No.' They admitted, exchanging guilty glances.

'Then all this other stuff is probably rubbish too. You won't know unless you go. Besides, you're a free woman, if you are unhappy you can always return. We'll miss you, Mae, but I'm sure you've made the right decision. There are no ladies here for you to serve.'

Mae wailed again. 'But I don't want to go, my place is here with Prince Offa and Edyth and - I want to serve you, Lady Tanwen.'

It was the first time Mae had called her Lady Tanwen. Although perfectly polite Mae and Edyth tried to avoid calling Tanwen by name, she imagined they saw her as an interloper and called her "the fosterling" behind her back. It seemed that at last they had accepted her.

'Why?' She asked.

'It's Lady Rowena.' Edyth answered for Mae. 'She's a strange one that Lady Rowena.

You never quite know where you are with her.'

Mae nodded in agreement. 'It's not for us to say, I expect she has her reasons, but she hardly ever speaks.'

'And she didn't like Queen Aelfrun,' Edyth piped in.

'Edyth!' Tanwen wondered why she was shocked she had often thought the same herself but had never mentioned it to anyone.

'Well, she always just - looked at Queen Aelfrun in that strange way, as if she was thinking - I'll get even with you for this.'

Tanwen had noticed that expression on Rowena's face when she learned that Aelfrun was pregnant. Now that she looked back on it, it made her shudder, but she could not have the servants talking about it.

'Then you must tell Lord Hengest that you have changed your mind.'

'I can't Lady Tanwen - what if he gets angry and tells the king and the king makes me go - or sends me back to Waernas?'

Tanwen smiled with relief, 'would you like me to speak to him?'

'Oh, would you Lady Tanwen? I'd be so grateful if you would.'

Tanwen was suddenly aware of how little she knew about the two women facing her. Mae was middle-aged, possibly twenty-two or twenty-three winters old, plain-featured with honey-coloured hair, which was always neatly tied in one long thick plait. Edyth was nearer Aelfrun's age, with a pretty face, pointed chin and hazel eyes. Her glorious coppery-gold hair was usually worn in two plaits, one over each shoulder, but today it hung loose with green braid circling her crown and hanging down either side of her face. They came from Waernas with Aelfrun, and Tanwen had never taken much notice of them, but from today she would make it her business to get to know every servant in the queen's hall.

'How long did you serve Queen Aelfrun?' She asked Mae.

'All her life, Lady Tanwen. Our mother was her wet nurse. I miss her terribly.'

Tanwen was aghast. *Our mother. They are sisters and I had no idea.* 'We all miss her, Mae, but we have to move on, and nothing would please her, and me, more than to have you stay here forever to care for the prince and keep the rest of us in order. I'll speak to Lord Hengest tonight, on one condition.'

'Oh, anything, Lady Tanwen, anything you say.'

'Please stop calling me Lady Tanwen. I am no more a lady than you and Edyth, just plain Tanwen will do.'

'Yes, yes, of course, Tanwen.'

***

It was Haligmonath, the "Holy Month" when thanks were given for the fruits of the haerfest and the safe return of the ships from the sea. It was almost a year since Aelfrun's death and Tanwen missed her every day. To help her better care for the prince she continued to live in the queen's hall. Mae and Edyth were still with her and had been joined by Leofrun, the wet nurse and Hilde, the nurse. Offa was thriving. He was a fine, lusty boy and everyone loved him. The king visited him daily and even Thorndor called in once or twice a week to admire him.

The Myrging raids had ceased for the winter and the king and his companions spent more and more of their time hunting. Sometimes they were away for several days at a time and Thorndor hunted with them. He left strict instructions that Tanwen was to persevere with her learning in his absence by practising Latin and word-craft and studying the runes and the Old Ways every day. She was to help Wynn in the healing chamber whenever necessary and to supervise the care of the baby prince at all times. Other than that, she was free to do as she pleased. 'A slave would have more free time,' she complained to Mae.

After their argument on the day Offa was born, Tanwen did not see Hunlaf again until he turned up unexpectedly at the hall. He was a true warrior now taller and broader than she remembered with a covering of fine golden down on his chin. He was carrying a red and white shield on his back and a sword and hand-seaxe on his belt. He brought her a gift, a dagger, its hilt decorated with green enamel fused onto crisscrossed gold wires.

'It's stunning, Hunlaf,' she said slashing it through the air to test its balance. 'It's perfect. It could have been made for me, where did you get it?'

'I bought it from a Geat merchant.'

'I love it. Thank you, I'll treasure it always. But why have you brought me such an expensive gift?'

'Because I'd like us to be friends again, Tanwen. You are the most irritating person on earth but I've missed you, and our sparring sessions.'

Tanwen laughed. 'I doubt if my sparring will be up to your standard any longer.'

'Then perhaps we should get you back into training as soon as possible.'

'And what would Arild have to say about that?'

'Arild has started weapon-training in earnest. He has sparring partners of his own now and won't trouble us. What do you say, Tanwen? Shall we meet on the hill tomorrow?'

Tanwen could barely conceal her excitement. She was so happy she could have kissed him. She had been stuck in the hall for ages and she was beginning to take an interest in spinning and needlework. 'Just try to stop me. But I can't leave the prince, he will have to come too.'

Hunlaf grinned. 'Who am I to object to the company of a prince?'

Hilde came along to look after the prince, and he played happily at her feet while Tanwen and Hunlaf practised their moves. Tanwen was out of condition, her footwork was terrible, and her shoulder ached from the effort of wielding a sword, but worst of all she found herself accepting instruction from Hunlaf.

Six

Hunlaf struck Tanwen with the pommel of his single stick, at the same time grabbing her hilt to prevent a strike. He followed through with a slash and Tanwen leaned back to avoid it. As she did so she glanced up into a nearby tree and spotted a warrior hiding on a branch. She dropped her weapon, pointed into the tree, and yelled 'Myrgings. Run for it.'

Hilde instantly scooped up the prince and ran to raise the alarm. The Myrging dropped from the tree and wrestled Hunlaf to the ground. Another grabbed Tanwen from behind. He clasped one hand over her mouth and held a dagger to her throat with the other. Hunlaf was on his feet, he thrust his opponent off, and he lay a few feet away momentarily stunned. Two more Myrging's came from nowhere. They charged at Hunlaf, he grabbed them both and banged their heads together, one fell away moaning, but the other grappled him to the ground. They rolled around, grunting and swearing at each other until Hunlaf managed to get back on his feet. He lifted the Myrging by the throat and hurled him against a tree, he fell face down with his neck twisted.

The first Myrging was back in the fray. He flung himself at Hunlaf knocking him to the ground, then sat on him while his companion tied his hands and feet.

Their leader came out of the wood on horseback, followed by two men on foot. One of the men holding Hunlaf pointed to the prostrate figure. He drew his hand across his throat and clacked, indicating a broken neck. The leader curled his lip in disgust.

Hunlaf's attackers lifted their dead companion and put him over the back of a horse. The two new men sauntered over to Tanwen. One came so close she managed to knee him, aiming for his groin. She thought she had missed the spot, but he buckled and the man holding her winced, sucking air through his teeth. Realising that the Myrging she kneed had lost concentration she bit deep into his fingers. His unharmed companion dealt a hefty blow to her head and she passed out.

When she regained consciousness, she was gagged and lying across the back of the horse, alongside the dead Myrging. Two more Myrgings were approaching with a fully laden wain. One addressed the leader. 'Lord Halfdane, we have taken grain, ale and oil and left them four wardens with headaches and broken teeth. Hagar says there a few sheep and a couple of scrawny oxen down there, but we'll be seen before we reach them. Shall we …?'

'No, Waermund's men are on the way, let's get out of here, we've done enough damage for one day.' They tossed Hunlaf, who was also gagged, into the cart and made a hasty retreat.

Tanwen and Hunlaf were taken to a hunting lodge several miles away. Two Myrgings carefully laid the dead man on the ground and covered him with a blanket. Another two pulled Tanwen off the horse before turning their attention to Hunlaf. They dragged him from the cart and propped him next to Tanwen. He head-butted one of the men who staggered around dazed, the other one brought the back of his hand across Hunlaf's face. Blood spurted from his nose.

The leader approached Hunlaf and Tanwen noticed he kept a safe distance. 'Mmm. I like a man who puts up a fight.' He spoke with a low drawl and without warning, he punched

Hunlaf in the gut knocking him backwards, almost causing the Myrgings holding him to lose their footing. He then pointed to the dead warrior. 'But you'll pay for this, English dog.'

He removed Tanwen's gag and looked her up and down making her flesh creep. 'Very nice,' he said, brushing her cheek with the back of his hand. She hissed. He grabbed her hair and allowed it to run through his fingers. His eyes rested on her amulet. 'And what have we here? Beau-ti-ful. Let me look after it for you, sweetheart. I'd hate you to lose it while we are - otherwise occupied. He seized it and squealed. He immediately dropped it and withdrew his hand crying out in pain. 'Well, well,' he said when he recovered his composure. It seems we have a witch in our midst.' He sneered at Hunlaf. 'A witch, a warrior and a warlord, it promises to be a very interesting night.'

His men were mumbling amongst themselves. The one holding Tanwen loosened his grip. She jerked free and glared at him, making a low, growling sound.

'Get hold of her.' Halfdane shouted at him.

'I'm not holding on to any witch.' He retorted.

'Do I have to do everything myself?' Halfdane moved towards her. She spat at him, stared into his eyes and spoke slowly through clenched teeth. 'Lay one finger on either of us and I'll turn your manhood into dust and grind it into the ground to feed the worms.'

He spun away. 'Tie and gag the witch. If she utters one word cut out her tongue. I'll have no more of her spell casting.' Tanwen growled and the Myrging ran off.

'Call yourselves warriors?' Halfdane bellowed. He took one step forward. Tanwen glared at him and hissed, he raised his hand to slap her.

'I'd be careful if I were you, that's Thorndor's daughter you're messing with.' Hunlaf warned him.

The hunting lodge was one large room. It was a dark, dank, airless space and Tanwen and Hunlaf were forced to sit on filthy rushes that smelled as if they had not been changed in years. The remains of partly eaten animals were strewn around a smouldering fire. One of the Myrgings tossed a lump of something resembling sheep fat onto the embers, allowed it to sizzle for a while, then piled damp logs on top of it. Its hissing and spitting did not appear to bother them, they settled down with what was left of the food and a barrel of ale to discuss their day's work.

The nauseating stench of burning logs, rancid meat and stale ale turned Tanwen's stomach and she began to retch. Halfdane removed her gag. 'One word from you and you are dog meat - understand?' She nodded.

Talk gradually turned to singing and the singing to raucous laughter as the ale began to have an effect and, one by one, the warriors began snoring, only Halfdane was left awake.

He swaggered towards Tanwen and Hunlaf, dagger in hand, ''sss fun time,' he slurred then collapsed over their legs.

'Now what do we do?' Tanwen asked.

'You could cast a spell.' Hunlaf suggested, and they both laughed.

Tanwen began pushing and shoving Halfdane with her knees and feet to get him off her. He woke up in a drunken daze and screwed up his face as if trying to bring her into focus.

'Don't shhtruggle, witch - it won't hurt if you don't shhtruggle.'

Tanwen froze. Her mind flashed back to that awful day in the boat, and she heard her brother, Rhufon, calling 'Don't struggle, Gwynedd. You'll be all right if you don't struggle.' And she screamed and screamed and screamed.

The bleary-eyed Myrgings were on their feet in an instant, the door burst open and Waermund's men charged in. There was no killing. Waermund would not take advantage of their drunken state. He had them bound, stole their weapons and horses, reclaimed his stolen goods and left it to Wyrd to determine their fate.

They travelled slowly, hampered by the dark and the wagon. The king apologised for not coming to their assistance sooner. He explained he was afraid that Tanwen and Hunlaf would be hurt if he closed in, so they followed at a safe distance ready to attack at the first sign of trouble. They hid in bushes waiting for the cover of darkness but acted the moment they heard Tanwen's scream.

Tanwen, embarrassed and furious with herself for screaming, apologised to the king.

'Think nothing of it Tanwen,' he said. 'Any woman would have done the same under the circumstances.'

That was no consolation. Poor Aelfrun, who had never raised a hand to anyone, had endured the horrors of childbirth without a sound, yet she, who dreamed of leading men into battle had screamed at nothing more than a distant memory.

***

Dawn was breaking by the time they reached the forest, and the hounds came across a boar snuffling about among the fallen leaves. This was not a hunting party, but his men were eager for a kill and the king agreed the opportunity was too good to miss.

Nine men spread out in a ring to block the beast's escape and the other three were sent in as beaters. The king ordered Tanwen and Hunlaf to get well back before the beaters flushed the beast out. But they were too slow. The boar tried to dash through the ring of men. Despite its great bulk it was amazingly fast and brought down a beater before anyone was quick enough to do anything about it.

It panicked and turned abruptly, slashing open the foreleg of the king's horse with its tusk. The horse screamed, then reared, and the king fell.

The hounds were baying, the startled boar turned to face them. The king was lying in its path. Hunlaf jumped from his horse, grabbed the king's spear and stood in front of him holding the spear at a downward angle. The boar quivered and flattened its ears to its head, signalling its intention to charge.

Hunlaf stood his ground. The boar rushed at him impaling itself on the spear. It squealed and tried to shake itself free but Hunlaf held firm. The ring of men closed in. Unable to escape, the boar ran round and round in a frenzy, dragging Hunlaf with him. Hunlaf fell and the boar was on him. Without dismounting one of the men drove his sword into the boar's throat. In no time the hounds were tearing at its hindquarters and the king's men moved in for the kill.

Tanwen covered her eyes with her fingers and did not see the end. When the thrashing, tearing, yapping and swearing noises ceased she let them drop. The king was safe, and on his feet, but Hunlaf had been laid out on the ground, the beast's tusk had gutted him.

The king knelt, closed Hunlaf's eyes and put the bloodied sword in his hand. 'He died a true warrior,' he said, and Tanwen turned away to hide her tears.

Seven

Tanwen was dressing after an early morning swim in the pond when she heard the murmur of voices and the crunching of fallen leaves underfoot. Not sure who it might be she decided to remain out of sight behind the bushes until they had passed. As they approached, she recognised the voices of King Waermund and Thorndor.

'The wretched Myrgings are becoming more of a nuisance every day. I lost another four men to them yesterday,' the king complained.

Thorndor agreed. 'They are a troublesome tribe to have over the border.'

'Now that they have the Saxons behind them, they think they can do as they please.'

'So, the stories are true then, they've taken King Witta as their overlord?' Thorndor asked.

'Only when it suits them. They do as they please most of the time. They're an evil lot, restless and rebellious. Witta may be young and foolhardy but at least he always follows the warrior's code. I can't understand why he tolerates them. They shouldn't even be raiding at this time of year, yet they come back day after day.'

'Witta wouldn't be foolish enough to start a war with us.'

'No, but he will allow his underlings to probe and pick at our defences until they find a weakness.'

'Then King Witta will move in, finish us off and push the underlings aside to get to our treasure-hoard,' Thorndor mused.

'My men are itching to get at Halfdane after his treatment of Tanwen and Hunlaf, I wouldn't like to be in his shoes when they catch up with him.'

'He'll get what he deserves.'

There was a long pause before the king spoke in a hushed tone, 'Freawine has agreed to take the boy; he leaves at first light.'

'A wise move. The atheling's safety is paramount,' Thorndor replied.

Their lowered voices were a clear indication that they did not wish to be overheard. Tanwen wondered if she should reveal herself and risk the king's anger or lie low until they had passed.

'He's a good man, a fierce warrior with two sturdy sons and a goodly wife. Who better to raise the atheling of Angeln?'

'Who indeed, Waermund?'

'His sons will help protect Offa during his childhood, then when he is a man, they will fight at his side.'

Tanwen was dismayed. Offa sent away to live with strangers, Aelfrun would never have allowed it.

'There is also a daughter. The hint of a betrothal may have swayed him. I'm sending an escort of twenty men, they will stay along with his nurses,' the king continued, 'but he needs more, a companion, someone to keep Angeln alive in his memory and to school him in the Old Ways.'

'A lot to ask, Waermund.'

'True. Few could fill the role. But I do have someone in mind.' The king stirred the bush with his sword. 'Why don't you join us Tanwen?'

Flushed with the embarrassment of being discovered and trembling with fear because she had overheard their private conversation, Tanwen scrambled through the bushes and stood before King Waermund and Thorndor.

'Who pays you enough to spy on your king?' Waermund asked, pointing the tip of his sword at Tanwen's chest.

'No one my lord king, I swear.' She looked to Thorndor for support, but he was staring at her through narrowed eyes, his fingers covering his mouth, in that studious pose she had seen so often when he was considering a problem. 'I had been bathing and just finished dressing when I heard you approaching.'

'And you lay in wait to eavesdrop.'

'No, my lord.' Tanwen said, regaining her composure. 'When I realised you were engaged in a private conversation, I tried to keep a discreet distance. But you came so close I was unable to move without being seen, so I thought it prudent to remain out of sight until you moved on.'

The king raised an eyebrow.

'So prudent you didn't hear a word, I dare say,' Thorndor said accusingly.

Her head dropped. She had long since learned that there was no point in lying to Thorndor. He knew everything and could even read her mind. 'No, my lords, I heard it all.' She confessed nervously.

The King and Thorndor exchanged a solemn glance and then, as if to a signal, they both let out a guffaw of laughter. It was the first time she had heard the king laugh and although she had no idea what he found so amusing the deep hearty roar warmed her heart and she found herself smiling.

'Prudent.' The king repeated when the laughter subsided, 'it is a fortunate king who finds a prudent companion for his only son. Prepare for a long journey, Tanwen. You leave at dawn,' he said as he walked away.

Tanwen was horrified. 'He doesn't mean it, Thorndor, does he?'

'A king always means what he says - when he says it.'

'He can't send me away. I haven't done anything wrong. I wasn't eavesdropping, I swear it. I tried to get out of earshot so I wouldn't hear any more of your conversation.'

'A king can do whatever he chooses, but a girl must do as she's told.'

'Speak to him please, Thorndor. He'll listen to you. I couldn't bear to be parted from you and Wynn.' *And the time for raising my army is almost upon me.*

'Your departure will leave a void in our lives that will never be filled. But leaving us is not what truly disturbs you, daughter. The time has come for you to consider past promises and future aspirations. Waermund is a fair man. He will not force you to go.'

Tanwen threw her arms around the old man's neck, 'Oh, Thorndor, you've both been so good to me I don't know how…'

Thorndor patted her shoulder. 'Shush child, time is short. Sit here quietly and collect your thoughts. You have an important decision to make, and the decision must be yours alone.' He kissed her brow set off after the king.

***

'I'm not surprised Waermund is sending the prince to Freawine. I've been expecting it, we've all been expecting it.' Wynn scrubbed mercilessly at a protesting child in the bath tub.

'What does surprise me,' she continued, pouring water over the unfortunate girl's head causing her to splutter and gasp for air, 'is that Thorndor is allowing you to accompany him.' She helped the girl from the tub and wrapped her in a warm towel then signalled to two nearby beastlings to remove the tub and asked them to burn the rags the child had been wearing.

'Thorndor said the choice was mine. I could have refused.' Tanwen replied. 'But I promised Aelfrun I would look after the prince as if he were my own. I can't do that if he goes to live with Lord Freawine and I stay in Angeln, can I?'

Wynn dismissed the problem with a flutter of her fingers. 'A silly childhood promise, that's all. No one would hold you to it. I doubt if anyone even knows about it.'

'I know about it.' Bitten back tears burned her eyes. 'And you taught me the importance of keeping my word.'

'And what will you be when you get there, a nurse, a servant?' Wynn shook her head. 'No, it won't do Tanwen, you weren't brought up to be a servant. We had such high hopes for you, Thorndor and I. He has said on many occasions what a fine handmaiden you would make for The Lady - a priestess even.'

'I'll be no servant or handmaiden. I'm going to be a shield-maiden, a great warrior.'

'A shield-maiden. Has the girl lost her wits? A shield-maiden indeed, whatever next. I've never heard such foolishness. Thorndor would never agree. And neither would I.'

'It makes little difference now that the Wyrd sisters have done their work and woven this for me. I'm to be a companion to the atheling of Angeln, and I'll do the job well. I'll honour my promise to his mother to teach him the Old Ways and word-craft and I'll make him a proud and worthy king.'

The little girl let out a piercing scream as her clothes were about to be thrown onto the fire.

'Fine words indeed.' Wynn retorted. But her ill-humour was instantly dispelled as she wrapped her arms around the child. 'There, there dear. Don't fret. You don't want those nasty smelly clothes. Look, Tanwen has some nice new ones ready for you.'

Tanwen shrugged off a pang of jealousy as she recalled the warmth that emanated from those plump arms. She did not want to quarrel with Wynn, not now. She wanted tonight to be special. She was too old to be embraced like the interloper but oh, how she longed for the comfort of her foster mother's bosom.

She held up a linen under tunic and a blue homespun dress for the child's inspection.

'Take it away. I don't want your horrible homespun. I want my dress, the one mama made for me.'

She spat at Tanwen. Fortunately, her aim was short, and the spittle missed its target. Tanwen was in no mood to deal with the tantrums of an ungrateful usurper and instinctively raised her hand to retaliate, but she glimpsed Wynn's tight-lipped expression and dropped it. Wynn nodded her approval, signalled not to burn the clothes and turned her attention to the girl.

'You, my darling, are very welcome to share our home. Your fleas and lice, however, are not. Therefore, I'm afraid you will have to decide whether you wish to remain here, accept our standards of cleanliness and become part of our family, or to live alone skulking in the forest with the wild animals, begging and scrounging for scraps of food and clothing. The choice is yours.'

The girl pouted and kicked sullenly at the floor rushes. 'Come along, we haven't got all day. What will it be, a roof over your head and all the food you can eat, or ...?'

Without looking up the girl snatched the clothes from Tanwen.

Always delighted to get her way without too great a confrontation, Wynn beamed and embraced the child. 'Good girl, a wise choice. Just look at Tanwen, barely a whisker's width taller than you when she came to us.' Her eyes glazed and an unfamiliar sadness crept into her voice as she slowly helped the girl into the dress. 'There she was, abandoned on the beach. And how she cried. Day and night, night and day. Wouldn't eat, wouldn't sleep. Inconsolable. We didn't know what would become of her.' She suddenly shook her head as if to cast out the memory then kissed Tanwen's brow before adding, 'every day we thank Nethrus for bringing her safely to Angeln.

'I also thank The Lady. For if it hadn't been for you, Wynn, I probably would have died or become one of the wildwood urchins,' she added with emphasis, as a warning to the child.

Wynn spoke to the little girl. 'Poor Tanwen, it's a wonder she survived. And now here she is, a grown woman, off to the southern marches to educate our future king without as much as a second thought for the folk who reared her as if she were their own flesh and blood.'

Her eyes met Tanwen's and lingered for a heartbeat. Was Tanwen mistaken or did her foster mother's lip quiver?

'How proud of her we are, and how sad we will be to see her go.' Wynn sighed, gently pushing the girl aside and stretching out her arms to Tanwen. 'But she goes with our blessing, cloaked in our love and we wish her well.'

Tanwen rushed to her embrace, relief washing over her like a wave of warm water. The tears she had fought for so long finally flooded her eyes and overflowed.

'Oh, Wynn, I'm going to miss you and Thorndor so much and when Offa is grown to manhood and has no further need of me, I'll come back to see you before I go searching for my family. I promise.'

'Nonsense. I've already seen forty winters; do you really think I'll be here when you return in another fourteen? No, Tanwen, I'll be long gone. Think of me often my love but don't waste precious time returning to Angeln. When Offa no longer needs you, follow your dream, go back to your homeland and find your family.'

'Don't say such things. You'll still be here. You will always be here. The Lady will protect you. She needs you to care for the sick and the orphans. Who else can do her work?'

'You can, my darling, Thorndor and I have trained you well, and perhaps you will, in your new home. Who knows? Perhaps this is Wryd's doing. Perhaps Freawine and his lady need your skills more than we do.'

While the town still slept: Tanwen; Prince Offa, Leofrun, Hilde, Mae and Edyth, clad in heavy cloth and furs to ward off the cold, were assembled in the great hall ready for the perilous journey to the home of Lord Freawine. Only the king, Thorndor and Wynn came to see them off.

King Waermund brought parting gifts; for the little prince a rare white bear fur, a finely spun woollen blanket and a gold brooch to fasten it. For each of the nurses and servants a woollen cloak and a silver pin but for Tanwen, nothing. She coughed hoping to draw his attention to the oversight, but the king seemed not to notice. Even Thorndor and Wynn were oblivious.

Tanwen was peeved. She was sacrificing her ambitions to care for the king's son, yet she was the only one who had not received a gift from him.

Wynn and Thorndor hugged her, said how much they would miss her and warned her to mind her manners in her new home. They had each brought her a gift. Wynn had made her a leather belt finely engraved with interlaced animal patterns to carry Arild's dagger. Tanwen stared at it.

'It's all right dear, it is stag hide,' Wynn said patting her hand. Tanwen sighed with relief and threw her arms around Wynn's neck. 'I'm so sorry, Wynn. I just couldn't have borne it if it had been from that despicable boar.'

Thorndor gave her a polished yew box containing a complete set of carved rune sticks. 'Use them wisely daughter and they will serve you well,' he said.

The king kissed his son, wished them all well and departed. He had gone no more than a dozen paces when he stopped and turned back. 'Oh, Tanwen, I almost forgot.' As he spoke a groom came from behind the wagon, leading Starlight. 'There is no one to look after Aelfrun's mare. Could you find it in your heart to care for her, as well as my son?'

Tanwen thought her heart would burst. 'Oh, yes Lord King,' were the only words she could find.

Mae, Edyth, Hilde and Leofrun climbed into the wagon. Within a heartbeat, they were shrieking with delight. Every need and comfort had been carefully considered and provided for. The interior of the wagon was draped with embroideries and the floor was thickly carpeted. All around the edge were wooden pallets topped with straw-filled mattresses and cushions covered in embroidered cloth. And wolf, fox and badger furs were scattered around to provide warmth. They revelled in the prospect of five days with nothing to do but care for the young prince and enjoy the sumptuousness of the wagon.

At the first glimmer of light, the great wheels of the wagon turned, and they set off, accompanied by twenty of King

Waermund's most trusted guards led by Hafoc. Tanwen wanted to ride Starlight but Hafoc insisted that she stay in the wagon until they reached the open plain in case of a Myrging ambush.

**

The rain began as soon as they passed through the stockade, a fine drizzle at first becoming steadily heavier until it fell like water over a weir.

They cut through the eastern tip of the forest and followed the meandering Eider south to its confluence with the Schwale, then turned west for a short distance and crossed the Schwale at a narrower point. After five gruelling days, they reached the plains and still it rained.

Offa wanted to play outside and was becoming fractious. Leofrun missed her husband and wanted to go home. Hilde wailed that the world was about to end and Mae and Edyth muttered constantly that it was an omen, and they should turn back.

Tanwen yelled at them to shut up, or she would throw them all out of the wagon and leave them to the wolves. Even the guards were miserable, they wanted to hunt but could not because the rain would soften their bowstrings.

On several occasions, the wagon became stuck in the mud and the passengers had to alight and trudge through the sludge in driving rain while the men tugged and pushed the wagon to drier ground. The weather worsened and the road became a quagmire. At one point it was flooded so badly Tanwen was sure they would need to find an alternative route, but Hafoc's experience shone through. He took the reins and urged the oxen forward, driving the wagon through the water without mishap.

At last, on the sixth day, the rain stopped but the sky was heavily overcast and a thick grey mist limited visibility to a wagon's length. Tanwen wondered how they could possibly find their way across the soggy plain without the sun to guide them, but once again Hafoc's skill won the day, and for that Tanwen thanked him and said she would be forever in his debt.

They crossed the Stör in glorious sunshine in the early evening of day seven and set up camp on the grassy slope. Offa toddled around on the sandy riverbank, happily collecting stones and picking flowers to give to anyone who held out a hand to accept them. The water was too cold, too deep and too fast for them to paddle or bathe in, but two of the guards managed to spear enough fish for the evening meal and for the first time since leaving home they would sit around a campfire and eat freshly cooked food.

While supper preparations were underway two footsore strangers hobbled into camp, one leading an overloaded ass on a rope. Tanwen could see by its overgrown feet and plodding shuffling gait that the animal was in dire need of rest. The men fared little better. Their shoes were in tatters and their long, homespun garments were stiff with dust and grime. Their faces were weather-beaten, and their short dark hair clung to their heads in tight curls.

All three looked as if they had not eaten for days. They introduced themselves as Vodine and Cadoc from a place called Dumnonia and said they were not beggars but pilgrims, whatever that was, who had travelled on foot from Rome to spread the word of their great Lord and Redeemer. Tanwen longed to ask why such a great lord had not provided them with better shoes and transport but held her tongue.

Despite their hunger and fatigue, their eyes were lively and their smiles warm and friendly. They enthusiastically accepted Tanwen's invitation to supper, welcomed Hafoc's offer of water and sweet hay for the ass and promised to pray for eternal grace for the guard who volunteered to trim its feet and groom it.

Mae offered them blankets to cover their bodies while Edyth washed their clothes. They thanked her for her kindness but insisted there was no need as their ass carried clean robes. They would bathe and wash their soiled garments in the river while supper was being cooked.

While they feasted on fish, flatbread and apples roasted over the fire, the pilgrims told them stories of their great Lord and Redeemer, who lived in the sky and somehow managed to be himself, his own son, a white dove and a lamb all at the same time.

'A shape-shifter,' Tanwen suggested, but Vodine silenced her with a frown. The Sky God's son was a carpenter or a shepherd who lived on earth with his mother and foster father and he performed miracles, like making the blind see, making cripples walk and raising his friends from the dead.

Tanwen thought miracles sounded suspiciously like magic tricks but not wanting to offend her guests she kept her thoughts to herself.

One of The Sky God's favourite miracles was to allow the pilgrims to charm bread and wine into his own body and blood. She listened intently to Vodine and Cadoc chanting over the bread and wine without admitting she understood Latin, and she stored the spell in her memory for future reference. But when she tried it the spell did not work. In the end, it was still bread and wine. Nevertheless, the pilgrims scoffed it down and seemed to enjoy it.

'Why do you call your great lord a redeemer?' Edyth asked.

'Because Our Lord, Jesus Christ, sacrificed his own life on the cross to pay the ransom for our sins,' Cadoc explained.

'Who did he pay the ransom to?' Tanwen wanted to know.

'To God, His Father in Heaven,' was the reply.

She thought this was a very odd thing to do and found the whole story confusing. 'Oh,' she said, unable to think of anything else to say, then quickly changed the subject. 'What is a pilgrim, exactly?'

Vodine smiled. 'A pilgrim is someone who goes on a journey to a holy place to prove his devotion to God,' he told her.

'And does the Great Sky God reward you for this?'

Vodine smiled. 'The only earthly reward is the gift of God's grace, but the ultimate reward, the one we all strive for, is everlasting life in Heaven. Brother Cadoc has already made one pilgrimage to Jerusalem and this was his third to Rome. He is a man of great sanctity and is almost assured of a place with the Heavenly Father.'

Cadoc blushed. 'Brother Vodine is much too generous in his praise,' he said with his head lowered. 'My duty is to serve the One True God.'

Tanwen wondered what Woden, Thor and Tiw would have to say about that. 'Have you been to Bryneich?' She asked attempting to sound nonchalant.

Cadoc frowned. 'Not that I recall.'

'It's somewhere over the sea, behind a woodland. It is my home, and my family is there.'

'Ah, yes, Bryneich sounds familiar. Perhaps we will come upon it soon,' Cadoc replied, 'and when we do...'

'My father is Cunedda, King of Bryneich,' Tanwen interrupted, 'if you meet him please tell him where I am. Please tell him you have seen me, and I am safe, and I want to go home. Please tell him that more than anything in the world, I want to go home.' Then she turned abruptly and walked away so they could not see her tears.

The following morning, they were all in high spirits. They washed in water warmed overnight in a cauldron over the fire and dressed in clean clothes ready for the last stage of their journey. Tanwen invited Vodine and Cadoc to travel with them to Lord Freawine's town, but they declined. 'We thank you for your kind hospitality but we must continue our journey. We must carry The Word to Saxland.' Tanwen wished them good fortune, *they would need it in Saxland.*

Vodine gave the prince a rope of prayer beads with an icon of their redeemer on the cross. Offa grinned and immediately put the icon into his mouth. Cadoc smiled indulgently, used his thumb to draw a cross on Offa's head and said 'God bless the child, he is taking the Lord God straight to his heart.' The pilgrims blessed the travellers, said their goodbyes and went on their way.

Offa wanted to stay. He had re-discovered the delights of playing with sand and water and screamed and fought as fiercely as a berserker when they tried to get him back into the wagon.

It was not until Tanwen filled one pot with sand, another with water and a third with stones and carried them onto the wagon for him to play with, that he eventually calmed down and they could get underway.

They had travelled about ten miles when two riders were spotted coming towards them. Hafoc instructed the women to stay inside and lie low in case of trouble, but Tanwen could not resist lifting the corner of the tent and peering out. Hafoc and one of the guards rode out to meet the strangers but there did not seem to be any sign of trouble. They exchanged a few words and all rode back to the wagon together.

Hafoc opened the tent. 'It is safe to come out now, Tanwen. These are Lord Freawine's sons, Wigheard and Cedd, who have been sent to escort us to the town.'

Wigheard came forward, he was tall and lean with long light brown hair and his gear was immaculate. 'Greetings, we welcome Prince Offa and his companions to our home. We trust you had a trouble-free journey. We are here to escort you into Hedeby where accommodation has been prepared for you and my parents are waiting to greet you.'

Wigheard was well-spoken and his manners impeccable. Cedd was silent and surly.

'Thank you, Wigheard and Cedd,' she replied, holding Offa up for them to see. 'This is Prince Offa, Atheling of Angeln and I am his companion, Tanwen, foster daughter of Thorndor.'

Wigheard smiled at the Prince. Cedd lowered his head courteously but said nothing.

***

Lord Freawine, and his wife, Lady Hebeke, welcomed them enthusiastically while their daughter eyed them suspiciously from the arms of her nurse. Tanwen guessed she was approaching her third winter. Her hair, which was extraordinarily abundant for one so young, was a tousled mass of ringlets, curls and frizz the colour of a blazing fire. Tanwen wondered if it had ever had a comb run through it. 'This is our dear daughter, Modpruth. We call her Honey because she the sweetest of children.'

The travellers were offered warm mead and tiny almond tarts. Lady Hebeke insisted on holding the "darling prince" while they enjoyed their refreshment, and promptly proceeded to remove all his garments. Offa screamed in protestation, Leofrun and Hilde exchanged horrified glances and Tanwen attempted to retrieve him without causing offence.

'It's rather cold out here, Lady Hebeke, perhaps we should take Prince Offa inside,' she suggested.

'In a moment dear. First, I must satisfy myself that the prince is in full working order, with no lumps bumps or missing fingers or toes that can be attributed to our mishandling.'

Tanwen flushed, this was the atheling of Angeln Lady Hebeke was discussing, not a pot she had ordered from a merchant. 'Prince Offa is in perfect working order, my lady,' she retorted.

'Yes, I can see that now. And he has a fine pair of lungs. What a joy he will be to us and what a wonderful playmate he will be for my beautiful Modpruth.' Lady Hebeke thrust the squalling, naked infant into Mae's arms. 'I expect he's hungry, dear.' Shocked, Mae shoved the prince at Leofrun. It happened so quickly Tanwen was amazed Offa did not end up on the ground.

'Leofrun is Prince Offa's wet nurse, not Mae, Lady Hebeke,' she explained, suppressing a giggle.

Tanwen had brought a gift for Modpruth, a small doll, carved from bone, that Aelfrun had brought from Waernas. On their journey Hilde, Mae and Edyth had made clothes for it from scraps of fabric leftover from Aelfrun's wedding dress and other clothes.

Modpruth snatched it from Tanwen's hand and threw it to the ground. One of Lady Hebeke's ladies retrieved it, wiped it on her tunic and offered it back, but Modpruth spat on it and swiped it away. Disgusted, Tanwen picked it up and slipped it under her cloak.

Seemingly unperturbed by this appalling behaviour, Lady Hebeke smiled indulgently at her daughter. 'She's a little tired,' she said.

The travellers were invited to join Lady Hebeke in her day room for a light meal of roast duck with pear and herb tart after they had unpacked and rested.

'It will be a perfect opportunity for the children to meet and get to know each other. Dear Modpruth has been so looking forward to meeting the prince. King Waermund has hinted that they will be betrothed when they are of age. What an honour.

What a fine marriage they will make. Did the king mention we are cousins? We shared the same grandmother and were constant childhood companions.'

'He may have mentioned that you and he were kin, Lady Hebeke,' was Tanwen's polite reply.

A hall had been built to accommodate the prince and his retinue. It was a rectangular, timber-framed building, daubed with a mixture of mud, straw and dung and thatched with reeds. It comprised one large day room and three small sleeping chambers. It was not up to the standard of the queen's hall in Angeln, but it was clean and comfortable. The new arrivals wanted for nothing and had no complaints.

The morning after their arrival Tanwen saw people assembling for a hunt. She slipped out, prepared Starlight, and tagged onto the end of the group. No one noticed, or if they did nothing was said, so she resolved to join them whenever she could.

Eight

Their new life in Lord Freawine's household was idyllic. Lady Hebeke had servants and slaves of her own, so Mae and Edyth had few demands made upon them and were free to spend most of their time as they pleased. The obnoxious Honey objected violently to having Offa around and slapped, kicked, or bit him at every opportunity, but Offa soon learned to avoid her and happily toddled around winning the hearts of Lady Hebeke and her ladies who indulged his every need; while Leofrun and Hilde were happy to sit back and leave them to it. Tanwen hunted, rode Starlight whenever she wanted and told Offa stories of his mother and Angeln at bedtime.

Lady Hebeke loved to listen to Tanwen's stories. 'You have a wonderful word-hoard, dear. It is many years since I visited Angeln, yet you describe it so beautifully I feel as if I've spent most of my life there,' she whispered one night when the prince had dropped off to sleep.

Tanwen judged Lady Hebeke to be approaching her thirtieth year. She was shorter than Tanwen, well rounded but not fat, her brown hair flecked with silver and braided under a headband of the same pale green as her eyes. She called Offa "her darling prince" and everyone else "dear".

'You must tell your stories to Honey, in my bower, when she is resting after her noon meal. She must learn all she can about my cousin, King Waermund, to prepare her for her new life as the future Queen of Angeln.'

Thinking there was nothing she would enjoy less than spending time with Honey, Tanwen agreed with little fervour.

The following day, when Tanwen returned from the hunt, Edyth was waiting in the doorway fidgeting in agitation. 'Oh, do hurry Tanwen. Lady Hebeke wants to see you in her bower.'

'Why?'

'Don't know, but she told the ladies to leave the room when you arrive.'

'The prince is all right?'

'Yes. Hilde has taken him to see the cygnets on the pond.'

'Is it urgent, or should I change first?'

Edyth shrugged. Tanwen was uneasy. Had she done something wrong, or had someone objected to her taking part in the hunt? Deciding it could not be anything too serious or Lady Hebeke would have sent a guard, not Edyth, she washed her hands and face and changed into a red linen tunic and fine woollen underdress.

'Ah, Tanwen dear.' Lady Hebeke clasped both of Tanwen's hands when she entered the room. The ladies immediately stopped what they were doing and smiled as they filed out.

Her heart fluttered. She hoped it was not bad news from Angeln.

Lady Hebeke offered her a silver-rimmed, oaken cup of warm ale sweetened with honey, and they sipped in silence for several heartbeats before Lady Hebeke spoke. 'My dear Wigheard will be leaving me tomorrow and taking his place in the men's hall.'

'Really?'

'Yes, can you believe it? And he still a boy. I have spoken to Freawine, pleaded with him, but he won't be swayed. He insists that Wigheard is a man now and must take his place in the men's hall before my women make him soft.'

'It must be very difficult for you, my lady, but I'm sure he will be a frequent visitor to your bower.'

Lady Hebeke snorted. 'This is my reward for providing strong sons. Daughters would not be taken from me at such a tender age. How cruel of Freawine to steal a son from his mother. How will my dear Wigheard bear it?'

The men's hall was only a few yards from Lady Hebeke's hall. Tanwen cast her mind back to Aelfrun, who had been taken from her family to live in Angeln at a similar age and never saw them again, and she glanced at Honey, who was playing on the floor, but would one day suffer the same fate. She believed Wigheard had little to complain about but kept the notion to herself.

'However, if my dear Wigheard must take his place with the men and become a warrior, he must be a very good warrior, the very best in the land. I insist upon it.'

'Naturally, my lady.'

'It was so good of my cousin King Waermund to send the prince to us. He will grow up looking upon Wigheard and Cedd as brothers so when he is king, he will trust them to fight at his side.'

'Yes, my lady.' Tanwen stifled a yawn, she had already heard similar words from the king.

Lady Hebeke sighed. 'That is why I have called upon you, dear.'

'Me?'

She patted Tanwen's hand. 'I understand you were specially chosen by the king to tutor Prince Offa. Is this correct?'

'Well, yes, I suppose it is, in a manner of speaking.'

'And that you were a pupil of Thorndor, are very learned and even know Latin.'

'My mother taught all her children to speak Latin, but that was a long time ago and since then I have used it only very rarely, in the learning chamber, with Thorndor.'

'The learning chamber? You actually had a chamber set aside for learning?'

'Lord Thorndor did, in his hall.'

'How extraordinary.' Lady Hebeke shook her head in disbelief and seemed to be considering it further. 'I want you to teach Wigheard,' she said at last.

Tanwen was alarmed. 'Teach him what?'

'Everything: word-craft; tally-craft, Latin, and everything he needs to know to make him a great warrior.'

'But my lady, surely weapon-training would be more appropriate for a warrior?'

'All warriors can use weapons. But a great warrior needs to be able to exchange information and ideas with his lord, to speak to his lord's allies and enemies in a common language and to ensure his lord's tally-men are honest men.'

Tanwen was overcome with admiration for Lady Hebeke. She was not the flutter-wits she had always appeared to be. She was an intelligent woman who recognised the importance of learning and the advantages it would bring to her sons over other men.

'I'm sorry, Lady Hebeke, I can't do that. I'm not a teacher, not a real teacher like Thorndor. I'm only here to tell Offa stories about his mother and father and The Old Ways.'

'Nonsense. Of course, you can do it. It's merely a matter of repeating the things Thorndor told you, and that cannot be too difficult, can it? It shouldn't take up too much of your time, Wigheard is a very bright boy.'

'Yes, my lady.' Tanwen sighed with resignation. Wyrd had struck again. Lady Hebeke wittered on but Tanwen had shut her out and did not hear another word until she realised the ladies were returning.

'Now, do tell me if there is anything you need, dear.' Lady Hebeke was saying as Tanwen awoke from her reverie and realised she was being dismissed.

'Yes, Lady Hebeke,' she said.

Wigheard was an uncooperative and incompetent pupil. He would saunter into the dayroom whenever it suited him and criticise and question everything Tanwen said. He did not remember anything she taught him from one day to the next and had an infuriating way of smiling through his brown eyes that sent an irrepressible rush of blood to her cheeks and a strange flutter to the pit of her stomach.

Despite this, Tanwen looked forward to his visits. She roughly carved some tally-sticks and painstakingly went through the numbers with him, over and over again, but he would give a casual shrug and tell her it was a waste of time, he had enough fingers to help him do all the sums he would ever need to do. It was the same with runes. She used a goose feather quill dipped in a small pot of ground charcoal, bound with yew tree gum and thinned with vinegar to draw runes on a piece of calfskin stretched over a wooden frame. He did show a slight flicker of interest, but it appeared to be more for the process than content.

'Why calfskin?' he wanted to know. 'Runes are usually carved on wood.'

'Because wood is cumbersome, whereas skin is easily rolled and carried. Besides you can fit many more runes on a skin than you can on a similar-sized piece of wood.'

He snorted. 'What use have I for runes, on a skin or otherwise?'

'You may need to send a message to someone. For instance, when you are in the midst of a great battle and the king sends a messenger with your orders written on skin, how would you reply?'

'I would tell the messenger the words to say or call on a word-smith.'

'How can you be sure either of them will use your words and not his own?'

Wigheard hesitated. 'You are being silly it would never happen. If we were at war I'd be fighting at the king's side. There'd be no need for messengers.' He picked up the skin and examined the marks she had made on it. 'What does it say?'

'Your name: the names of your father; mother, brother, and a charm.'

He looked up sharply. 'What kind of charm?'

'To protect you and to warn your enemies that should any harm befall you they will have to answer to the king.'

She could see the familiar laughter in his eyes as he said, 'Then I shall keep it always, and go into battle without fear, knowing I have your charm to protect me.'

If Wigheard had little interest in learning, he had even less in Offa, except for the status he brought the family. At their mother's insistence, the brothers visited Offa in the dayroom every evening. They pulled faces and dangled their arm-rings at him, but Offa always seemed overawed by them and only gaped in wonderment.

'He's feeble-minded,' Wigheard commented.

Cedd sniggered. 'That's because his father was too decrepit to do the job properly, old men always turn out feeble-minded babes.'

'Don't you dare say that. Offa has more wit in his little finger than you have in your whole body.' Tanwen said, rushing to Offa's defence.

When Cedd smirked and thumbed in Tanwen's direction saying, 'typical vixen defending her cub,' he reminded Tanwen of Arild in Angeln, strutting about in Hunlaf's shadow, imitating his every move and constantly trying to cause trouble, and she realised for the first time, how much she disliked him. She stiffened. 'You had better leave, both of you, it's time for the prince's nap. And don't come back until you've learned some manners,' she said.

The following day when Hilde took Offa for his walk, she heard rumours that the previous night Wigheard and Cedd had been drinking heavily in the harbour alehouses and Lord Freawine had confined them to quarters as a punishment. Tanwen was delighted.

Nine

It was Yule, the time of the winter solstice. Hovels and halls were decorated with holly and ivy. Mistletoe hung over doorways to ward off evil spirits and Offa watched in awe, as his great-grandfather, the God Woden led the wild hunt through the night sky.

The Yule boar had been slaughtered, roasted and eaten, washed down with copious amounts of mead and ale, and there had been rejoicing in the streets thanking the Earth Mother for an abundant haerfest. But now the festivities were over, and the Yule log was slowly burning on a huge fire in the centre of town. It would smoulder for weeks and its ashes would be saved to ignite next year's Yule fire.

The days were short and cold and the nights long and colder. The ground was thickly covered in ice, the pond was frozen solid and a dense, frosty, fog hung in the air. All but the most essential outdoor activities had come to a halt.

Even inside the hall, it was freezing. Mae brought a jug filled with hot water, but only moments later, Tanwen had to smash the ice that formed on the surface before she could pour its contents into a bowl. It was already much too cold for Prince Offa's morning wash.

Last night Tanwen had taken Offa into her own bed and Mae and Edyth slept on pallets in her chamber. There was warmth in numbers. Tonight, she would ask the house churl to bank up the fire in Offa's day room and they would all sleep there.

Offa would have to forgo his wash this morning. Instead, she took him to the day room and gave him a quick wipe down with a warm damp cloth. If Lord Freawine found out she would be reprimanded. Princes were not to be pampered. They were supposed to be strong. By the time they reached manhood, they were expected to be impervious to weather conditions and to lead men into battle regardless of the elements. But Tanwen had no intention of allowing the prince to fall victim to winter ills.

Later that day she was sitting on the floor in Lady Hebeke's bower playing with Offa and trying to keep Honey at bay when Wigheard and Cedd strode into the room. 'Salvē. Matrem, Tanwen, et quam tibi?' *Hello, Mother and Tanwen, how are you both?*

Tanwen stared in astonishment. 'Si autem bene, quid agis? *We are well, how are you?*

'Ego uti Roma Latine.'*I am going to Rome, to practise Latin.*

Tanwen was amazed. For weeks she had accused Wigheard of not paying attention, yet his Latin was flowing as comfortably as his native tongue. 'Well done, Wigheard. I'm impressed,' she said before repeating the conversation in English to Lady Hebeke.

His mother rushed to embrace him. 'My dear Wigheard, how clever you are. See, Tanwen, did I not tell you he would learn quickly? Did I not say how effortless teaching my boys would be? Lord Freawine will be overjoyed. As soon as the weather changes, we will have a learning chamber built adjoining my hall. Or should it be in the hall?' She frowned. 'No,' she said with conviction, 'concentration is not Cedd's strong point, he would be too easily distracted.' She chuckled. 'But a little learning will sort that out, do you agree, Tanwen?'

'Cedd. I'm sorry, Lady Hebeke, I can't possibly teach Wigheard and Cedd. I don't have the time. My first responsibility is to Offa.'

Cedd was equally unenthusiastic about the idea. 'I don't want to waste my days in a chamber learning Latin when I could be …'

'Ignore him dear,' Lady Hebeke said to Tanwen. 'Cedd will not encroach upon your time with Offa and you will find teaching two boys no more time consuming than teaching one, and twice as rewarding.'

Tanwen spotted Wigheard shaking with suppressed laughter and threw him a frosty glare.

He blew her a kiss, went down on all fours and lifted his sister onto his back to play horse. Honey grabbed his hair, dug her heels into his sides and squealed with joy as he rode around the room making neighing noises. Offa, wanting to join in the fun, tried to climb up behind her but Honey kicked him away.

'Don't be mean, he only wants to play. Help him up, there's ample room for two,' Wigheard said.

Honey scowled but held out a hand to the prince. Offa grabbed it. Honey leaned forward and bit deep into his arm, drawing blood. Offa yelled, Wigheard scolded Honey and thrust her to the floor as Tanwen rushed to Offa's aid. She paced around, comforting and trying to quieten the prince, while Honey lay on the floor kicking and screaming for attention. Wigheard roughly dragged her to her feet and called her a wicked creature. He held her in a firm grip as if about to give her a shake, but his mother leapt to her feet and intervened, pulling Honey into her arms.

'Wicked Wigheard. Can't you see our precious baby is overtired?' she asked in a childish voice, before handing Modpruth to one of her ladies.

Livid, Tanwen clutched Offa to her chest and stormed out without a word but Offa, apparently unconcerned, stopped crying and wanted to be on the floor the moment they left the room. Later, while he was sleeping, Tanwen made wings from duck feathers and a silk dress for Aelfrun's doll and hung it from a beam over his head.

***

Wigheard and Cedd were bored and rumours about their appalling behaviour were spreading. Edyth had become attached to the younger son of the hall thane and came home night after night with stories of how the brothers strutted around the town, bragging that their father was now the most important man in the kingdom after the king. They were also drinking heavily and causing disturbances. The latest gossip was that Wigheard had taken advantage of the daughter of a visiting Frankish merchant. No real harm was done but her father had demanded wergild.

Eventually, the fog lifted, the ice thawed, and many normal winter activities were resumed.

The days were already lengthening, soon the raiding season would be upon them again. Wigheard and Cedd had not been around for days, so Tanwen set herself the task of preparing salves and poultices to store ready to treat battle wounds.

'There you are, dear. I've been searching everywhere for you.' Lady Hebeke hurried up to the table where Tanwen was grinding herbs. 'Whatever are you doing?'

'Preparing salves and poultices, my lady.'

'Truly? How clever of you. But leave that for now, you can finish it tomorrow. Ask the guard to find Wigheard and Cedd, will you please?'

'Tomorrow? But my lady …'

'Hurry, Tanwen if you please. Lord Freawine is about to visit us, and I want to speak with our sons before he upsets them.'

Tanwen bit back a protest. She would not have time to make salves and poultices tomorrow, she would be out hunting. However, being wise enough not to argue she passed the message to the guard.

Edyth was massaging a salve made from precious oils and ground lavender flowers into Lady Hebeke's hands when Wigheard swaggered into the hall closely followed by Cedd.

'Wigheard, my dear son, and Cedd. How handsome you both are.' The boys greeted their mother with a peck on the cheek. 'Come, sit beside me,' she continued, patting the cushioned seat, 'and tell me what you have been up to. Wigheard, how are you enjoying your weapon training? Hafoc tells me you learn quickly.'

Wigheard puffed out his chest. 'I was born to be a warrior. Next year I'll join father's war-band on Myrging raids and bring you fine jewels for Mae to weave into your hair.'

'Goodness, Wigheard, so soon?' She gently smoothed his cheek with her slender fingers.

'And still no sign of a beard.'

'I'm fourteen.'

'That old?' She shook her head in mock amazement and smiled. 'And to think, Tanwen, I thought him still a child.'

Tanwen raised a haughty eyebrow. 'We will all sleep easier in our beds, my lady, knowing we have Wigheard to protect us.' Wigheard shot her an irritated glance. Lady Hebeke held out her hand to her youngest son. 'And you, Cedd, are you enjoying your word-craft?'

'I hate word-craft. I don't want to be a stupid girl like Tanwen. I want to be a soldier, a fierce warrior, like Wigheard.'

Unseen by Lady Hebeke, Tanwen curled her lip and stuck her tongue out at Cedd.

Lady Hebeke smiled indulgently. 'I know you do my dear and indeed you shall. But first, you must learn word-craft, just as Wigheard did and you must apologise to Tanwen, she is not a stupid girl, but a very clever one and you would do well to learn from her. Remind us Tanwen, how many languages do you speak?'

'Only English, my lady and some Frisian.'

'And Latin. Did you not teach Wigheard a little Latin?'

'Very little, my lady. My mother was half-Roman and encouraged all her children to speak Latin. Lord Thorndor also knows a little.'

'You survived a Roman mother?'

'My lady?'

'I have heard that Roman women leave their girl children to die on rubbish heaps.'

'Lady Hebeke. My lady mother would never have done such a thing. She loved all her children equally.'

'Then tell me, how many sisters do you have?'

'I had five brothers, but no sisters before I came to Engle Land'

'Then perhaps that proves my point.'

Tanwen would have retorted, but Lady Hebeke continued without a pause. 'Now, Cedd, see how clever Tanwen is? Three different languages and a fine word-hoard in each of them.'

'How many of father's war-band learned word-craft?' Cedd asked in a truculent voice.

'They are old men, Cedd, from an old world. This new world of ours presents new challenges. Lords Hengest and Horsa have discovered a vast new land in the west, a rich fertile land, worth fighting for.'

Tanwen's ears pricked. 'Has there been word of Lords Hengest and Horsa? 'She asked, instantly forgetting the insult.

Lady Hebeke appeared surprised at the question. 'Not recently, but we know they found such a place some time ago and its king invited them to return. One day my kinsman, King Waermund, will send an army to conquer this land. Warriors led by brave war-lords, who can not only fight and lead their men to victory but also check the tallyman's records and be sure the king gets all the wergild due to him.'

'I'll go.' Cedd danced across the floor slashing the air with an imaginary sword. 'I'll be a great general. See how well I fight, mother? I've been watching Wigheard, and I practise every day. See how easily I could kill Tanwen with my single-stick.' He lunged at Tanwen.

Startled, Tanwen jumped back and knocked over a horn of mead, spilling its contents over her tunic. She glowered at Cedd but quickly entered into the spirit of the game.

'Alas my lady, I am done for, this great general has pierced my heart, avenge me, Lord Wigheard.' And she crumpled to the floor, her body quivering with concealed laughter.

'Ah-ha, you imp of Hel. Your single-stick may kill a beautiful maiden, but it won't protect you from a grown man skilled in the nine strokes of a sword.' He unsheathed an imaginary sword and threw himself into a mock battle with Cedd.

Wigheard's daily weapon training had made him fit and nimble on his feet and soon Cedd was struggling to keep up with him. His eyes burned with humiliation. He pursed his lips and hurled himself at his brother, knocking him to the floor and landing on top of him. Their imaginary weapons were discarded and Wigheard, helpless with laughter, tried in vain to shield his face from the blows raining down on him.

Lady Hebeke tried to separate her sons, but a stray blow caught her off guard and she collapsed in a heap of laughter beside them, with her headband almost covering her eyes.

At that moment Leofrun entered carrying Offa fresh from his nap. She gaped at the heap of bodies on the floor, too surprised to prevent the young prince from wriggling out of her arms. He toddled across the floor to the tangle of limbs 'Wiga hurt, Wiga hurt …'

Lady Hebeke's eyes narrowed, 'Wiga?' she said in her deepest, sternest voice.

Undaunted Offa pulled off her headband, gave it a quick chew and offered it back with a toothy grin. She accepted it without a glimmer of a smile. Then she beamed and swept him up into her arms and tickled him. 'Long may, Nethrus, bless my home with the laughter of children,' she said kissing him fondly, and everyone joined in the laughter as the giggling infant kicked and struggled to be free.

In the commotion, no one heard Lord Freawine enter. 'Lady Hebeke.' he roared. 'Do you always keep such an unruly hall?'

Tanwen sprang to her feet and dusted herself down. The boys jumped to attention and Offa scampered back to Leofrun's arms.

Lady Hebeke replaced her headband and, still laughing, embraced her husband enthusiastically. 'Oh Freawine, what a pity you did not come sooner, we have had such an enjoyable game. And Offa's new name for Wigheard is Wiga. Can you believe it Freawine? Offa is such a bright child. What a fine prince he will make. Goodness me, I swear I have not laughed so much since our boys were small.'

Lord Freawine was not amused. 'Perhaps we should have spent less time laughing with our sons and more time chastising them, my lady.'

He was heavily built with steely eyes and a face almost obscured by unkempt grey hair and a scraggly beard. Tanwen had seen very little of him since her arrival for although he sometimes led the hunt, she always rode at the rear and avoided the kill, so she never came into contact with him.

'It shames me to say,' he continued, 'that our sons do us no credit. I am plagued by daily complaints about their exploits. They are drunkards and braggarts and Wigheard's lack of honour, with the daughter of a visitor to the town, was both costly and humiliating.'

Lady Hebeke was visibly shocked. 'You are too harsh, Freawine. They are only boys, with the exuberance of youth.'

'They are a disgrace, Hebeke, their behaviour has been inexcusable, and I'll have an immediate end to it.' He turned on the boys catching them unawares. 'Well, what do you have to say for yourselves?'

'It was all Wigheard's fault ...' Cedd whined.

'Enough.' Lord Freawine silenced him. 'I'll have no tale-telling in this family, and you will accept responsibility for your own actions.'

'I'm sorry, father, but Cedd is right. He was only following my lead. It won't happen again.'

Lord Freawine gave a long, low growl. 'See that it doesn't, young Wigheard, or I'll feed your balls to the crows.'

He kissed his wife on the cheek and pinched Offa's nose. 'A fine prince indeed,' he agreed before returning his attention to his sons. 'You will not join the hunt tomorrow, instead, you will spend the day caring for your prince. You will treat him kindly with all the respect due to the atheling of Angeln. You will not let him out of your sight, not even for one heartbeat, and you will guard him with your lives. If any harm befalls him, you will answer to me - do you understand?'

They blushed and hung their heads. 'Yes father,' they said in unison.

Tanwen did not trust the boys with Offa and even though Leofrun and Hilde swore they would keep him safe in his day room, she decided not to join the hunt but to stay home where she could keep a watchful eye on the prince.

The boys stormed in as soon as the hunt set off. Wigheard was in a foul mood and it was evident he would have disobeyed his father and followed the hunt if he had had the courage. He had bought a bow from a Hunnish merchant and brought it along to show Tanwen.

'It's superb. Have you tested it yet?' she asked smoothing her hands over its fascinating shape. She was truly envious. It was made of horn, wood and string, with a double curve above and below the grip.

'No. There's an art to it and I won't have anyone laughing at me while I'm learning to use it. I want lots of practise before I show it off in public.'

'We could go down to the river and test it on the waterfowl,' Cedd suggested.

Wigheard agreed. 'Father is out hunting, he'd never know.'

'He said you weren't to leave Offa,' Tanwen reminded them.

'We won't leave him. We'll take him with us,' Wiga said, with a mischievous grin.

'You're mad. Leofrun will never allow you to take him out,' Tanwen insisted.

'She won't know. She always sleeps after his morning feed.'

'But I would know, and I won't allow it.'

Wigheard put an arm around her shoulders. 'Oh, come on sweetheart, what harm can it do? We won't be disobeying father and if anyone reports us, we'll say we were taking him to feed the ducks. You can come with us to see he comes to no harm and you can try out my new bow. I know the perfect place, a secret place, where no one ever goes.' He lowered his voice and whispered into Tanwen's ear. 'We can make it our place, somewhere to go when we want to be alone.'

'Idiot,' Tanwen replied elbowing him in the ribs to push him away.

'We can't trust her. She's just a soppy girl and girls will do anything to save their skins. As soon as anybody asks an awkward question, she'll burst out crying and tell on us.'

'Oh, stop belly-aching, Cedd. Tanwen's all right, she won't betray us.'

'If Offa goes, I go end of discussion,' Tanwen snapped. 'Neither of you has any idea how to look after a child.'

'That's settled then,' Wigheard said. 'You fetch the atheling, Cedd and I will bring the weapons.'

Despite Wiga's protestations, Tanwen insisted on carrying Offa. 'You'll only drop him,' she said derisively.

'Suit yourself,' Wiga said without interest.

They slipped out of the hall unseen, cautiously made their way through the herb patch, across the pasture and into the forest. They slithered down a muddy slope to the riverside, but from there they made slow progress as their feet sank and squelched along the stinking, marshy, ground at the water's edge. Offa was good and barely made a sound except to say 'bird' every time one flew overhead.

When they reached a clearing, a woodcutter was crouched with his back to them, chopping logs with his hand-seaxe. His panting, foam-covered horse stood nearby.

'I thought you said this was a secret place and no one ever comes here,' Tanwen said.

'Who can it be?' Cedd whispered.

'A Myrging churl,' Wigheard announced pompously.

Cedd frowned. 'How do you know that?'

'Because only a Myrging would be witless enough to wear his hair in that ridiculous Swarbian fashion.'

Tanwen noticed that the man's hair was drawn tightly back and knotted on the crown of his head. 'I like it,' she said. 'It makes him look …'

'Stupid.' Wigheard interjected.

Tanwen pulled a face and slid Offa to the ground. 'It doesn't make sense. What would a Myrging woodcutter be doing on this side of the river? There aren't even any trees here.'

Cedd shuffled nervously and his left eye twitched. 'Let's go back, Wigheard,' he pleaded.

Wigheard hesitated. 'Not until we've chased him from our father's land.' He crept forward signalling to Cedd and Tanwen to follow. As they approached the stranger Tanwen could see that it was not wood he was chopping but the carcass of a boar that was lying in a pool of blood.

Wigheard and Cedd were transfixed, but Tanwen scooped Offa into her arms and drew him back to the bushes. 'Now, sweetheart,' she whispered, sitting him on his woollen wrap. 'I want you to wait here as quiet as a mouse until we come back for you.' She gave him a hug and one of his favourite fruit tarts. 'And if you are very, very, quiet you can have another to eat on the way home.'

Offa nodded but his bottom lip trembled. She kissed his head and slowly backed out of the bushes. She stepped on a twig that snapped, alerting the hunter to their presence. He looked around and sprang to his feet gripping his bloody seaxe.

He was a giant of a man, powerfully built and dressed in plain clothes of leather and wool.

'What are you doing here?' Wigheard shouted.

'I'm slaughtering a boar,' the man cheerfully replied.

'Well, Myrging, your place is on the other side of the river.'

'A Myrging always follows his quarry, wherever it leads.'

'This is Lord Freawine's land. You have no right to be here.'

The stranger looked amused. 'Then you should have arrived earlier and explained that to the boar, no doubt you speak excellent boarish.'

'If you don't leave immediately, you'll end up in pieces, just like your boar.'

The hunter glanced at Cedd and Tanwen. 'Run away and play with the other children, boy, and leave the fighting to warriors.'

Wigheard's face swelled with indignation and turned so red Tanwen was afraid it might rupture. 'You are right, fighting is for warriors. Pick up your sword, churl, because you are going to die, whether you fight or not.'

Tanwen jerked his hand away from his hilt. 'Lack-wit. Can't you see he's teasing you? Come on, let's go before he loses his temper and accepts your challenge.'

'Get lost, Tanwen, this is man's work and I'll handle it my way - the way of the warrior.'

Cedd tugged frantically at his brother's tunic. 'Wigheard, please don't fight. He'll kill us all.'

The man was clearly losing patience. He swapped his seaxe to his left hand and drew his sword. 'All right boy, if that's what you want, I'll fight. But I'll take the pair of you together, it'll be fairer and quicker that way.'

Cedd closed in to guard his brother's back, but Tanwen pulled him away. She could feel his arm trembling and knew he was terrified. 'No, Cedd, you're too young. Let Wigheard fight his own battles - tell him Wigheard.'

'She's right, Cedd. Don't get involved. I claim a warrior's right to single combat. He's mine.'

With that Wigheard lunged his sword at the man's chest, but the Myrging dodged it effortlessly. Wigheard tried again, this time aiming for the throat, but the hunter raised his sword to block it.

'Come on boy, you'll never win a fight if you don't put some effort into it.'

Wigheard's face was streaked with sweat and contorted with fury. He tried a quick undercut to the belly, but his opponent parried it with ease. It was soon apparent that the hunter was a skilled fighter.

Tanwen became aware of Offa's hand in hers. 'I told you to stay out of the way,' she snapped dragging the crying prince back to safety. 'I'm warning you, Offa, if you leave this spot for even one heartbeat …'

'Offa come with Tanwen, Offa come with Tanwen,' he wailed.

'Oh Offa, my love, you can't. So please sit still and be quiet. I'll come back for you as soon as I can.' She hurried back to the fight, clenching her teeth in an attempt to shut out Offa's cries. *I'll make it up to him as soon as this is over*, she promised herself.

Cold sweat trickled down Tanwen's spine. Wigheard was in trouble. The Myrging was confusing him with a hail of blows. Wigheard was hitting back in a mindless frenzy but he lost his balance and fell, dropping his sword. The quick-thinking Myrging paused in mid-stroke to avoid slicing the youth in half. Instead, the tip of his sword wavered then flashed as he shifted his grip and lowered the blade straight down towards Wigheard's throat.

Cedd's hand went to his seaxe but Tanwen grabbed his arm. 'No, Cedd. Wigheard chose single combat, you mustn't interfere.'

Cedd broke free. 'It's all right, I haven't taken the sword yet, I'm not a warrior, I'm not bound by the warrior's code.'

'No, keep away. Leave Wiga to fight his own battle.'

Wigheard was on his feet again, breathless and unsteady but still refusing to yield. He hurled himself at his enemy like a madman, but his blows were parried. He lashed out with single strokes, letting his shoulder take the Myrging's blows. His sleeve was slashed. Tanwen held her breath but there was no gush of blood. Wigheard's breathing was loud and rasping and Tanwen could see he was tiring. Over and over she called to him to yield, but he ignored her and staggered around, barely able to lift his sword.

With an unexpected twist of the wrist, the Myrging knocked Wigheard's sword from his hand. Wigheard stumbled and fell to the ground. He scrambled for his sword but the Myrging kicked it out of reach and stood over him. He paused then dipped his sword three times. A warrior's salute to his opponent.

With a cry of relief, Tanwen dashed forward to help Wigheard to his feet but from the corner of her eye, she saw Cedd clasping his seaxe in both hands, high above his head.

'No. Cedd.' she screeched. 'Don't.'

Too late. Her heart sank as Cedd's seaxe came down and smashed through the Myrging's skull with a sickening crack.

She watched in horror as the man staggered forward a few steps. He crashed to the ground, spewed blood, shuddered and died. Cedd swayed then vomited over the corpse.

Wigheard rose slowly. All three stared at each other in horror. The terrible realisation of what they had done washed over Tanwen in icy waves.

'Lack wit. You've broken the rules of engagement. You stupid, stupid, lackwit. What were you thinking of?'

Cedd's eyes were brimming with tears. 'It wasn't my fault. He didn't leave me any choice. He was going to kill Wigheard. He would have killed us all.'

'No, he wouldn't. He'd given the warrior's salute. He was about to let Wigheard go.'

'He would have taken Offa hostage.'

'Fool. How would he know that Offa is an atheling and worth a ransom?'

'Because you'd have blabbered it everywhere. You're just a silly girl. I hate you Tanwen, and I wish Wigheard had never let you come.'

Tanwen curled her fingers into tight fists to prevent herself from slapping his face. She wanted to kill him right now, but instead, she vented her rage on Wigheard, who was still staring trance-like, at the corpse.

She followed his gaze. There was a strange familiarity in the hunter's sharp features and that mark on his left temple was not a wound, it was a mother-spot, and she had seen it before. On Eadgils. The son of the Myrging king. He was older, of course, a grown man, and she would not have recognised him, but that unmistakable fiery patch of raised flesh left her in no doubt, this handsome warrior was the king of the Myrging tribe who, as a gangling atheling, she had last met at Aelfrun's wedding.

Her mind was in a spin. If she revealed the identity of the victim, the boys would panic. They might even be dim-witted enough to brag about it around the town and the consequences of that were too dire to imagine. She would have to keep the secret. There was no other way to prevent them from ruining all their lives.

'Don't stand there like a tree stump,' she snapped at Wigheard. 'You'll have to bury him.' She glanced around the clearing. 'Over there, behind the thicket.'

Wigheard tried to wipe the vomit and blood from the dead man's face but only succeeded in smearing it all over. Without speaking, or any sign of emotion, he picked up his seaxe, made his way to where Tanwen was pointing, sank to his knees and began cutting turfs.

Cedd reached out to retrieve his seaxe from the hunter's skull but recoiled, picked up the dead man's seaxe instead and scuttled after Wigheard.

When they had cleared enough ground, they began the laborious task of hollowing out a grave. Blood and sweat dripped from Wigheard's face and Cedd's hair clung in damp clumps on the back of his neck, but neither spoke nor paused until the job was done.

Meanwhile, Tanwen laid out Eadgils' cloak alongside him and, suppressing a shudder, rolled his body onto it and wrapped it tightly around him. Next, with eyes closed and lips tightly sealed to hold back the threatening vomit, she pulled Cedd's seaxe from his head, then called Wiga and Cedd. Together they dragged the corpse to the grave and carefully laid him out with his hand-seaxe, hunting spear and sword at his side. Finally, they piled the earth over him and re-laid the turfs, stamping them down as hard as they could, before scattering fallen leaves over them.

Tanwen was tired and her muscles ached, but she summoned every last shred of energy to help the boys haul the boar's carcass into the undergrowth before they all collapsed, exhausted, onto the warm grass.

But Cedd could not rest. 'It's no good here, somebody's bound to find it.' He ran around looking for a better hiding place and pleaded with them to move it further away, but Wigheard told him to settle down, there would be nothing left but scattered bones by morning.

Behind them, the horse snorted and pawed the ground.

'The horse. What on earth are we going to do with him?' Tanwen cried.

Wigheard forced himself to his feet. He ran his hands over the horse and murmured into its ear. 'He's a grand horse. Any warrior would be proud to ride him. Why don't we take him home and pretend we found him?'

'Because someone will recognise him. We'll have to send him back where he came from,' Tanwen replied.

Ears pricked and nostrils flaring, the horse was rigid and breathing heavily. With kind words, clicking tongues and sharp slaps to the rump, they tried to urge him out of the clearing, but he would not budge. He snorted and cantered to the water's edge, splattering mud in all directions, until he finally plunged into the water. They watched in dismay as the strong current swept the poor animal downstream, unable to swim.

Tanwen hated seeing it struggle in the water. 'He was a fine horse,' she said sadly. 'Let's hope he gets home safely.'

***

Tanwen held Offa close, gently stroking his head and crooning in his ear until his sobs subsided and his eyes closed.

A dozen paces away, Cedd was throwing stones aimlessly into the river. 'Come on, Wigheard, let's go.'

'No. We wait for Tanwen and Offa.'

Tanwen's ears pricked at the mention of her name.

'Why should we wait for her? She'll only betray us. No woman was ever to be trusted. Let's cut her throat and bury her, too. We can say she deserted the prince and ran off with a farmer.'

The spineless runt, I'll grind his liver and feed it to the cats. She wrapped the bear fur around the sleeping infant and gently laid him on the turf, turning just in time to see Wigheard jerk his thumb in Offa's direction.

'Tanwen's a good girl. She won't talk about it any more than he will.'

'But how do we know he won't tell when he starts to talk? Tanwen says he understands everything we say and do.'

'If he does, we'll laugh it off. We'll say he was dreaming about one of Tanwen's stories of monsters and river sprites.'

Tanwen joined the boys. The panic on Cedd's face reminded her of a trapped animal. Guilt and fear would make him capable of any treachery. If the story got out, he would blame her. She would have to find a way …

'Cedd, we have to stand together on this, or we'll ruin all our lives and the lives of your parents,' she warned.

Cedd's eyes narrowed.

'Don't you see?' She carried on. 'The king chose your father to teach Offa warriors' honour and swordplay. You and Wigheard were to be his guards, and later when he's grown his brothers-in-arms. If word gets back to the king that you axed a hunter in the back, for no reason, you'll be called a craven. The king would have no choice but to call Offa home and Freawine will be disgraced.'

The boys exchanged silent glances.

'Think about it, Cedd. Waermund is old. If he dies before Offa is old enough to rule, your father will be king.' She paused, just long enough to let it sink in. 'You don't want to spoil his chances. Do you?'

Cedd seemed to mull it over. 'How do we know we can trust you? You're not kin,' he said at last.

'No. But we must swear to be as true to each other as if we were kin.' Tanwen looked to Wigheard for support, but he was engrossed in tearing up leaves from the alder bush and remained silent. She eased the dagger Arild had given her from its sheath and with a sharp sweeping stroke cut through the vein in her arm. Blood spurted and spattered Cedd's face; his mouth fell open. All three watched the blood ooze over her wrist. She staunched it with her other hand and could feel the warm blood trickle through her fingers.

'We'll share our blood and make ourselves kin,' she said. 'We'll swear an oath to each other.' She thought for several heartbeats. 'And while our blood mingles, we'll say, I swear in the hearing of Nethrus, that I will be true to you both, and that no other oath or law will ever come between us.'

Cedd backed off, shaking his head. Wigheard said 'She's right, we must do as she says.'

Tanwen sighed with relief and handed Wigheard the dagger. Cedd's arm shot behind him, but Wigheard snatched it back.

'No. Leave me alone.' Cedd struggled but could not escape Wigheard's iron grip. 'Keep still, you little craven,' Wigheard barked as he slashed his brother's arm. Cedd yelped. Tanwen ripped a strip from the hem of her tunic, placed her cut arm on top of Cedd's and bound their arms together with the cloth. They solemnly spoke the words.

Wigheard slashed his arm and tied it to Tanwen's. For a moment he stood perfectly still without speaking, his colourless face a cold, hard, mask. She wondered if it would crack like ice or melt away. She tried to escape, but Wigheard pulled the cloth tighter. He grabbed her arm and stared into her face. 'Do you understand that these scars will bind us together for all time and from this day on we three are blood kin?'

'Yes,' she whispered, and Offa cried.

Ten

At four winters old, Offa was growing rapidly. However, Tanwen noticed that he no longer made any attempt to speak and the few words he had already learned seemed to have been forgotten.

Lady Hebeke pooh-poohed the idea, 'you worry too much, Tanwen. It's just a phase he is going through, it will pass. Of course, I had no such problems with my children. They were all very early speakers and were capable of holding a sensible conversation at Offa's age.'

Leofrun sensed she was no longer needed. Tanwen assured her that there would always be a place for her with the prince, but she was homesick, missed her husband and wanted to return to Angeln. Lord Freawine announced that it was time Wigheard was introduced to the king. They would be leaving Hedeby in the next few weeks and that Leofrun was welcome to travel with them. Leofrun was elated.

Tanwen begged Lord Freawine to allow her and Offa to join them for a short visit. 'I'm sure Wynn will have a spell or potion to help Offa find his voice again,' she pleaded. But Lord Freawine would not hear of it. 'There's nothing wrong with the child. I'm sure Cedd didn't utter a word until he was five. And what's more, it's much too perilous a journey for one so young.'

Disappointment must have shown on Tanwen's face for Lord Freawine's voice mellowed. 'Don't despair Tanwen, the boy will speak when he's ready, and by the time I return, I expect he will be chatting so much you will be seeking a potion to silence him.'

***

While his father and brother were away, Cedd was left in charge. Tanwen had avoided him as much as possible since the murder. He was a warrior now but had not seen battle. He had gained a reputation for being an ambitious braggart and had become known as the demon for his cruelty, yet his companions spoke highly of him and admired his skills in weapon craft. And Hilde loved him.

Tanwen had finished lancing a boil on a boy's thigh and was squeezing pus into a pot when Hilde appeared in the healing chamber doorway.

'He refused to marry me,' she said.

Mystified, Tanwen drew herself up and wiped the hair out of her eyes with her forearm. 'Who did?'

Hilde blushed but said nothing.

Irritated with the interruption, Tanwen returned to the extraction of pus. 'Hilde, this is not the most convenient time to play riddles. May we discuss it later, please?' The boy whimpered as she rinsed the wound with a solution of salt and willow bark in boiled water.

Hilde nodded and in a trancelike state passed a wad of moss to Tanwen, to fill the cavity, and a linen bandage to hold it in place.

'You were a brave boy,' Tanwen told him when it was all done, and rewarded him with a dish of sauce made from honey, vinegar, butter and hazelnuts and some pear slices to dip in it. He whooped with glee and hobbled out.

'Bless him, he must have been in agony and didn't make any fuss at all. Now, who refused to marry you, Hilde?' Tanwen asked as they cleared up the mess.

Hilde lowered her eyes. 'Cedd,' she whispered.

Tanwen dropped the bowl of pus. 'Cedd. You asked Cedd to marry you?' Hilde nodded.

'But why would you want to marry Cedd? Why would anybody want to marry Cedd?'

Tanwen waited patiently for a reply. 'Because I'm pregnant and now he doesn't want me.'

'That could be a gift from Wyrd,' Tanwen said as she flopped onto a nearby pallet and wondered how she was going to handle the situation without hurting Hilde's feelings. 'Are you sure it's Cedd's baby?' she asked.

'Yes,' Hilde insisted, 'of course I am. I've never been with anyone else.'

Tanwen believed her. 'Did he deny it?'

Hilde hesitated. 'No, he just told me to get lost; he didn't want me or the baby.'

'Well,' Tanwen said, 'we can all be thankful for that.'

'But what am I going to do?' Hilde cried.

'Exactly as you have been doing, but with a baby in tow.' Tanwen knew her words were harsh, but in her opinion, anyone foolish enough to get involved with Cedd deserved little sympathy.

'He'll have no father, he'll be a ...'

Tanwen rushed in before Hilde upset herself with the dreaded word and began wailing even louder. 'But he'll have Mae and Edyth, and me, and he'll be better off without Cedd.'

'You know nothing of love,' Hilde snapped and ran out sobbing. Tanwen sighed and threw the pus-soaked rushes onto the fire.

***

Three days after Leofrun's departure Tanwen was helping Offa count the eggs they had been collecting when Cedd unexpectedly joined them. He had brought a rod with a net tied to one end and spent some time trying to teach Offa how to catch fish in the pond, although Offa clearly thought thrashing the water with the net and soaking the adults was much more fun, and this sport kept him amused for the remainder of the morning.

While Offa played, Cedd removed a gold torque and handed it to Tanwen. 'Accept this as my bride gift to you.'

Tanwen laughed. 'What kind of jest is this?'

'No jest, you must agree that it is time we married.'

'It's Hilde you should be marrying,' she replied with a scornful smile.

'Hilde? Even if she meant something to me you know we could never marry. The blood oath we swore binds us as legally and morally as a betrothal.'

'The oath bound us as kin. If it meant we were betrothed, I would also be betrothed to Wiga and Wiga to you, and a right fettle we would all be in. Also,' she added, her voice suddenly hard and cold, 'I loathe you, Cedd, and wouldn't marry you if you were the only man on earth.'

He grabbed her arm and making a swift movement forward, he lifted his hand as if to strike her. His eyes emanated a strange cold fury she found disturbing, but his anger quickly subsided, he called her foul names, thrust her aside and staggered to the town to get drunk.

Later that night she was woken by Edyth violently shaking her. 'Tanwen, Tanwen, you must come, quickly,'

'Is it Offa?' Tanwen asked as she threw a cloak around her shoulders and grabbed her dagger. 'Is he ill?'

Edyth was gesticulating wildly. Her hair was loose, and her face flooded with tears. 'Oh, do hurry, Tanwen' she cried, sobbing so much she could hardly get the words out.

'Please, you must come at once.'

The stench of fresh blood and dung hung heavily in the still night air. Tanwen ran with Edyth to the stables. Mae was already there, with Lady Hebeke and her women. Cedd, covered in blood and entrails and holding his bloodied seaxe, was being restrained by two guards.

Tanwen gasped and fell to her knees, the bloody mass on the ground was the remains of her beloved Starlight.

Lady Hebeke glared at her son. 'Your father will hear of this,' she said and walked away. At the entrance, she turned back. 'Let him go and see that this horse is given a warrior's funeral,' she commanded.

Tanwen salvaged Starlight's tail and rigid with rage left without looking at Cedd or saying a word. Alone in her chamber, she washed the tail and spread it out on the floor to dry.

'I'm sorry Aelfrun, so sorry. It was all my doing. I should never have mocked him,' she cried out loud. 'Poor Starlight was trapped with no possibility of escape.'

She had no idea how long she had been crying, but dawn was breaking, and now invisible knives were piercing her brain so violently the pain overwhelmed her until, clutching the back of her skull with both hands, she collapsed onto her bed and surrendered to the blackness.

Six weeks later, Hilde announced she was going to marry Cedd after all.

'What?' Tanwen screeched. 'Have you lost your wits?'

'No, but what else am I to do? Prince Offa no longer requires a nurse, I am expecting a baby and I have no other home.'

'That's not true. You know there will always be a home for you here with us.'

'A woman needs to be mistress of her own home. She needs a father for her children and a safe place to rear them.'

'Hilde, you can't possibly believe that your children would be safe with that monster?'

'He's not a monster. He's a good man, the son of an earl and a great warrior.'

'Son of an earl he may be, but he is also a drunkard and an evil craven who hasn't got it in him to make a decent husband.'

But Hilde would not be moved and wed Cedd the following day. Lady Hebeke, her ladies, Tanwen, Mae and Edyth watched the simple ceremony in silence. When it was over Lady Hebeke gave Hilde a frosty welcome to the family, Hilde retreated to a hut Cedd had acquired for them and Cedd and his raucous companions went to town to celebrate.

***

When Lord Freawine and Wiga returned from their journey they joined Lady Hebeke; Cedd, Honey, Tanwen and Offa for refreshments, and to tell them the exciting news from Angeln.

King Waermund was still in good health, but his sight was failing. Thorndor and Wynn were well and sent their love to Tanwen along with a box of unguents, balms and mixtures for her healing box. The Swarbians had a new over-lord, King Witta. The Myrgings, now under Eadgils' brother, King Friogar, were behaving themselves, although a couple of outlying villages had been raided and burned. Tanwen remembered Urith and Gaeta and hoped they were safe.

Lord Freawine saved the most exciting news till last. The king had confirmed the betrothal of Prince Offa and their daughter, Modpruth. Lady Hebeke shrieked with delight. She was ecstatic. 'My beautiful, sweet, Modpruth, to be Queen of Angeln. Who would have thought it? And he such a darling prince. What a match. 'Did I ever tell you that King Waermund and my mother shared the same grandmother, Tanwen?'

'Not that I recall, Lady Hebeke,' Tanwen lied.

Lady Hebeke's face suddenly dropped. 'Oh, my goodness. Freawine, the bride-price. How are we going to raise a suitable bride price? Did my cousin give any indication of what he would expect?'

Lord Freawine pulled a louse from his beard and crushed it between his fingers. 'He suggested five hundred hides of land next to Fifledor,' he said avoiding eye contact with his wife.

'Five hundred hides.' Lady Hebeke cried. 'We do not have that much land to spare. If we give away five hundred hides, we will all starve.'

'My sentiments exactly, Hebeke. However, Prince Offa is very young, so we have time to accumulate more land. We would only need one good war with the Myrging and ...'

'Oh no, Freawine. We can't have our boys going to war at such a tender age. I couldn't bear it. There must be another way. You must speak to Waermund.'

Wiga caught Tanwen's eye and winked. The swine knows something. She thought trying to stifle a giggle.

'I did.' Lord Freawine found another louse, flicked it into the fire and nonchalantly examined the stains on his tunic.

Lady Hebeke was bursting with anticipation. 'And? What did he say, Freawine?'

'He said,' Lord Freawine replied, at last, that what he would like is many strong, intelligent sons from Modpruth and Offa. Wigheard and Cedd to help Offa govern when he is gone and as a special gift for himself, the head, sword and armour of Friogar.

Modpruth glared at her father, apparently unimpressed.

***

If Cedd was punished for the slaughter of Starlight, Tanwen did not hear about it. But three days after his return, Lord Freawine sent her a stunning, dappled grey-gelding with a black flowing mane and tail. He stood two hands taller than Starlight with impeccable manners and he whickered softly while Tanwen stroked his neck.

'A replacement for Starlight,' Lord Freawine said avoiding eye contact. *As if anything could replace Starlight,* Tanwen thought.

Her eyes smarted as she thanked the earl for his kindness. 'He's a handsome horse,' she admitted, *but not Aelfrun's horse.* She called him Storm.

Severe gales and unrelenting, torrential, rain had curbed all but the most essential outdoor activities for almost a month and the forced confinement gave the ladies time to catch up on cloth making.

Lady Hebeke's ladies, who were rarely seen without their wooden spindles, spent their time spinning as usual. Modpruth's nurse brought the ancient warp-weighted loom out of storage and taught Mae and Edyth to weave. And Lady Hebeke busied herself embroidering linen for Modpruth's tunics. Tanwen, uninterested in any of these occupations, made mordants from wood sorrel and stale urine and dyes from madder roots, weld plants and borage for Hilde to dye the spun yarn.

As soon as the weather improved and the equipment was put back into storage, Tanwen, with Offa seated in front of her, and Wiga, went riding together. The ground was heavy, but they were unconcerned by their slow progress for Tanwen and

Wiga had become close companions. They walked together, rode, hunted, discussed weapons and war and chatted comfortably about their dreams for the future. But they were friends, not lovers, and they never spoke of love or marriage, yet Wiga let it be known that they had an understanding, and for that Tanwen was thankful because it kept all other would-be suitors away.

To avoid ruts and furrows, they left the waterlogged road and meandered through the forest to evade the sodden meadows. They unintentionally came upon the spot where Wiga had fought King Eadgils. Offa made a whimpering noise and snuggled close to Tanwen.

'What's the matter, little prince, are you cold?' she asked not expecting an answer, but wrapping her cloak around him, just in case. True to their oath of silence, Tanwen and Wiga did not comment, although Tanwen dismounted, laid a stem of rue over Eadgils' grave and remounted without a word. When she remounted, she could feel the rhythmic contractions of Offa's chest and knew he was sobbing. Not understanding why he should be upset, Tanwen held him tighter, kissed his head, and eased Storm forward.

They rode on until they spotted a village known to Wiga. 'I once came here with my father. They are good people. Perhaps we should visit on father's behalf,' he suggested.

Tanwen agreed and they entered the stockade.

Within moments of passing through the gates, Tanwen realised that something was amiss. There were no churls to greet them, no children playing and no animals foraging around between the huts. She shivered. There was a cold eeriness about the place that made her feel uneasy. She glanced at Wiga who was staring at the sky where a dozen or more carrion birds were circling. Their harsh squawks made the hair on Tanwen's neck stand on end. Wiga loosed an arrow and the birds dispersed.

They dismounted and tied their horses to a stake. Tanwen sat Offa on a pelt. 'Now Offa, will you stay here and guard Storm for me, while Wiga and I go find out where everyone is hiding?'

Offa looked concerned. 'There's no need to worry, I promise not to go out of your sight,' she added hoping to reassure him.

'You're wasting your time, he can't understand you,' Wiga said impatiently.

'Yes, he can.' Tanwen snapped, 'he hears and understands every word you say, don't you Offa?' Offa's chin trembled but as usual, he remained silent.

Wiga tossed Offa a disdainful look before snatching Tanwen's hand and leading her off to investigate the huts. It seemed unlikely that there had been a raid, for although the huts were empty there were no tell-tale signs of fighting and no bodies lying around.

'Where have they gone? And why haven't they taken their possessions with them?' Tanwen whispered, gripping her pendant Wigheard shrugged.

It was a small village laid out in the shape of a horse's hoof. The largest hut, presumably belonging to the leader, was positioned centrally at the rear, with a crescent of huts on each side leading down toward the gates. The customary fire in the centre of the settlement had almost burned out.

A woman appeared in the doorway of the large hut. 'Go away,' she called to them, in a weak, croaky voice. 'There's nothing here for you.'

They slowly moved forward. 'Who are you?' Wiga replied, 'and where is everybody?'

'Do as I say and leave this place.' The woman looked exhausted and on the verge of collapse. Tanwen moved even closer. Tanwen guessed she was about Hebeke's age. With staring eyes and a pallid complexion. Her garments were crumpled and badly stained. She tried to stagger forward but fell against the doorpost and slid to the ground.

Tanwen rushed forward. 'Let me help you.' But the woman held up a hand. 'Keep away. I've warned you. There's disease in here,' she cried before fainting.

Tanwen and Wiga were at her side in an instant. Wiga gently lifted her in his arms and carried her through the door. He stopped, staring inside, wide-eyed in horror. Tanwen followed him and glared in revulsion at the dreadful scene. Bodies everywhere. Dead and dying. Whimpering and wailing men, women and children, a stinking mass of human flesh covering every inch of the filthy floor.

When Wiga regained his wits, he retreated and laid the woman outside on the ground. 'Where do we start?' he asked despondently.

'Let's carry the living outside into the fresh air and get the fire going. Then I'll search for blankets and water while you go for help. We have to get them away from this place as soon as possible.'

There were very few still alive; three women, four men, eight children and the old woman. The ground was muddy and probably tainted, but Tanwen believed they stood a better chance of recovery away from the festering bodies.

She leaned over the woman. 'Can you hear me? I'm Tanwen. Please wake up.'

Wiga had found two large iron pots. 'I'll fetch water from the well, it should be safer than the beck.'

'Yes - No – Yes. Oh, I'm sorry Wiga. I don't know what I'm saying. We will need water from the well for boiling, but I'll give them our drinking water in the meantime - at least we know it's safe.' She rose to fetch their water bag but Wiga put his hand on her shoulder. 'You stay, I'll get it.'

Wiga returned with the water bag. 'Is Offa safe?' Tanwen asked.

'Yes,' Wiga replied and hurried off to the beck to fill the pots. Tanwen trickled a few drops of the precious liquid through the woman's parched lips. 'The children ...' she said trying to raise herself.

'The children are being looked after,' Tanwen reassured her. 'I'll give them all a drink, while you rest. I'll be back in a few moments.'

Wiga deposited the water-filled pots and piled brushwood onto the embers to reignite the fire. 'Is there anything else I can get for you before I go?'

'No, I can manage - I hope. But will you take Offa back with you, please?' She looked pleadingly into his eyes, afraid he would refuse, but without argument, he lifted Offa onto his horse and swung up behind him.

Tanwen kissed Offa goodbye. 'Be good for Wiga,' she said. 'He is going to take you home, I'll follow shortly.'

'I'll bring a wagon,' Wiga said as he was leaving.

'The roads are waterlogged; a wagon won't get through. We'll need horses with stretchers - and bring men to burn the bodies,' Tanwen called after them.

While Wiga was away, Tanwen overcame her revulsion and set to work cleaning the sick and trying to make them comfortable. They rolled around on the ground clutching their bellies, insensible of the muck under them. The cries, especially from the children, were pitiful and no wonder. They had lost control of their bowels; their clothes were spattered in faeces and their pain-racked bodies were burning with fever. Tanwen offered the water bag to each of them in turn and they drank greedily. She heated water, lots of water, to bathe them, and rummaged through the huts for cleaner clothing and blankets. She knew there was a possibility that the huts were contaminated but accepted the risk. She could not leave them lying in filth.

The woman struggled to her feet and despite Tanwen's protestations wanted to return to the leader's hut. 'It's full of disease. If you catch it, you could be dead by nightfall. 'I am Swuste,' the woman said. 'My family is in there.'

'Then we can do nothing more for them,' Tanwen said firmly.

Swuste looked dismayed. Tanwen put a comforting arm around her shoulders. 'I'm sorry, Swuste, these are the only survivors. I'll find some herbs then at least we can give them a little something to ease their suffering until help arrives.'

She found earth navel, cinquefoil, cockle and yarrow, tore them into shreds and threw them into one of the pots of boiling water. 'The warm tea will draw out the fever and make them feel a little better - and this,' she said undoing a small pouch from her belt, 'is ground silverweed, to ease their cramps, I carry it with me always. If Nethrus is with us we may manage one dose each.'

The patients swallowed the powder and drank the tea willingly.

'Poor things are too sick to make a fuss,' Swuste said sadly.

Wiga soon returned with ten men and stretchers. 'Ten more are to follow,' he said. 'Mae and Edyth are preparing a place for the sick.'

They loaded the children onto the stretchers. Wiga wanted Swuste to ride in a stretcher but she refused. 'Let the sick use them, I can ride behind someone,' she said.

'I'll go ahead and be ready to receive them,' Tanwen said. 'Swuste can ride with me.'

Lady Hebeke would not allow Tanwen through the gates. 'I cannot have you bringing disease into the town,' she insisted.

'What if my dear Honey should become ill? She's betrothed to the atheling of Angeln, it could be a disaster.' Tanwen pursed her lips and rode to the woodland hut Lady Hebeke had designated as a healing chamber. It was dark, damp, and thoroughly depressing, even though Mae and Edyth had scrubbed it from top to bottom and prepared clean pallets for the invalids.

'Hilde wanted to be here to help.' Mae reported. 'But Lady Hebeke has confined Prince Offa to his chamber in case he infects Lady Modpruth, and we thought Offa would need her company.'

Tanwen thanked Mae for her foresight. 'Lady Hebeke was right not to let us in,' she said, 'but for purely selfish reasons.'

Wiga stayed behind with the men. On his return, he told Tanwen that they had built a pyre, burned the bodies and taken possession of the meagre village treasure hoard before razing the village. He decried the appalling conditions in the woodland hut and insisted that a proper healing chamber should be built for Tanwen, alongside the learning chamber.

One girl child, two women and two men did not survive the journey. Swuste was soon on her feet and helping with the care of the others. She was particularly fond of the children, especially the youngest, a little girl called Willow. 'I had two boys and a girl,' she said, 'and a fine husband, but now nothing. Not even a roof to keep me dry.'

'We can't replace your family, Swuste, but we will find you a hut with a roof and you will never go hungry.' Tanwen promised.

The others died one by one. Only two girls, Willow and Mati, a boy, Dan, and Herjan the basket-maker survived.

When they were feeling stronger, Herjan and Swuste married. Lord Freawine had a large hut built for them, no doubt with the proceeds of their village's confiscated treasure hoard. Swuste fostered all three children and Herjan made and sold baskets from their door.

Four months later, in the brand-new healing chamber, Hilde gave birth to twin girls, Eawyn and Cwenhild, and Edyth moved into Cedd's homestead to help with the babies. Hilde was seldom seen away from her new home, but Edyth visited Tanwen frequently, sometimes bringing the twins to Offa's day room to give Hilde a rest. Three weeks later, she moved in permanently. She complained bitterly to Tanwen that Cedd treated her worse than a slave, but she could not be persuaded to leave, because she said he treated Hilde even worse, and she believed Hilde would be unable to cope without her.

***

Tanwen was in an unusually pensive mood. She was seventeen and it would be another ten years before Offa was old enough to begin formal weapon training and two more before he would return to his father. The memories did not come so often now and her desire for vengeance was slowly diminishing. She had had no weapon training since leaving Angeln and doubted if she would have the stamina or inclination to lead a war band in twelve years, so she put her ambitions aside and devoted her time to educating Offa, who was growing rapidly.

He was tall for his age and strong with golden hair and clear blue eyes. He was an eager student and fast learner. He understood Latin and Frisian, was at ease with numbers and fascinated by her stories of the exploits of the heroes of the Old Ways: his great-grandfather Woden the god of war; Tiw the dark god, Thor the god of thunder, as well as tales of dragons, demons, wolves and bears. But most of all he loved to hear the stories Vodine and Cadoc had told Tanwen of The Great Sky God, his son and their wonderful Kingdom of Heaven. Tanwen gave him the prayer beads that had been given to him by Cadoc and he hung them on a nail by the angel, which still hung over his bed.

But Offa was a solemn child who rarely laughed and never spoke. Tanwen insisted that if he wanted something, he must ask for it. This way he learned to speak in short sentences but even then he spoke only in a whisper and only when he was sure they were alone. She devised a series of hand signals to make communication easier for him. The sign for his father, the King, was to turn his hand downward and touch the top of his head with all his fingers in the shape of a crown. For Lady Hebeke he stroked a finger across his brow from ear to ear, signifying a headband. For Mae he stroked the back of his head from the crown to the nape of his neck, representing a single plait and for Edyth, he stroked both sides of his face from ears to shoulders signifying two plaits.

There were many other signs but when the townsfolk saw him using them, they ridiculed him and labelled him the lack-wit. He was cuffed and kicked by the guards and mimicked by the children, so he rarely ventured outside the bower alone.

Even Wigheard and Cedd mocked him mercilessly. One day Tanwen overheard them calling him stupid. 'He's not stupid. Look at his eyes. He understands everything he sees and hears. He'll talk when he has someone sensible to talk to,' she protested.

'And he'll grow up none the worse for learning to think before he speaks,' Lord Freawine added. 'It's a lesson you would have done well to learn, young Wigheard.'

Wigheard and Cedd had long since started rumours that Offa would never be fit to rule. 'By the time he is a man, Waermund will be dead, my father will be too old to take his place and I will be the next king of Angeln,' Wiga boasted one day when Tanwen was within earshot.

'Why you treacherous turd ...' Tanwen scowled at him. Wiga was a blooded warrior now, but he winced at the venom in her voice.

Cedd rushed to his defence. 'Don't worry we will never need to resort to treachery. Wiga has every right to the crown, our mother and King Waermund shared a grandmother. And when Wiga is king there will be no place at court for the imbecile, or you, except perhaps in the kitchens, there's always a shortage of kitchen wenches.'

'There are times, Cedd when I detest you more than I ever imagined possible.' She turned back to Wiga. 'You'll never have the crown as long as I have a breath in my body. Offa is the rightful heir, and he will take his place when the time comes.'

Wiga smirked. 'Say what you will, idiots can't rule. Angeln will need a strong-minded, warlike king, not a weak-minded babe.'

'You make me sick. You are nothing but a pair of braggarts and bullies. Remember, Offa is a direct descendant of Woden and does not need to make conversation with underlings, but he will prove you wrong in his own good time and woe betide you when he does. I only hope I'm there to see it,' Tanwen retorted then walked away.

Lord Freawine and Lady Hebeke were distraught. The atheling of Angeln was deaf, dumb and a lack-wit. 'How could this have happened?' Lady Hebeke complained. 'He is such a handsome boy. Strong, healthy and energetic, he has never ailed for anything and swims every day, even when the river is ice-cold.' They told everyone they could not be blamed, a river-elf or one of those evil otherworld monsters, that came in from the ocean with the raging winter storms, had stolen his voice and there was nothing they could do about it.

They had Tanwen gather herbs and brew potions for him to drink. She made salves to rub on his throat and recited charms over him. Lord Freawine and Lady Hebeke had amulets made with runes carved into them to hang around his neck and offered sacrifices and gave treasures to the gods, but Offa could not be persuaded to break his silence. Tanwen insisted that Offa could understand everything that was said but they would not listen. They grieved for him and the king, but most of all Lady Hebeke grieved for the opportunity they had lost.

They warned the king that Offa was slow but were careful not to say how far he lagged behind other boys of his age, hoping that one day a sorcerer would find a spell to cure him, or the river-elf would bring back his voice.

When she was alone, Tanwen prayed to the Son of the Great Sky God, asking him to work one of his miracles on Offa. She tried to remember the Latin spell Brother Cadoc had used on the bread: Agnus Dei, qui tollis peccata mundi, miserere nobis. *Lamb of God, who takest away the sins of the world, have mercy on us. Say but the word and his voice shall be healed.* But he either did not hear or did not care. She felt cheated, Cadoc had said that he heard and cared about everyone. Perhaps the words were wrong, it was a silly spell, and who would ask a lamb for help anyway.

Offa was seven, the age when he should have been sent into the forest with other boys of his age; to learn how to fend for himself, hunt, run with the wolves and fight. But afraid he lacked the wit to keep himself safe Lord Freawine would not allow him to go or take part in any sport, weapon-training or swordplay with the other boys in the town, and the glum-faced prince could be seen day after day watching them from the window of Lady Hebeke's bower.

Tanwen tried to encourage him. 'Stand up for yourself, Offa. Speak to them, let them know you are as capable as any of the other boys.'

'I don't mind that they think me a lack-wit,' he replied the sadness in his voice tearing at her heart. 'What bothers me is that they despise me so.'

'Oh, Offa. They don't despise you. They despise themselves for failing you, don't you see? Of all the nobles in the land, Freawine was chosen to rear the future king. What an honour. What an opportunity for advancement. But it has all gone terribly wrong. You don't speak so they assume you can't hear. Because you neither speak nor hear, they believe you are a lack-wit. A lack-wit can't rule, therefore, in their eyes, they have failed in their duty. They have failed themselves, the king and Angeln, but most of all they've failed you, and for that they despise themselves.'

She took his hand in hers. 'Prove them wrong, Offa. Show them you hear and understand what they say. Prove you're not a lack-wit, speak to them Offa - please.'

Offa hung his head. 'I can't,' he whispered.

Remembering her promise to Aelfrun, Tanwen took matters into her own hands. Lord Freawine may have forbidden Offa to join in with the other boys, but he had said nothing about him sparring with a woman. She was older now and had not used her wooden sword since that terrible night when Hunlaf was killed, but she could remember all the moves and it should not take her too long to get fit again.

'Come, Offa. We are going for a walk,' she said. Offa looked reluctant but she did not give him time to object. She grabbed his hand and dragged him through the town to the wood-smiths house.

Old Hren was perched on a three-legged stool, whittling away at a lump of wood. 'Prince Offa needs a wooden sword,' she told him.

He peered at them through rheumy eyes. 'Then he's come to the right place, bound to be something on there that suits,' he said indicating to a board displaying more than a dozen wooden swords of varying sizes. 'Give 'em a try, see what fits.'

Offa was at the board in an instant. *Not much wrong with his hearing*, Tanwen mused. She had never seen him so excited. He grinned from ear to ear as he took each one down in turn, tossed it from hand to hand, slashed it through the air and scrutinised it for flaws.

Old Hren winked at Tanwen. 'Won't feel no burrs or flaws there,' he said to Offa. 'All made from the finest ash, yer won't get better - just need to find one that fits.'

When he had tried them all at least twice Offa, still grinning, offered his chosen weapon to Tanwen for approval. She smiled and paid Old Hren with a silver ring.

'It's time to start your weapon training,' she said and at dawn the following day, king-making began.

Eleven

Offa was not allowed to ride so Tanwen rode Storm and Offa ran alongside. Slowly, over short distances at first, then gradually faster and further until he could run for miles, keeping up with rider and horse without tiring. When she felt he was ready she allowed him to follow the hunt on foot.

Lord Freawine frowned in disapproval but did not comment until one day he put his hand on Offa's shoulder and said, 'well done, lad.'

From then on Offa followed every hunt, running tirelessly beside Lord Freawine's horse. Only chaining would have kept him away. He was also good at tracking and fearless at turning the game. Lord Freawine joked that he would make a fine hound one day.

Tanwen beamed. 'Tell Offa that, Lord Freawine, if you will,' she pleaded. But Lord Freawine shook his head, snorted softly and smiled pityingly at the prince, before turning away.

Tanwen began to teach Offa the simplest lessons of swordplay, not to swing too widely and waste his strength by missing his blows; thus leaving himself wide open to the enemy. 'You are already taller than most men and must use it to your advantage,' she told him. 'Hold your sword high over your head. Fast, powerful strokes from above are the most difficult to defend against.'

Offa could not get enough of it. He memorised every word and move and invented some of his own. In no time he knew how to grip a sword and where to aim his strokes. He was a born swordsman and Tanwen was overjoyed.

They trained every day with wooden swords, spear shafts and old shields. Tanwen was an excellent teacher. Competitive by nature she always played to win, telling Offa he would learn more by his mistakes and her blows than he would from a hundred words of undeserved praise.

'You are good,' she said. 'But not as good as your father, or the warriors of old, but keep working at it and you'll soon come up to scratch.'

The only problem was that Offa did not recognise his own strength and was quite capable of destroying a sword at one blow, so unless he killed his enemy with the first hit, he would be likely to find himself without a weapon.

'Never let men see how good you are unless you intend sending them into the otherworld,' she warned him. 'Only a fool tries to impress other fools. Show them you know which end of a sword to hold, but no more. That way you may live to be as old as your father.' Offa nodded to show that he understood and they fought again.

They spent long days and nights in woods and clearings where she showed him which roots, fungi and grubs were fit to eat, which berries to avoid and how to collect the honey of bees. He learned how to fish and trap, how to light a fire to cook the meat and how to weave branches together to make a shelter. In the learning room, using Mae as a dummy, Tanwen taught him how to bind a wound and set a broken limb. 'A king never knows when he may need to fend for himself or care for wounded men,' she said.

Remembering her lessons with Thorndor she taught him how to read the sky to foretell the weather and find his way by day and night.

Offa loved the water and whenever he had time to spare, he would throw off his clothes, wade out through the reeds and swim for hours and hours, much to the amusement of the townsfolk who took to calling him Offa the Otter. But for all Offa's prowess, Lord Freawine would not relent, and Offa was not allowed to ride.

Frustrated, Tanwen persuaded Hafoc, the guard who had escorted them to Hedeby, to have his men construct a wooden frame, the same shape and size as a horse, in the stables near the opening. The men were amused, but there was little to do at this time of year, so they happily set to work.

When it was finished, Tanwen padded the frame with blankets tied on with rope. She helped herself to an old saddle from the stables and threw a length of rope, with loops tied at either end, over the back of the 'horse'. Then she saddled up Storm, led him from the stable and summoned Mae and Edyth.

'You're going to learn to ride,' she told them.

The women were dismayed. 'Ride? Why should we ride? Riding is men's work; we do not need to ride.' Mae cried.

'I ride, and I'm not a man. Nor were Queen Aelfrun and Lady Rowena.' Tanwen expected an argument and was determined to remain calm.

'We have never been close to those evil, stinking creatures, why would we want to sit on them?' Mae asked.

'Horses are not evil, and they don't stink if you look after them properly,' Tanwen replied.

'We are servants, we look after people, not beasts.'

'They are not beasts. And everyone should be able to ride, you never know when it might be useful.' Tanwen was exasperated.

'I won't do it,' Mae insisted. 'It's not natural.'

'Mae, I promise you that after a few lessons it will feel so natural you'll never want to walk anywhere again.'

'Does it hurt?' Edyth spoke for the first time.

'You'll ache a little at first,' Tanwen admitted. 'But the benefits compensate for the discomfort.'

'What benefits?'

'Well, riding gives you a feeling of independence, you can cover a much greater distance on a horse than you can on foot.'

'We already have a feeling of independence, we are servants, not slaves.' Mae replied, sniffing and thrusting out her chin in a haughty manner. 'And we do not need to cover great distances,' she added and walked away.

'Wait.' Tanwen called after her. Mae turned her head but did not move. 'Please come back, Mae, I need to speak to you, to both of you.' Mae and Edyth waited politely. 'Come inside. There's something you should see.'

The sisters gaped at the wooden horse. 'Don't worry, it's for the prince. I've had it made to give him some idea of what it feels like to sit astride a horse.' As there was no reply she continued, 'Lord Freawine still refuses to allow Offa to ride. The idea is ridiculous, he's quite capable, and when did a king ever travel on foot? I plan to teach the prince the rudiments of horse craft by having him sit on this wooden horse and watch and listen to me teaching you both how to ride.'

The explanation sounded ludicrous even to her ears. She knew she could easily teach Offa to ride by demonstrating and describing her actions, but she needed him to experience the effort of using rope foot rings to pull himself onto a horse, as well as the sensation of stretching his thighs over its broad back. She had no qualms about deceiving Mae and Edyth. She truly believed that they should be able to ride because one day their own, or the prince's, life may depend upon it and that ultimately, they would thank her for teaching them. She also knew they would eventually concede, because they loved Offa, and wanted him to be a worthy atheling as much as she did.

Soon the lessons began and in no time Mae and Edyth could mount, somewhat inelegantly, walk, trot and jump over single logs. Although Mae was unconvinced about the advantages of riding, Edyth was soon converted and wanted to learn more. They had both overcome their fear and mistrust of horses.

'Who knows,' Mae said, with a mischievous smile, 'one day I may marry a wealthy lord and have a horse of my own.' Tanwen agreed and promised her she could practise on Storm every day.

As always, Offa practised repeatedly until he had perfected the art of springing gracefully into the saddle and leaping just as gracefully out of it, in little more than a heartbeat.

Mae and Edyth could ride a little, Offa had learned the basics of horsemanship, and Tanwen was well pleased.

Twelve

For several years there had been little trouble with the Myrging. Eadgils had left sons but Friogar, the eldest, was not old enough to rule and many uncles and cousins thought they should rule in his place. Consequently, the civil war kept them too busy for raiding.

Eventually, the marauding started again, around the borders at first but they soon began moving closer to Hedeby to steal the animals at pasture. Lord Freawine ordered that all animals be brought into the stockade. The bower was temporarily abandoned. The ladies stayed in the women's hall and Offa, now considered a man in body if not in mind, moved into the men's hall.

Lord Freawine and his sons were out patrolling the surrounding land when they discovered a hamlet of ten families had been raided. All the men, including the leader, were dead and it was obvious from the bodies that there had been a battle. Their weapons had disappeared, the women and children had been taken and the treasure hoard was missing. The trail led south to Myrging land. Lord Freawine immediately sent a message to King Friogar demanding an explanation, but Friogar denied all knowledge of the massacre and shortly after bought another hundred men for his war band.

King Waermund had been visiting the islands of Fyn and Falster to inspect his property, collect taxes, and dispense justice and was on his way to Lolland when Lord Freawine's messengers intercepted him. He immediately turned his fleet around and headed for Hedeby arriving several weeks later.

Lady Hebeke was in a spin. As soon as Lord Freawine sent his message to the king she began issuing orders. Everything was to be thoroughly cleaned. Animals were to be slaughtered, cooks were to work day and night to ensure there would be sufficient food to feed the king and his retinue, and new clothes were to be made for Modpruth.

'I have an inkling that when the king sees our dear Modpruth's beauty for himself, he will demand that the marriage take place immediately to prevent another suitor whisking her away from our darling prince, and should he do so, Modpruth will be ready.' Lady Hebeke boasted to anyone who would listen. 'I know Waermund very well. We met many times when I was a child - and he was a guest at my marriage to Freawine. Tanwen, did I ever tell you that the king and I are cousins? Our mothers shared the same grandmother?'

'Is that so, Lady Hebeke?' Tanwen replied trying to stifle a yawn.

Tanwen was in despair. She would not eat and despite being constantly tired, was unable to sleep. She had spent days with Offa trying to persuade him to say a few words of welcome to his father, but without success. 'He will blame me, I know he will, he will say I neglected Offa's education,' she complained to Mae and Edyth.

'The king can't blame you; you did everything you could to get Prince Offa to speak.' Mae insisted. But Tanwen was not convinced and seriously considered running away rather than face the wrath of Offa's father.

As the king neared Hedeby Lady Hebeke organised the welcome party. Wiga and Cedd would meet King Waermund at the harbour and escort him into town. Lord Freawine and Offa would stand inside the town gates waiting to greet him and one of Hebeke's ladies would be at her side with a tray of refreshments ready for Lady Hebeke, as was the custom, to offer the king on his arrival. Tanwen, Mae, Edyth and Hilde, being servants, were to keep out of sight until summoned.

Mae and Edyth protested loudly. They were furious at the insult to Tanwen, but Tanwen, unperturbed stared vacantly into the distance. She understood that they were angry and could hear what they were saying, but their words made no sense to her. Feeling cold, isolated and utterly despondent, she watched the king's arrival, with Mae, Edyth and Hilde, from the window in the women's hall.

The king was old and frail and later Wiga told her he needed his men to helped him from the longboat.

'Welcome to Hedeby, Lord King, your son, Prince Offa, is impatient to greet you.' Lord Freawine said bowing low and motioning to Offa to follow his example. But Offa ignored him and seemed to direct his attention to a buzzard circling above them.

'Is he always this disobedient?' the king wanted to know.

'No, Waermund, he generally obeys without question.' Freawine answered, truthfully.

The king grunted. 'Don't you have a greeting for your father, boy?'

Offa was silent.

'Well, can't you speak, has that buzzard nipped out your tongue?'

Freawine spoke on his behalf. 'Prince Offa is not long out of his sickbed, Waermund. A terrible fever and sore throat, even his ears were affected. He has been reluctant to use his voice for some time, but I'm pleased to say he is on the mend now. I'll have his nurse take him back to his chamber, to rest.'

'That's a lie.' Tanwen exclaimed.

'But easier than admitting the truth,' Hilde replied.

'Hmm,' was all the king had to say on the subject.

After the Waermund had drunk his wine, Freawine led him and his companions to the guest hall. Before entering the king peered around the enclosure and asked why Tanwen was not here to greet him.

Freawine glanced at Lady Hebeke who appeared flustered and at a loss for words.

'Tanwen, cousin?' She said at last. 'She is in the women's hall, with the other servants.'

'Servant. Since when has Tanwen been a servant?' The king demanded.

Lady Hebeke was visibly shaken. 'Tanwen is certainly not a servant, cousin Waermund. She is a companion. A highly respected member of our household. She is in the hall to supervise the servants and make sure everything runs smoothly during your visit.'

'Liar.' Edyth said.

'Wriggled her way out of it nicely though,' said Mae.

'Hmm, give me time to bathe then have her join me.' The king said.

* * *

Tanwen was quaking as she crossed the courtyard to the guest hall. She had expected to join King Waermund at the same time as Lord Freawine and his family, but the king had requested a few moments alone with her to talk about Angeln and her family, and knowing he would ask about Offa's affliction, Tanwen was very afraid.

She decided that unless the king intended taking Offa home with him, she would support Lord Freawine's story. Not from loyalty to the Freawine's, nor from fear of the king's reaction, but purely from her love of Offa and her desire to protect him.

Offa was an unhappy child. There was no doubt of that. But the people of Hedeby, heartless as they were, were familiar to him. He had learned what to expect from them and how to avoid their cruelty - most of the time. Furthermore, the Freawine's expected nothing of him, and he did not have to prove himself as a prince. Angeln would be different. He would know no one but Tanwen, and the jeers and taunts would start all over again. If she could take him to Thorndor's homestead Wynn would help keep him safe, but he would be sent to the men's hall where Tanwen would no longer be able to protect him.

When Tanwen entered the hall, Hafoc and some of his men were already there. Hafoc was in conversation with the king, who was sitting in front of the fire, ensconced in a well-cushioned chair Lord Freawine had paid Old Hren to make for him many years before.

He bade Tanwen welcome and beckoned her closer. 'My eyes are not so good these days, and I want to take a good look at you. Thorndor will never forgive me if I don't give him a full account of what I have seen.'

'Where is he my lord, is he well?'

'He is in Leire, collecting taxes, I hope. We were to meet there, but I was unexpectedly diverted, and yes, he is very well. Far too well for a man of his age if you ask me.' Tanwen tried not to smile.

The king's bones creaked as he eased himself to his feet. 'If Thorndor had known I was coming to Hedeby, he would have sent a kiss and his love. As his king, I claim the right to act in his place.' He took Tanwen by the shoulders and planted a kiss on her cheek. 'From your father, you understand,' he said with a frown.

Tanwen felt the colour rise in her cheeks. 'Thank you, lord king, and may I enquire about …'

'Yes, yes, the tireless Wynn is also well, and her motley family continues to grow. One of these days there will be no room for Thorndor in his own house.'

Tanwen laughed. She had forgotten how amusing and good-humoured the king could be. Waermund, apparently suffering from a wound or painful joint, limped back to his chair and groaned as he lowered himself into it. He drained his horn of wine. 'Now, what's all this nonsense about Offa? Is Freawine's story true?'

Tanwen swallowed nervously before she spoke. 'The prince is indeed obedient, my lord, and seldom objects to or argues about anything. He has had a cold recently, which has affected his voice, but he is also very shy. He is going through that difficult stage when boys feel awkward in company.'

'Shy?' The king blinked his rheumy eyes in surprise.

'Hedeby is a quiet place. Apart from occasional scops passing through we have few visitors.'

'Hmm. I suppose that's not always a bad thing.'

Lord Freawine arrived with his family and Offa in tow. The king indicated that Offa should sit at his side. Lord Freawine bowed to the king. 'You have already met my sons, Waermund, this is my daughter, Modpruth, known to us as Honey, because of the sweetness of her character. She will make Prince Offa a good wife.'

Modpruth, now a beautiful girl of fifteen, was dressed in a deep-green, linen tunic, over a lighter green shift. Tall and slender, her luxurious, flame-red hair fell around her shoulders in loose curls and her brilliant green eyes blazed with determination.

She bowed before the king, straightened up slowly, and looked him boldly in the eye. 'I do not wish to marry the imbecile, my lord king. I would prefer to marry you. Be assured I would make you a perfect wife and queen,' she said confidently.

The court gasped. Lady Hebeke looked as if she wanted to strangle her daughter. Lord Freawine flushed, Wiga and Cedd squirmed with embarrassment and Tanwen lowered her head and chewed her lip to stop herself laughing. Offa stared directly at Modpruth but said nothing.

King Waermund smiled but his voice was hard. 'I am honoured, Modpruth, but alas I am too old for a beautiful young woman like you. You would send me to an early grave, but with a smile on my face, no doubt.'

His men roared with laughter, but the Freawine's remained silent. The king held up a hand to quieten the court. 'I agree with your father, Modpruth. You will make a good wife for my son - after you have learned manners and how to control your tongue.' He turned to Lord Freawine.

'You have a fine family, Freawine, but now we must discuss the defence of Hedeby.'

Freawine reported on military matters on the southern marches. 'Do you believe Friogar is preparing to attack?' the king asked.

'No, Waermund, he is aware that you have brought a hundred men with you, and that another two hundred are making their way by land. He is young, but not a fool, he won't do anything to engage him in a battle with the might of your combined kingdoms. I expect he will continue with raids on isolated villages because he knows he can get away with it. If you could spend the winter here ...'

'Not possible,' the king said scratching his beard. 'I must carry on with my rounds of the kingdom, reminding my chieftains and the Jutes, who holds power. If the Swarbians are going to be troublesome I will need a steady tribute of men and money.'

It seemed the king was mulling it over, and no one spoke. 'What if I called in the fyrd and together we eliminated Friogar? How would the Swarbians react?'

'I believe the Saxon tribes will band together if one of their kings is attacked without good reason.'

'Are you ready for a major war against the Saxons, my lord?' Hafoc asked.

The king shook his head. 'No. So we have to catch Friogar red-handed.'

'Yes, lord,' Hafoc agreed.

'How many men does he have?'

'Around one hundred and fifty men, fully armed and armoured.'

The king turned to Freawine. 'Are his newly purchased men equally well equipped, Freawine?'

'I doubt it, Waermund, probably only spears, shields and leather armour. But if you leave me one hundred men from your bodyguard we should be able to prevent Friogar from crossing the Eider in force.'

The king stood, stretched and sat again. 'Hmm,' he said. 'So be it. That will leave me one hundred to travel with and another hundred stationed about the realm. In the summer, I want you to call up the fyrd in your district and prepare them to defend their property if the need arises.' He grinned. 'Don't look so glum, Freawine. We have long been companions and will soon be kinfolk. You are known as a great warrior and an even greater drinker. Let me speak with Tanwen and Hafoc and then we will spend the night drinking to our future grandchildren.'

'Yes, Waermund.' Freawine replied. The prince remained silent.

***

When Lord Freawine and the men left, the king beckoned Tanwen closer. 'Hafoc tells me you can use a sword as well as any man.' Tanwen wondered what else Hafoc had said about her. 'It is no surprise; I recall you dreamed of being a sword-maiden.'

Tanwen smiled but did not reply.

'I want you to keep the women calm. There will be rumours of war, play them down. I don't want panic to spread. And Hafoc, lastly and most importantly, I want Friogar caught with blood on his fingers. Suspicion alone is not sufficient to start a war. Do I make myself clear?'

'Yes lord.' Tanwen and Hafoc replied together.

'Good. In the meantime, I'll send messages to my chiefs and the Jutes, to gather their men-at-arms and prepare for a great campaign.' The king left two days later, keeping his promise to leave one hundred men behind.

Months passed without incident, then several outlying villages were raided and burned. The women were nervous. 'The Myrging's are coming,' they wailed. 'They will destroy Hedeby and make us all slaves.'

'No, they won't.' Tanwen insisted. 'We have the combined might of Angeln and Jutland behind us they wouldn't dare attack.'

'And Friogar has the Swarbians,' she heard them mutter amongst themselves. 'And don't forget he also has the Saxons, and they would have done with us long before King Waermund arrives.'

At Tanwen's request, Freawine addressed the townsfolk. 'We have one hundred of King Waermund's best men, Hafoc and Prince Offa's bodyguard, as well the militia and our own fyrd to protect the town. The Myrging civil war has left them weak, and their militia depleted. Our spies have confirmed recent rumours that Friogar is dead, no doubt at the hands of his uncle, Meaca. But Meaca is no fool. He won't come into Hedeby. He will satisfy himself with attacks on small hamlets and villages. We'll catch him soon, then even that will come to an end.' He sounded confident, but the women were unconvinced and worried about their sons being killed, their daughters raped, and their animals stolen.

Thirteen

Tanwen awoke to a melee of flaring torches, clashing weapons, shouts, and screams. She leapt out of bed and grabbed her dagger. Her first instinct was to run to Offa, but with Wiga, Cedd and guards to protect him, he would be safe for a while. Instead, she hurried to Lady Hebeke's chamber where Hebeke and the servants were stuffing whatever gold and jewellery they could find into skin pouches before fleeing.

Hebeke turned, pale-faced, to Tanwen. 'Help us, Tanwen. The Myrging must not find our treasure.'

Tanwen shook her head. 'I must find the prince …'

She heard a piercing scream and ran to the door to see what was going on. She cursed. The guards had deserted their post, leaving the women unprotected.

A band of armed men, their helmets glinting in the dawn light, were charging toward the hall. She slammed the huge door shut, dropped the bar into its brackets then flinched as a seaxe thumped into the door. She muttered a quick prayer to Nethrus.

'Tanwen, what's happening? Have we been invaded?' Mae appeared, closely followed by a gaggle of female household servants and slaves.

Tanwen forced herself to sound calm. 'It's all right. A Myrging raid, that's all.'

Mae squealed. 'What, here? The Myrgings are here, attacking the town?'

Tanwen nodded. The door shook as more seaxes hit the wood. Lord Freawine had always insisted the Myrgings were too craven to raid the town, but now they were here, and the hall echoed with the crash of their seaxe blows.

'What can we do?' Mae asked, anxiously.

'Get knives, daggers, swords, anything you can lay your hands on. If anyone breaks through the door knock them to the ground and keep stabbing until they are dead.'

The older women were horror-struck. Some were crying, others were muttering among themselves. 'We can't do that,' one cried. 'We're not soldiers.'

'That's right,' another agreed. 'It's up to the guard to protect us.'

'Then do nothing.' Tanwen snapped. 'Just wait here to be raped and killed.'

Mae paled but quickly assumed the role of senior servant and took command. 'Go, search everywhere. Try the woodshed, there may be an old axe lying around. Frieda, light the torches - let us at least have a decent light to kill them by. Is there anything else we can do? Boil water, fetch dressings?' she asked Tanwen.

Tanwen had a fleeting image of her mother dousing fires on that day, many years ago, when she prepared the hall to protect her family from the Picts.

'No. Leave the torches and douse the fires. We don't want flame used against us. And just make sure you kill anyone who enters the hall.' Her heart was racing. What should she do? She knew she had to get out of here and make sure Offa was safe. But how? She peered through the arrow-slit. Surprised

English warriors were running from their homes with swords, axes and spears.

Myrging arrows were flitting across the roofs. She could hear them thumping into the thatch. The hall guards had not deserted. They were dead, a bloody tangle of limbs and weapons lying in a heap at the door.

Fur clad enemy warriors whooped through the town, hacking mercilessly at any unfortunate English folk who got in their way. But no one noticed Tanwen jump down into the yard, run to the ditch and wriggle through the thorn hedge, which brought her out near the men's hall. Hysterical women and children sped past her, while half-dressed English merchants scurried to find makeshift weapons to defend their families.

For a moment Tanwen could not move. The house guards were dead, the townspeople were in a state of panic and the enemy was slaughtering its way to Offa. Lord Freawine, with Wiga and Cedd at heel, was swinging his sword in a circle above his head shouting, 'kill the Myrging swine. Kill them all.' She dropped to her knees and begged Nethrus to keep them all safe.

The stench of fresh blood and human excrement cast Tanwen's mind back to the horror of the last day she spent in her homeland, the day she witnessed another bloody massacre and experienced for the first time, the terrible sounds and smells of war.

She sank back into the hedge and in stupefied fascination watched the swords and seaxes rise and fall; watched blood spurting and splashing the walls of nearby houses, watched three Myrging warriors hacking at a man to ensure he was really dead and listened to a woman screaming in the house he had been defending.

'Tanwen. Tanwen.' Hebeke gripped her arm, shouting over the deafening noise. 'Tanwen. The hall is on fire. I am taking the women into the forest. Come with us. Help us hide the gold.'

Instantly alert, Tanwen sprang to her feet, shaking her head vigorously. 'Offa - I have to find Offa.' She would have darted away but Lady Hebeke caught hold of her nightdress and hauled her back.

'I will find Offa. He is my responsibility and so are you. I will find him and bring him into the forest. You go with the women.'

But Tanwen struggled free and dashed for the men's hall, with Hebeke close behind. They dropped down behind a bush while a howling mob of Myrgings surged by. One grabbed a log from a fire and tossed it onto the thatch of a nearby hut. His companions laughed and followed his lead until the huts caught fire and their inhabitants ran screaming onto the street and waiting enemy spears. Someone bellowed an order to open the enclosure and soon horses and cattle were thundering through the streets adding even more chaos to the fray.

Taking advantage of the turmoil, Tanwen and Lady Hebeke ran on, but they were too late. The hall doors were open, the Myrging's had been and gone and there were no survivors. Sickened by the sight of so many blood-soaked bodies lying on the floor, Tanwen crept along the sidewall and slumped down in a corner, wishing she had gone to the forest with the other women. With her arms wrapped around her knees and her head down, she cried.

It was not until the harrowing wail of a woman permeated the wall that Tanwen realised Hebeke had not followed her into the hall. She craned her neck to look out of an arrow-slit and saw Hebeke on her knees, sobbing over the body of her husband.

She knew she should drag Hebeke away, in case the Myrgings recognised her and took her hostage. But Offa might still be alive, and he was her priority. She took a deep breath and braced herself to search among the corpses for him, at the same time praying that he would not be there. She retched every time she rolled a body over for inspection. Many of the faces were no more than lumps of mashed flesh and bone, but Tanwen was undeterred. She would recognise Offa, no matter what they had done to him.

There was a thunderous crash and a huge Myrging warrior hurtled through the roof, swearing as he landed on the corpse of one of his companions. Tanwen, petrified, could do nothing but gape as he dragged himself to his feet and lumbered toward her.

'So, what we got here then?' He leered at her. 'A fine lady worth a fine ransom, I should say.' He was a broad-shouldered, red-bearded brute of a man, dressed in stinking, blood-stained wolf skins and wielding a heavy seaxe. He was drunk, though Tanwen was unsure if it was looted wine or the frenzy of the bloodbath that had intoxicated him.

He wiped the blood and slobber from his mouth on his filthy sleeve and lunged forward to grab her, but by now Tanwen had gathered her wits and dodged out of his reach. She made a run for the door but he caught her arm.

'Not so fast, my lovely,' he slurred, as she struggled to free herself. She kicked out, aiming for the spot she knew would hurt most, but his furs protected him, and her effort was wasted.

'Oh, I see. Fancy a bit of a struggle, do you?' He used his great bulk to pin her against the wall and stroked her hair. 'Lovely hair, soft and scented, not English though, too dark. What are you then, Roman, Frankish?'

'I'm Tanwen, daughter, and pupil of Thorndor, Wizard of Angeln and if you don't take your filthy hands off me, I'll turn your balls to pus and render your manhood useless.

Unexpectedly, the Myrging was on the ground with Offa looming over him, holding him down with one foot on his belly and a sword at his throat. Relief flooded over her. She smiled broadly at her saviour and spat at the Myrging.

'Kill him, Offa. Now. Kill him while he's down.' She urged.

Offa removed his foot and flicked the tip of his sword, indicating he wanted the prisoner to rise. The Myrging, eyes darting from Offa to Tanwen and back again, cautiously raised himself to a crouching position. Offa thrust his sword aside, picked up a shield and seaxe, and signalled to the warrior to stand.

Tanwen frantically tugged at his arm. 'No, Offa. You mustn't. Watching other boys training is not the same as taking part. You don't have to fight. You're not a warrior.' But Offa shook her away and gestured his intention to fight.

The Myrging scrutinised Offa through narrowed eyes. 'What's the matter English dog? Someone pinched your tongue?'

'He's mute. That's what's the matter with him,' she snarled. 'He's nothing but a mute child. What kind of warrior are you, to attack women and sick children?'

She turned. 'Offa. I forbid you to fight. In your father's name, I insist you drop the seaxe. If we take him prisoner there'll be no shame.'

But Offa was concentrating on the Myrging who was now upright and preparing to fight by shifting his seaxe from hand to hand to find a comfortable grip.

The enemies glared at each other, neither wanting to make the first move. Suddenly they both ran forward until they came within an arm's length then each took a mighty swipe at the other. Each deflected the blow with his shield and then crouched and warily circled each other.

Tanwen watched in horror as the Myrging advanced and delivered a blow with his seaxe, Offa blocked it with his shield and retaliated with a swing, which missed because his adversary had jumped out of range. The Myrging tried again. Then Offa. Round and round, they circled, until the Myrging lost patience, cursed and cast his shield aside enabling him to raise his seaxe with both hands. Offa did the same. In a heartbeat they were charging at one another like mad bulls, each determined to deliver the killer blow.

The Myrging tried first, letting go of his seaxe as he swung. The weapon struck Offa's arm, exposing the bone. Tanwen screamed at him to yield but he shoved her away. He staggered and reeled as blood sprayed from the wound, but he hurled his body forward, and with a supreme effort, raised his seaxe and embedded its blade in his enemy's shoulder.

The Myrging fell to his knees, swayed from side to side then slowly toppled, face down onto the corpse of a fellow warrior.

They stared at the body for several heartbeats before Tanwen spoke. 'You're wounded.' It sounded flat and superfluous even to her ears. Offa shrugged, wincing at the pain caused by the movement.

Flaming arrows were raining through the damaged roof, starting small fires wherever they landed, the thatch was alight and the area was rapidly filling with smoke.

Soon the whole building would be ablaze.

Tanwen ripped a strip from her nightdress and hurriedly bound Offa's arm. 'I'll dress it properly later but now we have to get Hebeke to safety. I'll get her away from Freawine's body, you take her to the forest to join her ladies - and stay there until I come for you.'

Offa shook his head vigorously. He picked up a sword and indicated his intention to fight.

'Not now, Offa, the king will punish Wigheard and Cedd if anything happens to you, and you wouldn't want that, would you?'

Offa screwed up his face and slashed the sword at an imaginary foe.

'Your day will come. But today it's more important to get Lady Hebeke away from here.' Offa pouted and lowered the sword. Tanwen smiled and squeezed his hand.

Outside the fighting had almost stopped and the plunder and destruction had begun. The enemies were wrecking houses in search of gold and jewellery.

Tanwen and Offa gently eased Lady Hebeke away from Lord Freawine's body. 'Come along, my lady. Offa will take you to the forest. Your ladies will look after you.'

An old woman, red-eyed and face blackened by smoke, peered back at Tanwen. Her hair, which had been brushed so carefully a few hours ago, hung lank over her blood-soaked nightdress.

'Lady Hebeke, you must get Modpruth to safety. When they're satisfied they have all the gold they will be looking for hostages.'

Hebeke seemed incapable of speech. She just stood and cried.

'You must go, my lady. Please. Before they come for Offa and Modpruth.'

'My sons, my husband …'

'I saw Cedd and Wigheard a short while ago, fighting by the crossroads. Nethrus will protect them.'

It was obvious Hebeke did not believe a word, but she allowed Offa to take her arm and lead her away. She turned back, 'Tanwen, are you coming with us?'

'I'll fetch salves and poultices and join you shortly in the clearing.'

She set off, weaving her way between the dead and wounded until she reached the remains of the hall. It had been fired. The thatch had collapsed, and flames engulfed the wattle and daub walls. At the rear of the hall, Tanwen's healing chamber was unscathed. It was little more than a hut and from the outside looked like a cattle byre, except that the roof was higher and more steeply pitched than usual. It was supposed to be a replica of Wynn's healing chamber but had turned out smaller. Not that that mattered. That is, not until now. Where on earth was she going to accommodate all the wounded?

She pushed open the timber door and closed it behind her. Everything was as she had left it. Seven wooden pallets for the sick were spread on the bare earth floor. A round stone, very old and almost black, lay in the centre and its smooth surface was carved with runes. She dropped to her knees, pushed the stone aside, and delved into a deep hole to retrieve a deerskin bag containing the pots of precious oils, salves and unguents she had saved for just such an occasion. She took rolled-up strips of linen from a box and stuffed them, along with several bundles of dried herbs, into the bag. Then she wrapped herself in a coarse woollen blanket, closed her eyes, and thanked Nethrus for keeping the healing chamber safe.

She ran to the crossroads where she had last seen Wiga, hoping to see him alive before she fled the town but there was no sign of him. She prayed he was wounded and had made his way to the forest.

Two enemy warriors had slain the basket maker and his wife, Swuste. Having ransacked the meagre hut and found nothing but baskets, they had taken brands from the street fire and set it alight. Tanwen stopped abruptly. The children. Swuste still cared for the children. Where were they?

Smoke billowed from the doorway. More burning brands were thrown in. The men took swigs from nearby pitchers of ale and fell, laughing, to the ground, too drunk to notice Tanwen slip past them. She covered her mouth with the corner of the cloak and ran through the choking smoke into the house.

Inside, huddled behind a stack of baskets she found Dan, Willow and Mati, wide-eyed and speechless with terror after seeing their guardians cut down. Close by, in a small basket lay a baby of only two months old.

'Grab your cloaks and follow me,' she said. The children stared but did not move.

'Come along. Do you want the Myrging's to find you and throw you onto the fire?'

Only Mati, who was approaching her third winter, responded. She came forward and slipped her tiny hand into Tanwen's. Her bottom lip wavered. 'I want Mama. I want Mama come.'

The children were coughing. If they were here much longer, they would die. Exasperated, she thrust her precious bag into the arms of Dan and pushed him to the door. If she could get him out surely the others would follow.

'Take this to Mae. Go out of the door, turn left, and don't stop running until you reach the clearing. We will be right behind you.' Dan obeyed without a sound or backward glance and, as she had anticipated, the other children immediately followed their brother out of the burning hovel. Tanwen picked up the baby, snatched a bundle of cloaks, and escaped just as the roof collapsed. Dan raced ahead and was soon out of sight but Tanwen, struggling with the baby and cloaks and constantly stopping to chivvy Willow and Mati along, made slow progress.

When they reached the safety of the forest. Mae spotted them and rushed to help. Tanwen passed her the baby. 'We'll need a wet nurse,' she said.

'I'll send Edyth to find someone.'

'Offa?' Tanwen asked.

'He's safe, helping the men-folk.'

'And Lady Hebeke?'

'Much better. We've cleaned her up. The water was freezing but she didn't complain. And a forester found her some clothes to wear. Now she looks more like a woodcutter than a warlord's lady.'

'Where's Modpruth?'

'In the woodsman's bed. His wife gave her some broth to calm her and thankfully she fell asleep, the last thing we need is a display of hysterics from Modpruth.' Tanwen smiled. She could not have put it better herself.

Lady Hebeke emerged from a hut, pale-faced with gaunt hollows under wild eyes. She was dressed in the garb of a woodsman, dark leather breeches and a coarse woollen tunic. She looked terrible, and no wonder, after all she had been through. She threw her arms around Tanwen. 'Tanwen. Oh Tanwen, I am so pleased to see you alive and well after all that has happened.'

Tanwen returned the embrace. 'Thank Nethrus we are all here, safe at last.'

'Except for my lord husband and my dear sons,' Lady Hebeke added in a trembling voice.

'Tanwen nodded sympathetically. 'How is Modpruth?'

'She's resting. The poor darling was exhausted.'

Edyth and Hilde gathered the children and were sorting them into groups according to their needs. Older children were sent out to retrieve and distribute the large stash of blankets, furs and dried meat which was secreted in the wood for emergencies such as this. Calm, slightly younger ones sang to soothe the babes and Edyth and Hilde comforted the scared and screaming who had witnessed the slaughter of one or both parents. The townswomen scavenged about the wood by torchlight, looking for anything edible to add to the dried meat to make a broth to warm their bellies and Offa was working with the woodsmen, hauling logs and bracken from the forest to make shelters.

The looting had stopped, and all was quiet. Tanwen assumed the Myrging's were sleeping off the effects of the wine. Wounded men were making their way to the forest, many carrying or dragging companions with wounds much worse than their own. Tanwen glanced at the pathetic contents of her healer's box and her eyes filled with tears of dismay. Would she have enough medicine to treat them all, and if she did, would she have the strength to see her through the ordeal?

'What are we to do?' Lady Hebeke asked.

'The best we can,' Tanwen replied.

***

As dawn was breaking, two of the warriors who had escaped with minor injuries placed themselves on the roof of the woodman's hut to watch for activity in the town. Before long one called out that the Myrging's were stirring. By mid-morning, they had gathered up their loot and departed in their boats, with their prisoners.

The men took woodsmen's wagons and oxen to collect their fallen companions too badly wounded to walk to the forest and Tanwen followed on foot. The town was destroyed. Obliterated as if it had never existed. Nothing remained but bodies and heaps of white ash swirling in the breeze.

She slowly picked her way through the dead and dying, stopping to offer help or comfort where necessary, all the while searching for Wiga and desperately praying that she would not find him. Someone called out that they had found Cedd and Tanwen rushed to his side. An axe had crashed through his thigh and he had lost a lot of blood, but he was still alive. He groaned as they lifted him onto the wagon, before passing out.

Tanwen hoped they would be able to save him, for his mother's sake.

When the last of the survivors were taken away, she stayed behind and walked once more around the corpses forcing herself to look closely at each one. And then she found Wiga. Lying in a pool of blood an arm half severed and an axe in his spine. She cursed the Myrgings and fell over his body, weeping.

She spent the following days bathing wounds, setting bones and changing dressings and the nights making salves, poultices and infusions, or any other medication she might need the following day. There was little cloth left for making bandages and dressings, as it had all been burned by the Myrging's, so the womenfolk washed the used ones in the burn then boiled them in a cauldron over the fire ready to be used again.

Tanwen and Mae carried out the complicated, gruesome, medical procedures while Lady Hebeke and Edyth helped with the after care, but the unrelenting work left them little time for food or rest. Even when the opportunity arose Tanwen was too agitated to sleep. She worried that she might have inadvertently used poisonous herbs to ease pain or stitched something into a wound that should have been left out. She worried that it was her mismanagement that caused some wounds to fester, and not the terrible conditions she worked in that made infection inevitable. And she cried. She cried for Wigheard, she cried for Wynn, she cried for Aelfrun and she held her precious amulet close to her heart and cried for her mother.

In the dead of night, while the makeshift camp slept, Tanwen, accompanied by one of the night guards, wandered from shelter to shelter checking wounds and offering warm poppy leaf tea to help ease their pain.

Offa worked tirelessly. At fourteen he had the strength of three men and never baulked at a chore no matter how grisly or menial. Tanwen's heart missed a beat every time she glimpsed him felling a tree with a woodman's axe or lifting a wounded man from the wagon.

She was astonished when she saw him hand signing to two of Lord Freawine's men. He was asking them to go to seek help from the king, they seemed to have no difficulty in understanding the signing and would have departed without questioning his authority if Cedd had not commanded them to wait as he would soon have an important message of his own for the king.

Tanwen was cleaning an infected head wound when she noticed Offa with a group of men. Concerned that they might be bullying him she stopped what she was doing and moved closer to hear what was being said. The men were watching him intently. He was using hand signs to suggest the digging of a pit for a mass grave rather than wasting time digging many individual graves. Some of the men argued for a traditional pyre, but Offa demonstrated, by holding his hand over his nose and mouth, and indicating first to the fire and next to wounded and dying warriors that the smoke and smell of so many burning bodies would be intolerable to them.

'He's right. The smell would linger for days and they've suffered enough already,' one man shouted to his companions.

'The women and children too, let's not make life even more unpleasant for them,' another added.

The men muttered among themselves for several heartbeats until led by Offa, they set off to dig a pit.

Tanwen thought her heart would burst with pride. Offa was a born leader of men, even without a voice.

On the fifth day, Cedd, learning that his father and brother were dead, insisted he was well enough to take command, despite protestations from Hilde and Lady Hebeke.

'Don't fuss, mother. Has it escaped your notice that I am now next in line to be king? Except for the lack-wit of course, and he will never be fit to rule.'

Tanwen seethed. 'Prince Offa will make a fine king. He has already shown his worth by working as hard as any man in the camp.'

'What use is a king without a voice?'

'More use than a king without a heart.' Tanwen stormed off. Didn't she have enough to worry about without Cedd making a bid for the crown? She was hot and her head seemed to be filled with gushing water. She made her way to the burn to bathe her face, knelt on the damp grass and bent forward to drink the cool, clear water straight from the stream.

She recoiled in horror. It wasn't water. It was blood. It was red. Everything was red. No. It was black. The water was closing around her. The noise was deafening, she felt for her amulet.

She was swimming. She was cold, very cold. Her arms ached and her chest hurt. She wanted to stop and rest, but in the distance, she could see a ship with Horsa at its helm and his arms outstretched. He was calling out to her, 'Tanwen, Tanwen,' but no matter how hard she swam she could not reach him. She was nearly there. 'Tanwen.' Horsa was waiting, the pain was excruciating but she would not give up. Harder and harder she swam, gasping for breath but determined to reach the ship, then she was falling, down, down into the darkness. Seaweed brushed her face. She screamed and swiped it away. Water trickled down her throat.

She was lying on the soft, damp seabed, willing her aching body to raise itself. She could smell food cooking on a fire and hear distant voices, but not Horsa's. She remembered the battle. The dead, the dying, the screaming children. Her eyes were sore as if filled with sand and the lids would barely move. She hoped they were stitched together, she never wanted to open them again.

'Don't leave me, Tanwen,' someone whispered. The words were slow and deliberate, like Wiga's when he was learning Latin. A man's voice, but not Wiga's.

'Please don't die.'

Her eyes opened. Offa was at her side he kissed her brow and was gone. Had she dreamed it? Later he was holding her hand. How much later she could not tell, a heartbeat, a day, a year?'

'Tanwen.' Footsteps. Mae was standing over her. 'Edyth, fetch Lady Hebeke.' She lifted Tanwen's head and did something with her pillow. 'There's a fright you gave us all. The poor prince has been beside himself.'

It was all coming back now; the overwhelming weariness, the desperate need to sleep and the utter inability to rest. 'How long have I been here?'

'A full day, Prince Offa said you never opened your eyes once, and he should know, he's been at your side the whole time.'

Offa grinned and nodded enthusiastically and Tanwen mouthed 'thank you,' at the same time touching her lips with her fingertips and dropping her hand forward.

She was lying on a bedraggled bear fur under a three-sided log and fern shelter. Offa brought her a roughly hewn wooden bowl of thin broth. She eased herself into a sitting position and sipped it slowly, relishing each mouthful.

'You must be starving, you haven't eaten for days, not that there's been much to eat. And most of what we have goes to the men.' Tanwen noticed the resentment in Mae's voice.

'They need to keep their strength up,' she said.

'I agree,' Mae said, 'but the women and children have bellies too.'

Lady Hebeke arrived. 'The gods may have deserted us, Mae' she said, 'but thankfully the weather has been kind. The men have already built enough shelters to get everyone under cover at night and now they are rebuilding the town. They will soon turn their attention to hunting and we will all have full bellies.'

'Yes, my lady.' Mae replied with an ironic smile.

'We are so pleased to see you well again, Tanwen. We were beginning to wonder what would become of poor Offa if anything should happen to you. Is that not so, Offa?' Lady Hebeke turned just in time to see Offa disappear into the forest. 'Sometimes I simply do not understand that child's behaviour,' she said. 'My boys were so bright and cheerful; they never gave me a moment's concern.'

'Yes, Lady Hebeke,' Tanwen and Mae replied, with raised eyebrows and little conviction.

Fourteen

Rest, sleep and warm food had worked their magic and Tanwen was on her feet, ready to start work in no time. Mae begged her to rest, at least for the remainder of the day, but she was determined to check all her patients before dark. She did not mention her dream to anyone.

Offa returned in the early evening with a doe across his shoulders and two cows and a bull trailing behind. The children spotted him first, and their taunts could be heard throughout the camp. They thumbed their noses, bared their backsides and hurled insults at him until the women rushed out, boxed their ears, and sent them away.

'What's the idiot been up to now?' Cedd called to Tanwen as she ran past his pallet on her way to Offa.

'He's brought food.'

Excited women dragged the doe away to be skinned and gutted, while youths wasted no time in building up the fire and erecting a spit.

Two men tied the cattle to nearby trees, 'good lad. We'll start work on an enclosure tomorrow,' one said, patting Offa's shoulder. Tanwen gave Offa the thumbs-up sign.

For the first time in days, folk were laughing, chatting and singing as they went about their chores. The whole camp took on an air of festivity. With Hilde's help, Cedd had dragged himself from his pallet to see what all the fuss was about.

Lady Hebeke ordered one of her ladies to find the heart and liver of the doe to sacrifice to the Earth Mother. She was mortified. 'Me? I've never handled innards in my life.'

'Then go hungry, Frieda, I do not have the energy to argue. I will find someone with an appetite to do it.' Frieda scowled and clomped off in the direction of the slaughter.

'Where did the lack-wit find a deer carcass?' Cedd asked.

'Prince Offa brought the deer down himself.' Tanwen could not disguise her pride.

'Offa. Rubbish, that bungling fool can't ride and has no weapons.'

'He can run, and he has a dagger and hand-seaxe.'

'It's impossible. No one ever outran a deer or brought one down with a dagger. He's lying.'

'The Atheling of Angeln does not lie. He runs as well as a hound and could break a deer's neck with his bare hands. You will do well to remember that Cedd if you should ever be unfortunate enough to meet him in battle.'

Lady Hebeke and Tanwen built a small shrine to the Earth Mother and offered her the heart and liver of the deer in exchange for the food she had delivered. Tanwen also sacrificed an arm-ring and silently begged the Earth Mother to show her the way to restore Offa's voice.

Hilde, with Eawyn and Cwenhild in tow, came up behind them. 'Excuse me, Mother Hebeke, my lord husband asked me to fetch you.'

Lady Hebeke was on her feet in an instant. 'Is he ill? Has he relapsed? I ordered him to rest.'

'No, Mother Hebeke, my lord is well and in fine voice, he said he has something of the utmost importance to say to you.'

'Daughter, you really must not allow your husband to treat you like a servant. Tell my son I am at prayer and will come to him when I am finished.'

'But my lady, I was told it is urgent and I was to bring you immediately.'

'Hilde, show some spirit in front of your daughters. Are the Myrgings upon us?'

'No Mother Hebeke.'

'Then what can be so urgent that it must disrupt my prayers? Tell my son I will be along forthwith.'

When Tanwen and Lady Hebeke arrived Cedd was sprawled on a makeshift chair with the twins at his feet. He stood, pushed the children aside with his foot and offered his seat to his mother. Hilde was agitated and clumsily tried to conceal a red weal on her cheek by hiding behind the twins. The girls pushed her away and ran from the shelter. Cedd dismissed his wife with an impatient wave of his hand. She picked up soiled bandages and left without a word.

'You too, Tanwen,' he barked. 'This is family business.' Fuming, Tanwen turned to leave. 'Stay, Tanwen.' Lady Hebeke commanded. 'There is nothing in our family that cannot be discussed in front of you.'

'Suit yourself. She'll find out soon enough anyway.' Cedd paused for several heartbeats before speaking directly to his mother. 'I've been considering our situation. As you are aware, part of the agreement with Waermund was that if anything should happen to Offa, father would inherit his kingdom. It would then pass down our line to Wiga and, in the unlikely event of his death, to me.' He paused, waiting until his mother and Tanwen nodded in agreement. 'Well, Father and Wiga are both dead and something has happened to Offa. He's lost his wits - if he ever had any. He is an imbecile, and we all know the Engel folk will never accept him as king.'

'He is not an imbecile.' Tanwen cried.

'Shut up or get out.' Cedd bellowed. Tanwen threw him an icy, resentful stare but did not speak. Cedd continued, 'Waermund is in his dotage and can't have much longer to live. He will soon recall his son and heir. However, as we have already established, Offa is unfit to rule.'

Tanwen was about to interrupt but Cedd silenced her with a disdainful look. 'As yet, Waermund knows nothing of the raid. We'll tell him that Offa lost his wits during the battle, the king will then name me his heir.'

'And how do you suppose Offa will react when he learns you have stolen his inheritance?' Tanwen asked.

'Offa is too stupid to know what is going on around him. Besides, I have no intention of stealing his inheritance. I will act as regent until his death. I'm a patient man and imbeciles aren't long-lived creatures.'

'And what of Offa?' Tanwen asked through clenched teeth.

'Offa will remain here, receiving the same care and attention he always has. The king is too frail to pay us another visit, if he sends envoys, we will keep Offa out of sight as much as possible. No one will suspect. If anyone asks to see him, we can say strangers disturb him, it's not too far from the truth.'

'Don't you think Offa will object?'

Cedd snorted. 'Offa doesn't have the wit to object.'

Lady Hebeke beamed. 'All my prayers answered so soon. My son will be king, and I will never have to tell Waermund his son was born a lack-wit.'

Tanwen's body tensed with indignation. She glanced from one to the other. 'You'll never get away with it, you are mad, both of you.'

'We'll get away with it as long as you keep your mouth shut,' Cedd snapped.

'And are you witless enough to think I'll stand quietly by and let it happen?'

'Yes, unless you want to lose your head.'

'And how do you intend to get this message to Waermund? Who do you suppose you can trust enough to lie to the king for you?' Tanwen wanted to know.

Cedd smirked. 'I'll send a written message, runes, just like you taught me. No one will be able to read it but the king.' He nodded insolently in Lady Hebeke's direction. 'See, Mother, I will make the great general you wished for.'

Tanwen's heart leapt to her throat before plummeting to the pit of her stomach. 'Why don't you just kill him and be done with it?'

'Because I'm no child-slayer.'

Biting back an acid retort, she turned to leave. Cedd seized her wrist and pulled her so close she could feel his fetid breath on her face. 'I'm going to be king, Tanwen, and no one is going to get in my way. Not you, not the idiot nor anyone else. Do I make myself clear?'

Tanwen stared defiantly into his eyes. 'If any harm befalls Offa, I swear I'll make your pain so bad you will cry out to Hel's Steed to end your suffering and carry you off to the underworld.'

Cedd loosened his grip and backed off. 'Your imaginary powers don't scare me. When I'm king …'

'You'll never be king as long as I have a breath in my body.'

Cedd threw back his head and roared with laughter. 'That little problem can soon be overcome.'

'Not by you.' Tanwen stormed off, trembling with rage.

***

When Tanwen returned to the fire, Offa was missing. She found Mae and together they searched the camp for him, to no avail.

Mindful of Cedd's desire to be king and fearing for the prince's safety, they took torches and a pair of hounds and anxiously searched the surrounding woodland, calling his name over and over again until Tanwen eventually found him curled up in the hollow bole of an oak.

'Leave us a torch and a dog and take the others back to camp. Say nothing of this to anyone. We'll follow you shortly.' She waited until Mae had disappeared from view before saying, 'Come out Offa.' The prince turned his head away.

'Offa don't turn away when I'm speaking to you,' she commanded.

He did not respond.

Tanwen's voice hardened, 'the Atheling of Angeln does not cower in a tree, like a hunted animal. Come out into the open and face up to your problems like the king you are going to become,' the tone of her voice demanded obedience.

Offa crawled from the tree and sat on a fallen branch staring into the distance. Tears filled his red-rimmed eyes, and his misery brought an almost unbearable ache to Tanwen's heart, but she knew she must stand firm.

'Well, what have you to say for yourself?' she asked.

Offa began signing. 'And no signing,' she snapped. 'You have a voice, use it.'

The prince accepted her authority without question. 'I'll never be king,' he whispered.

'You will be king. I promised your mother you would be king, and I never break a promise.'

'I heard him,' Offa said.

Tanwen's stomach somersaulted. The wretchedness of his reply left her in no doubt he was referring to her conversation with Cedd. 'Oh. Offa, I'm so sorry,' she said crumpling on the branch beside him and taking his hand in hers. 'I had no idea you were nearby.' She paused, trying to find the right words. 'Well, now you know how precarious your situation is. The time has come for you to prove you are not an imbecile. Go to him, Offa. Stand in front of him and what is left of his father's war band. Make sure there are witnesses, and tell him you are the Atheling of Angeln, the rightful heir to your father's crown and that you will show no mercy to those who oppose you.'

Offa's lip quivered but he looked her in the eye and gave a forlorn smile. 'I can't,' he said.

Struggling to control her temper, Tanwen rose, took the dog lead and said, 'Come, they'll be looking for us.'

They walked back in silence. Mae had saved them each a generous portion of roasted venison, Offa refused to eat and went straight to his bed. Tanwen had suddenly lost her appetite and picked at the meat without interest. She was mulling over the events of the evening. Offa was in danger, she had to get him away from here as soon as possible.

'What happened back there?' Mae sounded more curious than concerned. 'I thought he'd be ravenous.'

Tanwen did not reply for several moments then she suddenly dragged Mae by the hand. 'It's time for action.'

Offa was cuddled into the dog pretending to be asleep. 'I know you're awake,' she said, pushing the dog aside, 'so listen to what I have to say and let me know if there is anything you don't understand, is that clear?'

Offa nodded.

'I'm going to do my usual late evening check of the injured. While I am occupied, I want you both to go in search of Hafoc. When you find him, it must look as if you have come upon him unexpectedly. If he is with companions entice him away, do not allow anyone but Hafoc hear what you have to say. Hafoc may be old, but he is loyal, and he knows his men. He will know who we can trust. Mae will be your voice. Tell him I need to speak with him in secret. After my round, I'll go to the shelter to prepare tomorrow's medications as normal. Bring Hafoc to me there, quietly and under cover of darkness. Don't use torches; rely on the light from the fires, but keep well away from them in case you are recognised. Do you understand?'

Offa and Mae nodded.

'Good. And Mae, while I'm talking with Hafoc, I'd like you to find Edyth and tell her I need help with dressings, don't give her any details, just tell her it's urgent.' Tanwen paused to mull over her instructions. Their lives depended upon Cedd being unaware of her plans, and he would surely have spies everywhere. 'Stay well away from Cedd's shelter,' she said at last, 'and from those of his cronies, and try not to let Hilde see you, she's bound to carry tales to her husband or his mother.' She touched her amulet *Dear Mother, I hope I am doing the right thing, please help me and protect the prince.* 'Do you have any questions?'

***

Hafoc was nearing fifty. He had lost his left ear in a skirmish with the Myrging several years ago and suffered a broken nose in the recent battle, but he still stood erect and trained as hard as any of the younger warriors. His grey hair was thinning and his beard a mixture of frizz and plaits decorated with silver and gold rings. He wore leather leggings and furs and carried a hand-seaxe and knife in his belt.

'Do you know why you are here?' Tanwen asked him.

'No, but I can guess.'

'Prince Offa is in danger. I fear another attack is imminent. He could be taken hostage or killed at any time. I need to get him to the king, in Angeln, without delay and I can't do it without your help.'

Hafoc nodded. 'There's an abandoned wain in the forest. I'll have my men do the necessary repairs …'

'There's no time for that, we must leave tonight.'

'In the dark?'

'Yes, and on horseback. We must put as much distance between the town and ourselves as possible before first light.'

'But the prince can't ride,' Hafoc exclaimed.

'He knows how to ride but lacks experience. He can ride close to me until he is confident enough to ride alone. Mae and Edyth have basic skills, they should improve on the hoof.'

'I wish I shared your conviction.'

'I'm sorry, Hafoc. I know I'm asking a lot, but we must make sure we do everything we can to get make the journey as fast and safe as possible. I'll bring food we can eat on horseback so we can ride with only the briefest of breaks during daylight.'

'I understand, Tanwen.'

'I would like to bring Swuste's children along. Is it possible?'

Hafoc did not flinch. 'The baby is extremely young and would be a hindrance. Its wet nurse would have to come, and we would need a basket of some kind to strap it on someone's back. Providing we have enough horses it will be difficult, but not impossible.'

'I'll speak with the wet nurse and let you know the outcome as soon as possible.'

'I hope Mae and Edyth are up to such a rigorous journey.'

'So do I, Hafoc, so do I.'

'Perhaps it would be more advisable to leave the servants behind.'

'I couldn't possibly do that. They came with the prince and they'll return with the prince, unless they choose to do otherwise, of course.'

Hafoc gave a courteous nod. 'I will order my men to take horses to the pond, supposedly to wash them. We will make our way to the kiln. Spread out and come to us on foot, in ones and twos, to avoid suspicion.'

'How long will it take to reach Angeln?' Tanwen asked. Hafoc shrugged. 'Four days, maybe five, or six if we take Swuste's children. And if the weather is against us, Wyrd will decide.'

The burden of responsibility suddenly weighed heavy on Tanwen's heart. 'If Wyrd has a use for us we will be safe in her hands,' she said. 'If not, may Nethrus have mercy on us.'

She was stuffing bandages into a bag when Mae and Edyth arrived. 'Mae, fill a pouch or two with food that can be eaten without being cooked, and ask the wet nurse to come and see me, will you please?' Mae nodded and left.

'Edyth, has your sister told you why I wanted to speak with you?' Tanwen asked.

'No, Tanwen, but it would seem we are about to embark on a journey.'

'I overheard Cedd and his mother planning to harm Prince Offa. We must get him away from here tonight.'

'How?'

'Hafoc will help us, he has horses waiting. You may bring any possessions that will fit into one of these bags, but nothing more, unless you have access to some food we can eat on the way.'

'I'll see what I can find. I must go, Hilde will need help packing for the children.'

'Edyth, Hilde can't come, it's too dangerous.'

'What do you mean? She's one of us, we can't leave her behind.'

'Hilde made her choice. She has a husband and family here; she belongs with them.'

'No. She must come with us.'

'I'm sorry, Edyth. We can't trust her. How do we know she won't betray us to her husband?'

'She won't, I know she won't. Please, Tanwen, we can't go and leave her alone with that - monster.'

'Enough, Edyth.' Tears burned Tanwen's eyes, through the blur she saw a little girl in a boat, begging her brothers not to leave her. She remembered the utter misery of being alone, among people who did not want her or care about her, and she knew that whatever the consequences, she could not leave Hilde behind.

'So be it,' she reluctantly agreed.

The wet nurse was adamant that she did not want to take the children to Angeln. She had lost her husband and baby son in the massacre and was determined to make a new home for Swuste's children. 'My father is re-building his hovel. It will comfortably accommodate us all. Mother is looking forward to having the children around and they will help me get over the loss of my family.'

Tanwen could not argue with that. She thanked the nurse, gave her a gold clasp for her belt, and wished her well.

They met up at the disused kiln a mile from the camp as arranged. One of Hafoc's men remained behind to ensure the camp was sleeping before he joined them.

'Where is Storm?' Tanwen asked.

'We've left him behind. Moving him would have attracted too much attention.'

Tanwen counted nine men, including the one still in camp. 'Is this all?' Her voice was an anxious squeak. 'Where are the rest?'

'It's been a long time, Tanwen. Two returned to their wives and families: two have died of natural causes; three were killed in battle, and the remainder settled here, married and raised sons, some of whom are nearing manhood.'

Tanwen gave a wan smile. 'Where have all the years gone, Hafoc?' But there was no time to brood. Hafoc sent two men ahead to warn the king that they were on their way. The others mounted up and set off behind them, slowly at first, until Hafoc was sure their noise would not carry back to the camp, before gradually building up speed. Hilde and the twins were unable to ride so they doubled up with some of Hafoc's men. Mae, despite her training, was too nervous to ride alone and shared Hafoc's horse, and Offa, who insisted he could manage, rode alone.

The journey was long and arduous but thankfully uneventful. Even the weather was kind. They slept only during the darkest hours and rode all day eating on the move whenever possible and stopping only when necessary. To Tanwen's amazement, no one complained, and the children remained in good spirits throughout the journey, singing cheerfully and giggling as they were bounced over rough ground, despite the discomfort.

They were approaching Angeln when a band of horsemen was spotted in the distance. Hafoc sent a man to investigate. The strangers stood motionless until he neared them, then a banner was raised. Hafoc's man glanced back, yelled something no one could understand, then galloped towards the band of men. At the same time, the band of men charged forward with the banner floating behind them. 'It's a wolf,' Hafoc cried shading his eyes with his hands. 'The silver wolf. Waermund's banner, they're Waermund's men come to meet us.' The twins squealed with delight and begged to be let down, but Hafoc ordered them to stay put.

They were safe. Tanwen was shaking and her heart beating so fast she thought she might faint. The bannerman addressed Offa. 'Welcome home, Prince Offa, Atheling of Angeln, your father, King Waermund, is looking forward to your safe return.'

He turned his horse to Tanwen and smiled broadly. 'Welcome home Tanwen, it's been a long time.'

Tanwen frowned. Did she know this warrior? He sat tall and straight in the saddle. His long brown hair was streaked with silver and tied back in two fine plaits. His short beard was unadorned, and he wore a fox fur over gleaming armour. He carried his helmet under his arm.

'It is good to be home, thank you …' She hesitated, hoping he would introduce himself, but he smiled, bowed his head then turned his attention to Hafoc.

***

They arrived in Angeln in the early evening. The king and Thorndor were waiting in the king's hall to greet Offa in private. A waving, cheering crowd had gathered for its first glimpse of the atheling and moved aside when he dismounted, clearing a path to the hall for him and his retinue. Offa appeared embarrassed, but after a nudge from Tanwen, he lifted his arm and waved at the throng.

A fire was burning in the centre of the hall and refreshments had been laid out for them. Warm mead, small venison pies, and cheese with freshly made bread. The twins tucked in as if they had not been fed in weeks. Chairs were offered, but the saddle-weary women preferred to stand by the fire, upright for the first time in days.

Wynn was missing. Tanwen's eyes scoured the room, but there was no sign of her foster mother. She tried to hide her disappointment but could not help wondering what would have kept Wynn away.

King Waermund embraced Offa. 'Welcome home my son.' He held Offa at arm's length then ran his hands over the broad shoulders and down the muscular arms of the prince.

'Freawine reared you well, Offa, and a fine warrior he has made of you. You are indeed a credit to Freawine and Hebeke.' He embraced Offa again, then stepped back with a questioning frown on his face.

Tanwen realised he was waiting for Offa to speak and although she had rehearsed the meeting over and over again in her mind, she now stood as rigid as a rock, unable to think of a word of explanation.

Thorndor cleared his throat to break the silence and Tanwen ran to his arms. He had worn well though he seemed shorter and bonier than she remembered. His hair was thinner and his beard, now almost reaching his waist, was decorated with even more bones, teeth and rings than ever. She was overjoyed to see him again at last.

'Oh, Thorndor, it's been so long,' she cried, afraid to squeeze him too tightly in case his frail body snapped. He kissed her cheek. 'We've missed you, daughter,' he said, patting her back as if comforting a child.

'Where's Wynn?'

'Wynn is - unwell. I'll take you to her soon,' he promised.

In an attempt to hide her concern for Wynn, Tanwen introduced the rest of the group to the king. 'I remember you well,' he said to each one, before thanking them all for bringing the atheling home safely. He summoned a servant and asked her to take them to the guest hall and make them comfortable. 'Then go into town and fetch playthings for the children,' he added.

When they had gone, the moment Tanwen was dreading arrived. The king fixed his misty eyes on Offa. 'And now my son, what have you to say for yourself?'

Offa's woe-filled eyes lingered on Tanwen's for a heartbeat before he hung his head. He made no reply.

Tanwen felt as if she had been struck by a mallet. Her arms ached to cradle him, to comfort him, to speak for him. *Say something, Offa, anything, please*. But he said nothing.

'Speak, boy,' the king bellowed. Offa remained silent.

'Perhaps the prince is overawed, Waermund.' Thorndor suggested. 'To the best of my knowledge he has never had the opportunity to speak with a king.'

The king grunted. 'That is not so, we met in Hedeby, did we not lad?' he asked, not unkindly. But still Offa did not speak.

Tanwen could stomach the prince's humiliation no longer. 'I'm afraid Prince Offa has an affliction, lord king,' she said moving to Offa's side.

The king raised one eyebrow and looked at her as if she were a stranger before repeating. 'An affliction?'

'He is unable to speak, lord king.' Another silence followed.

'Since when? Was he sick?'

'The prince has never been sick, my lord, nor has he ever been able to speak.'

'Never. Are you telling me that my son, the Atheling of Angeln, is mute?'

'Yes, my lord.'

'Rubbish. His lungs worked perfectly when he was born.'

'Yes, my lord, but he never learned to speak, at least, he did but then suddenly seemed to forget how.'

'Then why wasn't I told when I visited Hedeby? I was told he had a sore throat and was reluctant to use his voice.'

Tanwen flushed with embarrassment. 'The prince has always been reluctant to use his voice, my lord.'

'Then why was nothing done about it?'

'We tried to teach him, lord king. We told him stories and sang to him, without success. Later we prayed to The Lady, Nethrus, and offered sacrifices to her. We tried charms, herbs, and potions but sadly nothing worked.'

'Why wasn't I told?' King Waermund's voice was unnervingly quiet and Tanwen hesitated before answering.

'He was such a good-natured, thriving, child, everyone assumed he would speak when he was ready.'

'So why wasn't I told?' he repeated thumping his fist on the table.

Tanwen considered her answer carefully before replying. 'In the beginning, Lord Freawine believed that Offa would speak when he had something interesting to say and Lady Hebeke agreed. When they finally admitted to themselves that it was never going to happen, they decided not to tell you, because they couldn't bear to hurt you. Later they were afraid of your reaction, so they just kept hoping ...'

'Hoping I would die without discovering the truth,' the king roared jumping from his seat and banging his fist on the table again.

'No, my lord, not at all. They just didn't want to hurt you.'

'Why didn't you send me word?'

'How could I? I was little more than a servant.'

The king was furious. 'You could have sent a message through Hafoc, or Leofrun the nurse, but you chose not to.'

'I wanted to, I begged Lord Freawine to let me bring Offa back on a visit. I was sure Wynn would be able to cure him, but Lord Freawine wouldn't hear of it. He was afraid.'

'Afraid of what?'

'Afraid he would be held responsible. Afraid to face the wrath of the king.'

'So, you did nothing. You sat back and allowed Freawine to wallow in his fear and keep his terrible secret.'

'No, it wasn't like that, my lord.'

'There were rumours, rumours we chose to ignore. Rumours about the drunken behaviour of Freawine's boys and how they bragged about their father being the next king of Angeln, and rumours about their untoward behaviour with Prince Offa's companion.'

Tanwen gasped.

'Tell me, Tanwen,' the king continued. 'Where does your loyalty lie, in Hedeby with the Freawine's or here, in Angeln with your king?'

Tanwen breathed deeply and glared at the king. 'My loyalty, my lord, is and always has been to my king and his son, Prince Offa, the Atheling of Angeln. There never has been and never will be any untoward behaviour between either of Lord Freawine's sons and myself.' She was quivering with rage. She wanted to slap his face and storm out of the hall, but she knew better than to strike or turn her back on the king.

King Waermund flopped into his chair. 'Get out of my sight,' he said with a dismissive wave of the hand. Tanwen turned on her heels and walked away. From behind she heard Thorndor speak.

'That was unkind and unfair, Waermund. Tanwen risked her life, bringing the prince home.'

The king sighed. 'Let us hear what Hafoc has to say.'

***

Tanwen was outside taking deep breaths in an attempt to calm her nerves, before joining the other women in the guest hall, when Thorndor came along.

'How could he say that? How could he even think such a thing?' She cried.

'Kings can say what they like to whom they like. He's hurt. He'll have calmed down by morning.' Thorndor replied.

'But I may not.'

'You will. You have had a hard journey, you are tired, you'll feel better after a good night's sleep.'

'What about Offa, Thorndor? Where will he sleep?'

'Offa will be looked after. Waermund won't let any harm come to him. I expect he'll spend the night in the king's hall.' He wiped a tear from Tanwen's cheek with the edge of his sleeve. 'Now, are you ready to visit Wynn?'

Tanwen nodded. Thorndor smiled but could not hide the sadness in his eyes. 'You will find her much changed, and she may not remember you at first, but be patient. It will soon come back to her.'

The old homestead had not changed. Herbs were growing in abundance. Two sheep grazed in the enclosure while ducks and geese waddled around them. They were all so ancient they could have been there since before Tanwen left.

Wynn was propped up in bed, asleep. Tanwen hesitated at the door but a woman who had been sitting at Wynn's side stood and bid Tanwen welcome.

'Come in, come in. She's only dozing. She will be thrilled to see you.' She gently tapped Wynn's shoulder. 'It's Tanwen come to see you, Wynn. It's Tanwen, come home at last.'

Thorndor pushed Tanwen through the door. 'Speak to her, daughter, she'll recognise your voice.'

Tanwen doubted that after all these years, but she went to the bedside and took Wynn's hand. She jumped when it flopped, lifeless over the edge of the bed. The woman picked it up and carefully laid it over Wynn's chest. 'You'll find the other hand easier,' she said with a knowing nod.

'Wynn.' Tanwen spoke in a whisper.

'You'd better speak up, girl if you want her to hear. Her mind is a long way away.' Thorndor said.

'Wynn.' Tanwen repeated, louder and more confident now. 'Hello Wynn, it's Tanwen. I've come home, to help look after you.'

Wynn stirred. 'Tanwen?' She turned her head towards Tanwen and frowned, 'Tanwen?' She was awake now and offered her right hand to Tanwen, 'Tanwen? Is it really you? What a way to greet you, Wulfrun, help me sit.'

The woman leaned Wynn forward and fluffed up the cushions to help make her more comfortable. Wynn's speech was slurred, the left side of her ashen face drooped slightly, and the eyelid could not open, but the right side was unscathed, and her wits seemed to have survived intact.

Tanwen smiled and kissed her cheek. 'You look wonderful. Oh, Wynn, it's so good to see you again. You can't imagine how much I've missed you.'

'How you've grown child, I'd never have known you. You're quite a young woman now.'

Tanwen laughed. 'Wynn, I'm twenty-eight.'

Wynn seemed puzzled. 'Yes, I suppose you are.'

The woman brought goblets of warm, sweet liquor to refresh them.

'Wulfrun was little more than a babe when you left.' Thorndor said.

Now it was Tanwen's turn to be confused. Wulfrun was a comely woman, taller than Tanwen and considerably plumper, with a shock of fair curls and a ruddy, cheerful face.

'Wulfrun? I - I'm sorry, I don't remember …'

'I was here the night you told Wynn you were leaving.' Wulfrun chuckled.

Tanwen frowned as delved into her memory. 'Yes, of course, I remember. There was a child here, a scruffy urchin Wynn had found in the woods.'

'Right first time. Oh, how I hated you. You were so beautiful and confident - and loved.'

Tanwen laughed. 'Loved, yes. But in all my life no one has ever called me beautiful. My, how you've changed. It's good to meet you again, Wulfrun, and thank you for taking such good care of Wynn.'

'What happened to you, Wynn?' Tanwen asked, gently.

'Acorn nuts.' Wulfrun replied on Wynn's behalf. 'We'd gathered a bagful and tied them to a rock in the river. The fast-flowing water cleans them effortlessly in just a few days. Then we boil them and the strained liquid makes a wonderfully refreshing drink, you had some earlier.'

'And very good it was too. But what has this to do with …'

'It was the oak-elf, or possibly the river-sprite Wynn slowly raised her right hand to her left temple. 'The dart must have been aflame because I felt it burn deep into my skull.'

Tanwen was aghast. 'Oh, Wynn, that's terrible. Why would an elf or sprite do such a thing?'

'Picking acorns may have angered the oak-elf or cleaning acorns in the river may have disturbed the river-sprite, who knows?' Wulfrun said with a shrug.

'Evil little creatures.' Tanwen said bitterly before kissing Wynn's hand.

Wynn wanted to get out of bed but Tanwen insisted she stay put. 'I'm tired. It's been a long day and I need to sleep. But I'll be back tomorrow for a long chat.' She kissed Wynn and Thorndor, wished Wulfrun a good night, and left.

The young warrior who had escorted them into town was outside waiting for her.

'King Waermund would like to see you,' he said.

Tanwen was startled. 'Me? Why?' He gave a wry smile, 'Who am I to question the king?'

'I feel I know you,' Tanwen said, 'but it's been so long I'm afraid I …'

The warrior laughed. 'I thought perhaps you preferred to forget. I am Arild - we were sparring partners many years ago.'

'Arild. I should have known. How grand you look in your warriors' gear.'

'And how grand you look, in your lady's garments. I had expected to see you in battle gear. Did you ever raise your army?'

Tanwen grinned. 'Wyrd had other ideas, I'm afraid. Oh, how we have both changed since those halcyon days.'

They had reached the king's hall. Arild stood back while guards opened the door, 'I'll be waiting here to walk you back to the guest hall,' he said and then left.

King Waermund was alone, sitting at a table with a horn of ale. Tanwen glanced around the room.

'Prince Offa has retired,' the king said. 'Please sit, I have things to say.'

Tanwen sat and waited patiently until the king spoke. 'Hafoc speaks highly of you. He confirms all you said. I apologise for mistrusting you. It seems my son had few friends in Hedeby. Is it true, Cedd and Hebeke were plotting against him?'

'I'm afraid so, my lord, that is why we returned so unexpectedly.'

'And what was the condition of Hedeby when you left?'

'Dire, my lord, the town was razed. Those who were fit enough were rebuilding it, but when we left, many wounded and dying were sleeping rough on the ground in the woods. Most of the stock was lost or stolen. They have nothing, and if

Prince Offa had not built shelters and hunted for food, many would have died of cold or hunger.'

The king studied her for several moments. 'Prince Offa will remain in my hall until the queen's hall is rebuilt. When it is ready, you, Mae, Edyth and the servants will move in with him and care for him as you have done in the past.'

'But my lord …'

'It will be so, Tanwen. Until the queen's hall is ready you will remain in the guest hall.'

'May Hilde and the twins join us, lord king? They have nowhere else to go.'

'As you wish,' he said.

The twins were already abed when Tanwen returned to the guest hall. She related the events of the day to Mae, Edyth and Hilde while they ate their fill of the steaming, squirrel stew that had been prepared for them, and washed it down with copious amounts of warm mead. Later they lay around the fire, drank more mead, sang raucous songs and relived the events of the past few weeks.

'The shtrange thing is,' Hilde slurred, between hiccoughs, 'it sheems quite amushing now.'

'Yesh,' they all agreed then fell asleep where they lay.

***

Tanwen, nursing the first hangover of her life, along with Mae, Edyth, Hilde, and the twins, was invited to join Wynn and Thorndor to break their fast. She was relieved to discover that Wynn's condition was not nearly as bad as she had thought the previous night.

To Wulfrun's consternation they all, except for the twins, favoured fruit to the fresh herbed bread with salted pork and eggs she had laboriously prepared for them.

'Take it home, the children will enjoy it, take the remains of last night's meal too,' Thorndor insisted.

Wulfrun beamed. 'Thank you, Thorndor, the children have already broken-fast, but they will make short work of this at midday.'

'Wulfrun looks after all the children now,' Wynn spoke, slowly but fondly. 'I was getting too old to run around after the young ones.'

Tanwen smiled, unable to remember Wynn running anywhere.

'Aye, eleven of the little buggers,' Wulfrun said good-naturedly.

'Eleven.' Tanwen exclaimed. 'It was very brave of you to take them all on.'

'The poor loves had nowhere else to go, and I was glad of their company.' Wulfrun was wrapping platters of uneaten food linen cloth.

'Perhaps the twins would like to meet the other children.' She suggested. Edyth and Hilde agreed.

'I'll come too,' Mae said then whispered in Tanwen's ear, 'I fear all these visitors are too much for Wynn,' Tanwen nodded gratefully.

'Wulfrun's husband was killed in a Myrging raid,' Thorndor told Tanwen after they had gone.

Tanwen was taken aback. 'The Myrgings are still troublesome here too?'

'Extremely troublesome, Offa's condition could herald the demise of Angeln.'

'Thorndor, that's not fair, Offa's …'

Tanwen's raised voice made Wynn fearful. 'I didn't force the children onto Wulfrun,' she said, 'It was all her idea.' Although no longer slurring her words, Wynn's voice quivered nervously.

'Dear Wynn,' Tanwen said, taking Wynn's right hand in her own. 'You never forced anyone to do anything. That's why we all loved you and never wanted to leave home.'

The right side of Wynn's face smiled. 'Did you bring Aelfrun back with you?'

Tanwen blushed. She had not been prepared for this. 'No, Wynn …'

'Aelfrun died a long time ago, Wynn, don't you remember? Thorndor said rather harshly.

Wynn's face clouded.

'But I've brought Offa home, Aelfrun's son, the atheling,' Tanwen explained.

Wynn frowned, concentrating hard on Tanwen's words. 'A baby.' She exclaimed at last. 'A beautiful baby prince for Angeln.'

Tanwen gave her a gentle hug. 'That's right, and you brought him into the world. He's a man now, a true warrior …'

'Hardly.' Thorndor interrupted sourly.

'Yes, he is. He saved my life and has proved he can fight as well as any man.'

'Face the truth, Tanwen. A mute cannot rule.'

Arild burst in. 'Lord Thorndor, a party of Myrgings is approaching, their leader says they are here to meet the king in friendship, shall I inform the king? I don't trust them.'

'Nor do I, get some men together. I'll speak to Waermund.'

Fifteen

Tanwen watched Offa's jaw tighten as the Swarbians, led by Mearcweard the Myrging, strutted into the king's hall. He greeted King Waermund with an impudent smirk and said they had come in peace, offering friendship to their English neighbours.

'News has spread that you are ailing, King Waermund,' he said 'and we are afraid you will not be able to rule effectively. Knowing that your son, Prince Offa, is a mute imbecile and not fit to govern in your place, my brother, and your cousin, King Meaca of the Myrging tribe, proposes that you abdicate and allow him to appoint someone of noble blood to rule over Angeln.'

A wave of dissent from the English warriors and courtiers rippled around the hall. King Waermund raised his hand to silence them. 'Let the Swarbian speak,' he commanded.

Mearcweard smiled. 'Face the truth, King Waermund, your dynasty is over, and you are in your declining years. But King Witta of Swarbia will allow you to spend the rest of your days in peace, as tribal chief, if you accept him as your overlord and pay tribute. Your people can go on living in Angeln and Jutland and farm the land. In return, you must swear never to lift a hand against Swarbia or the Myrging. You must give us all the land up to ten miles north of the Eider and you must pay us whatever wergild we set for our blood you have shed.'

The room was silent. 'Well, have your warriors lost their voices too?' he asked. 'If you don't like our terms, send a champion of royal blood to meet me by the Eider at midsummer and we will settle this matter once and for all. King Witta and his warriors will have arrived by then.' He paused briefly. 'Well, what is it to be, fight or yield?'

Waermund sat alone and no one spoke for him.

'In the old days,' Arild whispered in Tanwen's ear, 'the hall would have been filled with the roar of warriors all claiming the right to be King Waermund's champion, but now look at them. Oh, they're loyal enough and willing to die with their king. But they want to do it properly in battle, not like this.'

Waermund rose slowly to his feet. Tanwen's eyes filled with tears for this once great king who looked as if his heart was breaking. He spoke out towards the jeering voice.

'All my life I have led my people with pride and honour. No Swarbian was brave enough to face me with a sword in his hand. I never shirked in battle as you well know. I am old and my sight is fading, but I am still the king and I will not fight underlings. Tell King Witta I will meet him in combat if he dares to face me.'

Mearcweard laughed. 'You. At your age. King Witta wouldn't stoop to fight you. Even if you could see what you're doing, you are too frail to lift a sword never mind use one. I'm not wasting any more of my time trying to reason with you, old man. King Witta will be here on Midsummer's Day to accept your surrender.' Without the courtesy of leave-taking, Mearcweard turned to go.

'One moment, Mearcweard. You haven't received our answer to take back to your master.'

Mearcweard glowered around for the speaker.

Tanwen's eyes darted around the room; her heart skipped a beat when she realised the speech had come from Offa. Offa, who had never spoken a word out loud in his life.

His voice was level and slow as if every word caused pain. 'Tell King Witta to save himself a journey, unless he wants a sword through his guts. That is all he, or you, will ever get from Angeln.'

Tanwen tugged his sleeve. 'Oh Offa, be careful. Think before you speak,' she pleaded.

The English murmured among themselves and King Waermund frowned in bewilderment.

'Who speaks for Angeln, I do not recognise the voice?'

'It is your son, Prince Offa, who speaks,' Thorndor informed him.

'Is it not enough to be insulted and threatened by foreigners without being taunted by my chief advisor? Your eyes must be as dim as mine.'

'But it is Offa speaking, Waermund. He has found his voice at last,' Thorndor insisted.

'Tell the King of Swarbia he will not get what he wants, for I will gladly fight his son,' Offa said.

'You are not Prince Offa,' Mearcweard replied scornfully. 'Prince Offa is an imbecile, unable to speak. You are a commoner and the Prince of Swarbia will not fight a commoner.'

'I am Offa, Atheling of Angeln, and I speak for my father in our people's hour of need. Tell the Prince of Swarbia he may either fight King Waermund's champion or stay at home with the women, where he belongs.'

Mearcweard sneered. 'You are only trying to impress your companions. You know I would never agree to single combat with someone too young to have completed weapon training.'

'Don't be afraid. I'm not asking you to meet me in single combat. I want a fair fight, so I'll allow you to bring a companion, and if I am killed the Swarbians will have won their right to over-lordship.'

Tanwen's head was reeling. and her stomach churned as she recalled that disastrous day when Wiga challenged the Myrging King to single combat. She took Offa's hand.

'Please Offa, leave it. No one will think less of you if you back down. They don't expect a child to fight their battles.'

A Swarbian envoy came forward. 'We agree to your terms. Our prince and his champion will tear your heart out and give it to your father - whoever he is.' The Swarbians sniggered. The envoy spoke to King Waermund. 'We will meet on Midsummer Day, with our respective armies and peoples. I trust swords are acceptable weapons? Although an axe would be better for hewing down a giant,' he said, smirking and thumbing at Prince Offa.

'Swords it is,' Offa replied, 'if Mearcweard has the strength to wield one.'

Mearcweard was purple with rage and a few moments passed before he spoke. 'Very well, whelp. If you think you are man enough. But there will be no quarter given for your youth and inexperience. You will get exactly what you've asked for.' With that, he left, closely followed by the other envoys.

No one else moved or spoke until Waermund broke the silence. 'Well-spoken young man. If you survive the battle you will rule as regent while my son, Offa, lives. I would rather give the kingdom to you, whoever you are, than yield it to the Swarbians.'

'But I am your son, Father.'

'Then prove it. Come to me, so I may run my hands over your features.'

Offa climbed the steps to his father's throne and leaned forward. The king's hands explored his son's face, his massive shoulders and his arms.

'It is my son. But Offa, why did you go all through your life in silence when you were able to speak?'

Offa kissed his father's hand. 'I will tell you, my lord, in your chamber, when we are alone with Tanwen and Thorndor.'

The king suggested they eat in Thorndor's house, well away from the exuberance of his men and the noise of the mead hall. Tanwen prepared a simple meal of fish stuffed with bread and herbs to be followed by pears cooked in ale, while Offa explained his silence to his father.

'When I was a child, I watched Wigheard and Cedd fight a Myrging who had strayed onto Lord Freawine's land by chance, following a boar he was hunting. He did not want to fight, but Wigheard goaded him until he had no choice. To make it a fair fight, the Myrging wanted to take them both on together. Wigheard would have none of it. He insisted on single combat. The Myrging got Wigheard down and offered the warrior's salute, but Cedd came at him from behind with a hand-seaxe.'

Offa stopped. The king waited in silence for him to continue but he seemed to have run out of words. Tanwen suddenly remembered Offa's distress when they passed Eadgils' grave with Wiga and it all became clear to her. Her heart ached for him. She went to his side, took his hand and held it.

'Tell your father the rest, Offa. You've gone this far it can't hurt to finish the story.'

But Offa shook his head. 'My lord king,' Tanwen began, 'I believe Prince Offa was in a quandary. If he spoke of other things and never mentioned the killing he thought he would have made himself a partner in it, and if he spoke about the killing, he would betray his foster-brothers and me and shame Lord Freawine. Am I right Offa?'

Offa nodded.

'He was little more than a babe. Too young to carry such a burden, lord king.'

'I decided not to speak at all,' Prince Offa added.

'It was my fault entirely, my lord. If I hadn't taken him away from the bower, he would never have seen the fight and …'

'No, Tanwen, you tried to protect me by hiding me in the bushes, but I wouldn't stay, I disobeyed, crept out and witnessed the whole horrid thing. But the worst of it was, that as I grew older, I realised that a brave and generous king had been killed and I felt that I was responsible. I saw Cedd lift the seaxe and knew what was about to happen. I should have cried out a warning, but my voice wouldn't come.' He hung his head and a tear fell on Tanwen's hand.

Thorndor spoke. 'So, you buried yourself in a living grave, without respect or friendship.'

'If I'd intervened, this terrible thing would never have happened. If I had spoken out, Edgils' body could have been recovered and buried with the honour rites due to a great king.'

Tanwen was moved to tears. 'Oh, Offa, you were much too young to know how to act. If only you had confided in me, I may have been able to help.'

'Tanwen has pleaded with me all my life to make myself heard, but I could not. However, when I heard Mearcweard threaten you and our homeland my voice took on a life of its own and came through unbidden.'

The king embraced his son. 'Dearest Offa, you paid Eadgils' wergild with your childhood. I can do nothing to bring it back, but I will do my best to protect you from now on. Midsummer is only two weeks away and you must be ready to fight. We need to find a teacher, suitable armour and have the best of swords forged for you.'

Waermund addressed Arild. 'The atheling will be fighting not only for his life but also for the future of our nation. We must prepare him well.'

***

When armour was brought not a single coat of mail was large enough to fit the prince. No matter how much he wriggled not even King Waermund's largest suit would slide over his shoulders. As a last resort, Angeln's best smith was summoned and ordered to modify the byrnie until a new one could be made. Finding Offa a suitable sword proved even more difficult.

No matter how much the king objected, Offa insisted on sword training with Tanwen. 'After all,' he said, 'Tanwen taught me everything I know about weapons. She is my true sword companion.'

The king relented on condition Tanwen would step down and be replaced if she proved an unsuitable teacher, and he spent an afternoon listening to Arild describing Offa and Tanwen's movements at weapon training.

'He knows how to use a sword,' Arild reported, 'but he takes too much time over it. Too much time thinking and not enough doing.'

'Well, Tanwen,' the king's voice was grim, 'if you have taught him that much you may as well carry on, but don't give him time to think, set two or three men on him at once.'

With Thorndor's help, Tanwen demonstrated to Offa that his best strategy in the duel would be to choose a corner of the duelling square and wait for his enemies to approach him one by one.

'If you allow yourself to drift into the middle of the square one of your adversaries could manoeuvre behind you and kill you while the other charged your front,' she explained. 'Much better to use your strength and reach, to take care of them one by one.'

Offa watched intently as Tanwen used her left arm to push Thorndor back with her shield then used her right arm to strike a blow that would cut through his shield and armour right through to the bone - if the sword were sharp enough.

She had a pig's carcass placed inside a suit of armour and an old shield put in front of it to use as a target. Then she offered Offa a selection of swords to test. The first sliced through the shield and armour and cut deeply into the pig's body, but the blade snapped due to the force of Offa's swing. The second cut through the shield then bent, and the third shattered on the iron band on the shield's rim.

Tanwen threw up her arms in despair. 'Be careful, Offa. Don't hit so hard or you'll find yourself weapon-less.'

She picked up the bent sword. 'Will the smith be able to straighten it?'

Thorndor slowly shook his head. 'There is only sword worthy of him,' he said.

The king nodded. 'Stedefaest. I had Arild bury it when I doubted my son's ability to rule. It is very precious to me and I didn't want Mearcweard to get his hands on it.' He signalled to a guard. 'Fetch Arild.'

Arild led them north to a thorn-bush covered hillside, then turned east and carried on for fifty paces until they reached an ancient oak. Arild then counted another thirty paces north to a bramble-covered mound. He chopped the brambles with his seaxe and revealed the Tiw rune etched into a rock.

The king reverently traced the shape with his fingers. 'Tiw, the War God, who sacrificed his sword hand to keep his word,' he said.

Offa and Arild heaved the rock aside and Arild began scraping at the ground with his seaxe until he reached the sword, encased in its scabbard and wrapped in oiled leather.

The blade was already beginning to rust and Offa was dismayed. 'Don't worry,' his father told him. 'The swordsmith will soon restore the shine. It was Weland's work and is precious to me because of the strength of its cutting edge. Its name is Stedefaest because it can always be trusted to cut through anything in its way, however hard, in one blow.'

The swordsmith worked on Stedefaest for three full days and when he returned it to the king everyone gasped at its beauty and brilliance.

The king forbade Offa to practise with Stedefaest. 'If Stedefaest is broken before the death blow, there's not another sword on earth that can help you.' So Tanwen and Offa continued to practise with lesser swords.

King Waermund sent messengers to King Witta to inform him that the battle was to be fought on Fifeldore, an island in the Eider halfway between the English and the Myrging lands. It was known as the Monster Gate because the current there was so fierce. There was neither bridge nor ford and the island could only be reached by boat, so there would be no danger of either side receiving help from friends on the riverbank.

When the English envoys met King Witta they swore, in the name of King Waermund and the English, to keep the terms. If Prince Offa was beaten, they would surrender their borderlands up to ten miles north of the Eider and pay wergild to the Myrging. If he won, they would keep their lands and take as much wergild from the Myrging as the Myrging had claimed from them. They would also take hostages for peacekeeping. King Witta would witness and judge the fight.

When they returned, they told King Waermund that King Witta had quickly noticed that the terms had changed. 'So, your king has changed the purpose of the battle from my claim of overlordship to a quarrel between Angeln and Myrging, with me as the wise and fair-minded judge. I like that,' he said. 'Tell King Waermund I will allow the amended terms to stand, for whatever terms he offers will make no difference to the outcome of the battle.'

***

On the eve of the battle, Tanwen, Mae and Edyth joined Wynn for the evening meal. As always, Wynn was delighted to see them and said repeatedly how fortunate she was to have them home at last and how she would love to be on the riverbank tomorrow to support Prince Offa. Unknown to Wynn, Thorndor had arranged to have her collected in a wain and driven to a spot on the riverbank where she would have a good view of the fight; Mae and Edyth had spent the afternoon furnishing it with cushions and skins to keep her warm and comfortable.

When Wynn tired and Mae and Edyth withdrew to their chamber, Tanwen made her way to the king's hall, hoping to see Offa before he retired. Women were not usually welcome in the king's hall, except to serve drinks to the king and his companions at mealtimes, but she hoped that tonight would be an exception.

She was too late: the meal was over; the king's companions had drunk their fill and were sprawled all over the floor, Thorndor had returned to Wynn, and Offa had already left.

The king was drinking alone in a huge chair by the embers of the fire. He welcomed Tanwen, told her to pull up a chair and offered her a horn of mead. 'It pains me to think that I may be sending my son to his death,' Waermund confessed. 'But I had little choice. The security of Angeln must be my first consideration.'

'Offa knows that, my lord, and understands your situation. He will bear you no grudge. What he does is for love of you and of Angeln.'

'It seems neither of us is overly confident of Offa's success.'

'I didn't say that my lord.'

'Not in so many words, but we know his chances are slim.'

'His weapon skills are excellent.'

'Yes, and he's big enough and strong enough to thrash the life out of his opponents, but he is young and inexperienced, whereas they are battle-hardened warriors.'

The king drained his drinking horn, 'Victory could go either way, but it will more than likely go to the Myrging.'

Tanwen nodded and refilled the horn.

'If Offa fails,' Waermund said, 'it won't diminish my love for him, but I'll never be able to face my people again.' As he spoke, Waermund's eyes filled with tears.

Tanwen wanted to wipe them away, to comfort him, but he was the king and had to deal with his misfortunes alone.

'I am going to ask, Arild to join me on the footbridge where the stream meets the river. Witta knows my eyes are bad, I've sent a messenger to tell him I've chosen this spot away from the noise of the crowd so I can hear Arild describe the battle to me as it happens. He won't object, he's a fair man. If Offa is taken …'

The king's voice faded, but Tanwen knew instinctively he had suicide in mind. She was speechless. She was not prepared for this. She had been so preoccupied with Offa's training she had not given any thought to what life would be without him - and under Myrging rule. Her heart was racing. She understood King Waermund's reasoning, but Arild must not be involved.

'Lord King, please, let me be your eyes, allow me to take Arild's place in the boat.'

'Dear Tanwen, I wouldn't dream of it. What kind of man would expect so much of a pretty young woman?'

Tanwen smiled at the compliment. The king's eyes were truly failing, nearing twenty-eight she was no longer young, but verging on old age.

'Lord king, I have cared for Prince Offa since he was a newborn babe. I promised his mother, on her deathbed, that I would see him take his rightful place as King of Angeln and everything I have done for him has been to that end. Please, let me come with you, to support him on the most important day of his life, just as his mother would if she were here.'

The king's eyes were full of sadness. 'Very well, it's little to ask. But you must swear to leave the moment I ask you. When Offa is beaten you must make your escape before the trouble begins.'

'If Offa is beaten, I will have failed him and Queen Aelfrun and I will be unable to live with my grief.'

Waermund stared at her through watery eyes for what seemed an eternity. Did he realise she knew what he had in mind?

'As you wish,' he said, at last.

***

Tanwen was unable to settle that night. She thrashed about drifting in and out of fitful sleep. She was falling, the ground rushing towards her at an alarming speed. A tiny Offa appeared in the distance, as she turned towards him, she began to plummet. She screamed and screamed but her throat was silent.

Down and down, she fell, knowing she was dreaming and that she must wake before she hit the ground.

She woke with a start, sweat-soaked and panting. The chamber was oppressively hot and humid. She stepped outside into the cool night air. The guards were playing at dice, they looked up, acknowledging her presence, then immediately returned to their game. She asked for a torch. One of the guards took one from the wall. 'Would you like an escort, Lady Tanwen?'

'No thank you, Gunnar, I'm just taking a breath of air, it's stuffy inside.'

'Can't sleep, eh?' He placed a bear fur around her shoulders. 'Mustn't let you catch a cold must we?' Gunnar was a kind man. A family man, more suited to playing with children than playing at war, and she liked him a lot.

'You'll feel better when the battle's over, my lady, you'll see.'

Tanwen smiled. 'I'll feel better when the battle's won, Gunnar. Give my regards to your wife.'

'I will my lady,' he replied.

Tanwen thanked him, took the torch and made her way to the queen's hall. She needed to be near Aelfrun's spirit tonight. She needed to tell Aelfrun how sorry she was for getting things so terribly wrong. She had tried her best, she had brought up Offa as she had promised as if he were her own child. Indeed, she loved him as if he was her own child and she had never been parted from him for a single day. She had even rejected Horsa rather than break her word. Would Aelfrun appreciate that?

Rightly or wrongly, Tanwen had taught the prince to fight and defend himself. And now he was preparing for combat a mere boy, just approaching his fifteenth winter, going into battle against two experienced killers.

She entered the overgrown herb garden and carefully picked her way through brambles and nettles. She stopped. A candle flickered in the birthing chamber. She froze. Who would be here in the dead of night? She thrust the torch into the earth and crept up to the window. She could see a dark form, possibly a man, but she could not be sure. She turned and stood with her back to the wall wondering what her next move should be. Could she escape without being seen?

'Tanwen?'

It was Offa's voice. He stood in the doorway, his huge frame filling the space.

'Offa. What are you doing here?'

'I could ask the same of you.' He collected the torch, took her hand and led her into the chamber. 'Come.'

'Offa, I ...'

'Hush Tanwen, there's something you should see.'

Inside, beside Aelfrun's bed, the table Tanwen had used to bathe and dress the baby prince had been converted to a shrine. It was covered with a milky white cloth and in the centre, a large candle burned in a small metal dish. To its right lay a group of three wooden carvings, each a hand high, the face of an old, bearded man, a body on a cross and a bird perched on a twig. Over the corner of the table, hung the prayer beads Cadoc had given to Offa all those years ago and the little angel she had made for him from Aelfrun's doll and a few feathers.

Tanwen gasped. 'The Great Sky God,' she whispered.

'The Holy Trinity,' Offa corrected.

'But - what? I - I don't understand.'

'The old Gods didn't seem to listen - or care, but I remembered your stories about the Great Sky God, and I started speaking to him in my mind. And He listened, He really did. One night I was sad and told Him I wanted to be a great warrior like my father, but as I was forbidden to join in warrior training with the other boys, I knew it could never be, I was destined to be an outcast.

The very next day you took me to Old Hren to buy a wooden sword and began teaching me warriors' ways. And the night you found me in the tree bole I'd been talking to Him; I told Him I wanted to end all this squabbling between tribes. That night you brought me home and now I've been given that opportunity.'

Tanwen took his hands in hers. 'Offa, aren't you afraid?'

'Yes, I'm afraid. Very afraid. But what kind of prince would I be if I turned my back on my father's people when they needed me?'

'Oh Offa, you don't have to do this. It's not too late to back down, you're still a child, no one will think ill of you, your father loves you and will always remember that you were prepared to go into battle on his behalf, and I will love you, whichever path you take.'

Offa kissed her brow. 'I must do this, Tanwen, for my mother's sake - and Angeln's.'

'Then good night, my prince.' Tanwen took the amulet from around her neck, kissed it and slipped it over Offa's head. 'May the Holy Trinity and my mother's amulet protect you.' And with a heavy heart, she made her way to her chamber, where she fell on her knees and prayed to The Holy Trinity.

Sixteen

On Midsummer's Day both banks of the Eider were crowded where they overlooked the island. King Witta settled himself on a high seat, looking over the heads of his war band. The Myrgings came in throngs and were chanting for the death of the English prince and the humiliation of Angeln.

On the English side, many nobles and warriors had come out of loyalty to Waermund, but the farming folk kept away, no doubt worrying about what would become of them when Offa fell.

Wild stories of Offa had spread, and strangers arrived from Waernas, Jutland and Frisia to see the battle. Tanwen sent Mae, Edyth and Hilde among them to listen to their gossip. It seemed they were drawn by curiosity, pity, or simply for the pleasure of seeing poor Offa done to death.

'Is he really a lack-wit?' They wanted to know. 'Is that huge young warrior really the old king's son, or Thunor, come to help the English?' Even the members of Waermund's household, who had seen him and spoken with him, admitted they did not know what to expect of Offa today.

After breaking-fast, Thorndor, wearing his hair long and straight and carrying the same carved staff as he had at Aelfrun's wedding, led Waermund and Offa, followed by

Tanwen through the heavy oaken doors of the hall, to the waiting, sad-faced, crowd that had been gathering since dawn.

Offa looked magnificent. Tall and muscular, golden-haired and bronze-skinned with armour and jewelled weapons glinting in the bright sunshine, every inch the prince, and Tanwen thought her heart would burst with pride.

A murmur rippled through the crowd. Thorndor stepped forward and tapped his staff.

He stretched out an arm to introduce Offa. 'I give you the son of Waermund, I give you a prince who will not fail. I give you Offa, Atheling of Angeln, who will stand fast and smite through Mearcweard, and Meaca, and shield you against the might of the Myrging and Swarbia.'

A loud cheer erupted. Churls raised their arms, waving their makeshift weapons in the air and chanting. 'Offa. Offa. Offa.' They moved aside, clearing a path for Thorndor. The king, Offa and Tanwen followed. They had gone only a few steps when someone shouted, 'Kill them, Offa. Kill the Myrging dogs.' The churls took up the chant, 'kill them. Kill them. Kill the Myrging dogs.'

Guards tried to move them on, good-naturedly nudging them to the riverbank for a better view of the battle.

Offa, Waermund and Tanwen stepped into the ferryboat. Thorndor wanted to join them but the king insisted that he would be more useful on the riverbank with the men, in case of trouble. The ferryman rowed them to the island. Offa embraced his father, kissed Tanwen on the cheek and strode off to meet his foes. The ferryman turned the boat and took the king and Tanwen to the base of the footbridge. The king rewarded him with a gold pin and dismissed him.

Engrossed in their own thoughts, Tanwen and the king walked to the brow of the bridge in silence. The king grabbed the rail to steady himself when she told him Mearcweard had brought his brother, King Meaca, to the island and that they would not move aside to let Offa through to the fighting circle. 'Offa doesn't stand a chance; Meaca killed Eadgils' son Friogar, and his younger brother, simply because they blocked his way to the crown,' he said bitterly.

Tanwen's heart sank. *Oh, Offa, what have you done?*

Offa stood patiently waiting until he was allowed to enter the fighting square. Then, without warning, the Myrgings struck. Offa parried their blows with his shield but did not strike back. Fear gnawed at Tanwen's stomach. 'They are trying to wear him down, raining blows on him,' she told the king. 'They're laughing. They think they are in control.' Tanwen paused for a while, concentrating on the fight.

'They're becoming frustrated because Offa is not tiring,' she said. 'They are goading him - calling him names.' The sadness in the king's face tore at Tanwen's heart. 'Don't worry my lord, Offa spent his childhood listening to insults. Words will not hurt him.' To her delight, the brothers seemed to be slacking. 'The fools have wasted their breath on insults, now they're tiring.' She reported, scornfully.

Offa was speaking, loudly and clearly. 'What's keeping you, Mearcweard? Are you waiting for your older brother to do your fighting for you? Are you hoping you will get a chance to strike me while I am killing Meaca? If so, you had better not make it too obvious, your future subjects are watching - and they despise cowards.'

Some of the English on the north side of the river heard and laughed. Mearcweard scowled but hung back. 'And you, Meaca,' Offa continued. 'A fine champion you are. You should be protecting your brother. If he dies, and you live, you will be dishonoured forever.'

The Myrgings advanced on Offa. 'Meaca is opposite Offa's sword arm, he's darting in and out of his reach. He could easily wound Offa but - he's hesitating.' Tanwen's voice rose shrilly, 'and Mearcweard is hacking at Offa's shield, trying to splinter it. He must be planning to attack from the left. Offa is preventing Meaca from closing in on his right by keeping his sword up and outstretched - I believe he's daring Mearcweard to come in and end the fight.'

But the waiting crowds on both banks of the river believed that the Offa was on the defensive. The Swarbians cheered and a low moan came from the English.

'What's happened? Why are the Swarbian's cheering?' the king asked anxiously.

'Prince Offa is staying on the defensive, my lord.' Tanwen replied. 'He's playing with them, making no effort to kill either of them.'

'If he doesn't act soon,' the king said, 'Meaca will kill him as soon as Mearcweard demolishes the shield.'

A feeling of foreboding washed over Tanwen. She watched with trepidation but could not find the words to describe the scene before her. On the north side of the river, the English were drifting away. Reluctant to witness the slaughter of their atheling and the fall of Angeln.

'They think he can't use his weapons.' Tanwen tried to swallow but her throat was dry, and she coughed instead.

'Rest Tanwen, save your voice. The sound of sword on shield and the roar of the Myrging crowd, tells me all I need to know. My son is doomed to failure.' The king sounded despondent. He began edging to the end of the bridge, but Tanwen took his hand. 'But they're wrong, my lord. I know Offa. He won't let them see how skilled he is with a sword until he goes in for the kill.'

The king stared down into the river where the water flowed deepest ten feet below where he stood. 'It's almost time,

Tanwen. Before I go, I want to thank you for devoting your life to the welfare of my son.'

Tanwen's chin twitched. She nodded. *Oh, Offa, my love, what have I done to you?* She took the king's hand and with tears in their eyes, they climbed onto the lower rail. Tanwen chewed her lip. *I'm sorry, Aelfrun, so very, very sorry.*

As soon as Offa fell, they would jump together. Bracing herself for the final stages of the battle, Tanwen looked over to the island. It took her a moment to grasp what was happening. 'My lord. Prince Offa has changed tactic - he's jumped to the right, away from Mearcweard, along the side of the square.' Her heart was pounding.

There was a screech of metal on metal. 'Stedefaest - Tanwen what has happened?' the king demanded.

'He has unsheathed Stedefaest at last.' she screamed excitedly. 'Stedefaest has sliced through Mearcweard's shield and armour.'

'Can it be true?'

'Oh, yes, yes, my lord. Mearcweard is slit.'

Mearcweard's still-beating heart drenched Offa with spurting blood. Tanwen saw him shudder. Still holding Stedefaest he stepped over the body and moved to the right where Meaca stared in horror at his brother's body. There was a moment of silence before the crowd realised that Mearcweard was dead. Then a great cheer erupted from the English on the north bank of the Eider.

'I heard the sound of Stedefaest,' the king shouted. 'Tanwen! What has happened?'

'Prince Offa has slain the Swarbian champion, lord king.'

'And my son, how does he fare?' Tanwen looked over to where Offa faced King Meaca. His side was bleeding heavily under the flapping loose links of his byrnie, but Tanwen decided to spare his father the news. 'Prince Offa fares well, lord king. One enemy is down, and only the weaker one remains.'

King Waermund clutched Tanwen's arm. 'Lead us back from the brink, Tanwen. It seems that we have something to live for.'

'Yes, my lord,' Tanwen said as she happily obeyed her king.

Offa stepped toward the centre of the square. King Meaca was looking at the body of Mearcweard as if he had been his only hope of victory over the prince, and now Mearcweard was dead.

'Why doesn't he strike Meaca while he is preoccupied?' Tanwen asked. 'Because it would not be honourable to deal with a preoccupied man,' Waermund replied.

The solemn mood that had hung in the air abruptly changed. The crowds on both sides of the Eider River now waited expectantly for the next act of the drama to unfold.

Offa spoke. 'King Meaca, it is time for you to avenge or join your brother and champion, and for one of us to win a kingdom.' Tanwen's hand went to her mouth. 'My lord, Meaca is moving toward Offa with an out-thrust sword.' Her voice rose shrilly. 'He's going to impale the prince in the gut!' She exhaled, 'Oh, my lord, all is well; Offa has leapt aside.'

Meaca's sword screeched across the chain links of the mail byrnie until the point of the sword came across the loose flap created by Mearcweard's death-stroke and went under the links. Offa had another cut that intersected the previous one on his abdomen, but Tanwen chose not to mention it.

'Now Offa has slashed Stedefaest's blade through Meaca's neck,' she screeched. 'And Meaca has fallen. He's twitching over the corpse of Mearcweard.' She paused, 'Offa is looking at King Witta and the Swarbians. The king's head is lowered. He's weeping. King Witta is weeping! And Offa is tearing up blades of grass.' She continued, 'why would he do that?'

The king smiled for the first time in days. 'It is customary for the victor to wipe the gore off his blade onto the leggings of his dead enemies. Offa is using grass as a mark of respect, to Witta.' Tanwen wondered how Offa would have known that. It had not been included in her lessons.

The prince lowered his head to the south bank then motioned for his countrymen to the north to cross the bridge. Quietly the English filed across the bridge, with King Waermund, being led by Tanwen, in front. They lined up behind their new leader as the Swarbians, led by King Witta, waded across the stream. The two tribes looked at each other across their respective sides of the duelling field as King Witta stepped into the fighting square with the victor. For a moment neither spoke.

'King Witta,' Offa said breaking the silence. 'You may take Meaca's and Mearcweard's arms and armour. One day you may need them to help defend against our common enemies.'

'You are generous, Prince Offa,' Witta replied in a hoarse voice. 'I thank you and accept your gift of honour.' He undid the huge gold brooch that fastened his woollen cloak trimmed with a collar of ermine. He cleared his throat and gave the cloak to one of his companions who began making a stretcher of it using two spears. Two more of the Swarbian king's companions placed King Meaca's corpse onto the stretcher. He hung his brooch in Offa's byrnie. 'In return, I will keep the agreement that was made earlier. I will not appoint another chief in Meaca's place, for King Waermund is their overlord now. We cannot be friends, but we need not be enemies.'

***

Offa stepped into the Eider and drew Stedefaest's blade through the water, washing away all traces of Myrging blood. He held the gleaming sword high above his head for all to see.

'I have drawn the borderline between our lands. The English will stay on the north side of the Eider and the Swarbians on the south side - forever.'

King Witta looked away from Offa and motioned his men into the fighting square to recover the bodies. Then the Swarbian army, with their grieving king at the rear, re-crossed the Eider and continued on south to their own territory.

'This is a great day for the Angeln tribe, and Engle Land, my son.' King Waermund said when the Swarbians were out of earshot. 'Never before has there been such a day of honour given to the House of Woden.'

Offa watched the Swarbians depart. His left hand rested on Stedefaest's pommel, while his right hand explored for broken or cut ribs where Mearcweard's sword had pierced his armour. He turned around at the sound of his father's voice. 'Not a great day, father,' he said, 'but a necessary one. We were fortunate on the field of honour today. The Swarbians paid the higher price.'

'How are you, my son. Do you fare well?' King Waermund asked anxiously. Offa embraced his father. 'I fare very well, lord king, a few cuts, that's all.' Offa turned to Tanwen, 'And you, Tanwen, my one true friend. Are you well?'

Tanwen bowed, 'I am well, lord prince,' she replied remembering that this hero of Angeln was no longer her own, sweet Offa, but a king in waiting. Offa stooped and kissed her cheek.

The English were rejoicing. Singing, dancing and drinking through the streets and cheering Prince Offa as they passed him. The prince and his father were deep in discussion about the battle, Offa explaining his actions in detail, and

Waermund listening, wrapped in admiration. Tanwen, feeling awkward and out of place, asked to be excused. The king and the prince looked at her as if she had lost her wits but before they replied Thorndor joined them, pale-faced and agitated.

'Ah, Thorndor, you're here at last,' Waermund said holding out his hand in welcome. 'It seems the revels have already begun. The English have much to celebrate today. Come, join us in the mead hall.'

Thorndor bowed his head. 'Please excuse me, lord king. I have matters of some urgency …'

'What could be more urgent than toasting the health of Angeln's greatest hero?' the king asked.

'Wynn is dead, my lord,' was Thorndor's sombre reply.

The king suggested that all festivities should be postponed until after Wynn's funeral, but Thorndor did not agree. 'The English have been under a cloud for too long. They need Prince Offa's great victory and Wynn would want them to celebrate.

Tanwen was too upset to take part in the celebrations; she asked the king if she might be excused to help Wulfrun with preparations for the funeral. 'Naturally, we understand,' he replied.

***

The king's popularity was swiftly restored and the prince, denigrated as an imbecile only a short while ago, was now the adored hero of Angeln. The king ordered the cooks to provide a great feast for the townsfolk and the ale flowed freely until the early hours.

Wynn's funeral was held four days after the battle. Tanwen and Wulfrun had bathed her, dressed her in her finest tunic and threaded flowers in her hair. They laid her on a trestle draped in white linen, and four men, all former beastlings, carried her to the pyre that had been prepared for her. Wynn had been well known and respected in Angeln and the surrounding villages and it seemed that everyone from miles around came along, dressed in their best clothes, to mourn her.

The shock had numbed Tanwen and after the funeral, she paced around the king's hall unable to settle. Thorndor's eyes were red and sore but he shunned sympathy. 'Wynn was a good wife who lived her life caring for others. We all have to die; Wynn was aware of that and would not want a fuss.' His words offered no comfort to Tanwen. Yet one more person she had loved had been taken from her.

'That proves it then,' Wulfrun said morosely, as she and Tanwen sat moping by the fire. 'Proves what?' Tanwen asked out of politeness rather than interest. 'It proves it was a river-sprite that did for poor Wynn and not an oak-elf.' Tanwen's mind was blank. Wulfrun clacked her tongue. 'She died by the river, didn't she? So, it was a river-sprite that shot her, not an oak-elf.' She explained slowly as if Tanwen's brain was addled. 'Oh, yes.' Tanwen replied flatly.

Seventeen

After Wynn's funeral, the king ordered an ox-roast, dancers and musicians took to the streets and the scop related the story of the battle over and over again, delighting, freemen, churls, lords and ladies alike.

When it was over, Thorndor told Tanwen to help herself to any of Wynn's possessions and he gave the homestead to Wulfrun and the children. 'You may make use of the healing chamber, but I will keep the learning room. I have accepted Waermund's invitation to join him in the king's hall,' he admitted to Tanwen when they were alone. Tanwen could think of nothing to say in return. She absentmindedly fingered the contents of Wynn's herb box, the only item she had chosen to keep.

A week later, Tanwen was summoned to attend the king without delay. Knowing instinctively that something was seriously amiss she grabbed her healing bag and rushed to the hall.

The king was lying on his bed when Tanwen arrived. He tried to raise himself on an elbow but winced with pain and fell back onto the cushions. 'It's nothing, a pulled muscle, that's all. A night's rest is all I need.'

But Tanwen knew better. He was running a fever and his joints were red and swollen. She quickly made him an infusion of willow bark to sip while she pounded cinquefoil into mutton grease, added woodruff juice and almond oil and smothered it all over his swollen joints.

'I don't want your willow tea. It's sleep I need; the pain keeps me awake night after night. Give me your strongest sleeping potion.'

'The inflammation is bad, my lord, the willow tea will help reduce it. When it's all gone you can have a potion of white poppy juice to see you through the night.'

The king grunted but swallowed the tea in one gulp. 'You are worse than Wynn - bribing your king as if he were no more than a stubborn child.'

Tanwen smiled. 'I'll take that as a compliment, my lord. You will need to rest for several days.' She warned. 'I'll instruct the hall-thane to have a servant sit with you overnight.'

'There will be no need for that.' Offa was in the doorway.

'Offa, you shouldn't creep up on people like that, you gave me a start.'

'Champions do not creep; they approach with stealth.' Offa replied with a grin.

'Well shed, my shon.' The king slurred, nodding approval.

'I'll stay all night and make sure father behaves himself.' Offa said.

'That's kind of you, Offa. I'll leave a little more willow bark tea in case he becomes restless.'

'Theresh no need to whish … wishper, I know whash going …' the king said and fell asleep.

'The slurring tells me the potion worked. I'll return before breaking-fast to reapply the unguent.' Tanwen said and then asked Offa's permission to leave.

But the king did not wake.

***

Thorndor arranged the immediate transfer of loyalty oaths from of all Waermund's men to their new chief, Prince Offa, while Offa prepared for trouble. He expected opposition from some of the tribal chiefs, who believed they had a greater claim than he to the crown, but to Tanwen's delight, none came.

Four weeks later Tanwen's heart almost burst with pride as she watched kings and chiefs come from afar to witness the king-making and all agreed that Offa would make a fine king. It was a great celebration, even greater than Aelfrun's wedding, and many brought along their daughters hoping to catch the eye of the new king, but Offa, although courteous to all, showed no interest in any of them and they left disgruntled.

At last, Offa took his rightful place in the king's hall and, for the first time in his life, he was treated with the honour and respect he deserved. He lived, trained and drank with the warriors, but was the gentlest and kindest of men. He never cursed, bullied, or belittled anyone, however lowly. Tanwen's eyes smarted when he said, 'I have suffered contempt, and will not subject others to it.'

Tanwen was bored in Angeln. There were plenty of things to do, but she had little interest in any of them. Thorndor had set her the task of educating Waltrude's children, but her efforts were futile. She did not want to teach they did not want to learn and the men in the town were unwilling to spar with a woman.

'It was different when you were a girl,' Arild explained. 'It was a game then and we were more or less equals, but now, well, you're a woman and it doesn't seem right.' Tanwen recalled a similar discourse some years ago but chose not to remind him of it.

Offa's visits to the hut were frequent but brief. They lived in separate worlds now and there was little room for an unmarried woman in the world of men. He roared with laughter when she suggested they should spar together.

'The king sparring with a woman. I would never be able to enter the mead hall again,' he said. However, he must have sensed her disappointment because he pulled her close to him and kissed her head.

'Dear Tanwen, you were almost a mother to me and I can refuse you nothing. You have my promise that as soon as it is rebuilt, we will have regular, secret weapon-training sessions in the queen's hall, away from the mocking eyes of my companions.' Tanwen was satisfied, Offa would never break a promise.

Determined to avoid the spindle at all costs, the next time Offa called, Tanwen asked if she and Edyth could borrow horses from the royal stable. 'Edyth enjoys riding and I thought we might hunt together.' Offa agreed. 'A good idea and hopefully the exercise will bring the colour back to your cheeks.'

Later that day three fine mares, a merlin and two hounds were brought to the hut by the king's groom. Mae, still distrustful of horses, sniffed and went out in a huff, but Edyth shrieked with delight. Tanwen grinned, 'we will soon need a proper homestead to accommodate us all.'

'Will you teach my girls to ride?' Hilde asked.

'With pleasure, and all of Wulfrun's fosterlings too.'

Tanwen and Edyth spent all their free time riding and hunting and before long, without knowing why or when it began, Tanwen was teaching Edyth how to defend herself with weapons. She was surprisingly good. Extremely quick and light on her feet, she moved effortlessly around a fighting square. She could handle a hand-seaxe and was adept with a dagger.

'A woman needs to know how to protect herself on a dark night,' she told Tanwen with a wink. She pulled a small copper brooch, in the shape of a fox's head, from her tunic to show Tanwen. It was about half the length of a woman's hand and resembled a needle filed to a very fine point. It fitted perfectly into a leather sheath, which was stitched onto the inside of her tunic. 'Serving girls can't afford fancy daggers to ward off unwanted advances,' she said with a grin.

'Amazing.' was all Tanwen could say.

Unfortunately, Edyth proved inept with a sword, finding them heavy and cumbersome, but her skill with a bow astounded Tanwen. 'Are you sure you have never used one of these before?' She asked.

'Never,' was the chirpy reply. She soon grasped the basic techniques of archery. Right eye dominant and always in control, she had a strong, steady stance, a smooth draw and a consistently smooth line running from the tip of her drawing elbow, through the arrow, all the way to the target. And she rarely missed.

Offa and Arild watched in awe. 'Perhaps you would like to join my war-band,' Offa teased. 'Good archers are always in short supply.'

'No chance of that, I have the first claim on her talents,' Tanwen countered good-naturedly.

'I'm going to be a sword-maiden, and join Tanwen's war-band,' Edyth said.

'Ah. Another sword-maiden,' Offa replied, ending the conversation. He invited Tanwen to join him in the newly completed queen's hall, for the evening meal. Before they ate, he took her for a look around. It was almost as she remembered it from Aelfrun's days. One large room with a thatched roof supported by massive tree trunks, a walkway around the edge and three sleeping chambers at each end.

'Will it serve, my lady?' Offa asked.

'It will serve very well, my lord king.'

'And is there room for weapon practise and all of your companions?'

Tanwen laughed. 'Ample room, my lord.'

'Good. Then from today, it will be known as Tanwen's Hall. You may move in tomorrow, but before we eat there is one more thing for you to see.' Offa led her to the rear of the hall to what had been Aelfrun's bower. It now contained a shrine with all the accoutrements necessary for the worship of the Great Sky God.

'It's lovely, Offa. I hope it gives you many years of pleasure.'

'I'm sending men to Rome to fetch brothers to help me. Hafoc has asked permission to lead them but sadly, he is too old to lead men so far into strange lands, although I have consented to his travelling with them. They will no doubt benefit from his expertise.' He paused and looked expectantly at Tanwen.

'Oh, yes. A good idea,' she said.

They ate a simple meal of duck and lentils, followed by roasted apples and cheese before Offa walked her back to the hut. She noticed two guards following them; a king could not even take an evening stroll without protection.

The following morning the women happily carried their meagre belongings into Tanwen's hall and spent the entire day moving things about until every item was perfectly positioned. Offa had provided them with a hall thane and house churl, so they did not need to concern themselves with attending the fire or lighting candles.

After the midday meal, Mae left for her usual afternoon stroll and it was almost dark when she returned, stone-faced.

'Why so glum, Mae, don't you like our new home?' Tanwen asked.

'It's a fine home, Tanwen, but it's not for me. I will not be moving in here with you.'

Tanwen gaped and Edyth dropped her spindle. 'Why not? Where are you going?' Tanwen asked when she regained the power of speech.

'I have married Hafoc.' There was a moment's silence broken by Edyth shouting, 'you've what? I'm your sister. You can't marry someone without telling me.'

'I did,' was Mae's curt reply.

'Why the secrecy?' Tanwen asked.

'Because we didn't want a fuss. King Offa gave his permission yesterday and we married immediately. The king said we can have Waltrude's hut when you all move into the queen's - Tanwen's hall.'

Edyth grimaced. 'But Hafoc's so old.'

'Well, I'm no longer young.' Mae snapped. 'You could at least pretend to be pleased.'

Edyth kissed her. 'Of course, I'm pleased, I'm thrilled for you, but you should have said
something sooner, or at least thrown out a hint or two.'

'Mae, last night, King Offa told me …' Tanwen began.

'That Hafoc is going to Rome,' Mae interrupted. 'Yes, I know, and I will be going with him.'

'To Rome.' Edyth screeched.

'Hafoc's bones are bothersome in the long cold winters. Thorndor said the weather is warmer and kinder in Rome and King Offa has given us permission to remain there if the climate suits and the Romans don't object.'

'Oh, Mae, what will I do without you?' Edyth asked. 'Rome is so far away, and we've never been apart.'

'You will do very well. You have Tanwen, Hilde, the horses and your war games. Everything you need.'

Tanwen embraced her. 'Dear Mae, we wish you both well. Hafoc is kind and will make a fine husband, but how will we manage without you?'

'You are not angry?'

'Certainly not. You've been a faithful companion all these years and I'll miss you dreadfully, but I wish you joy in your new life.'

'You should have told me,' Edyth said crossly at the same time hugging Mae, 'but I forgive you and I know you will be happy together, whereas I ...'

Hilde nudged Edyth aside, 'whereas you, Edyth, should pour us all a glass of mead, to toast the bride,' she said before kissing Mae.

When the news broke that Mae was to travel to Rome with her husband, the wives of Offa's men clamoured to accompany their husbands on the journey. 'I don't understand them,' Offa complained to Tanwen. 'Are they jealous? Are they afraid Mae will seduce their menfolk? Or have I made them so unhappy in Angeln they do not want to stay?'

'Possibly all three,' Tanwen replied. 'The men are going into the unknown and will be away for some months. Perhaps they are afraid The Great Sky God will harm them, and they will never see their menfolk again, or maybe they just want to find this glorious sunshine we've heard so much about recently.'

Four weeks later Mae, Hafoc, twenty of the king's men and five wives left for Rome and the whole town came out to wave them off. The townsfolk were used to seeing their men go off on raids or into battle: but this was beyond their comprehension; this was a small band of men going in peace, on a journey to the end of the earth and taking their wives with them, to find the brothers of The Great Sky God, whoever and where ever they may be.

Tanwen and Offa met regularly and true to his promise he occasionally sparred with her in Tanwen's hall. 'You're good, Tanwen, as good as some of my men and getting better every day,' he said one afternoon. 'A king would feel safe in your hands. It's a pity you are a woman, your talents are wasted.'

Inwardly, Tanwen was fumed, but she smiled and said nothing.

Sometimes Offa would watch Tanwen and Edyth at swordplay and offer Edyth advice, but she was never truly comfortable wielding a sword and concentrated on improving her archery skills.

***

Tanwen was sitting near the pond watching ducklings taking to the water for the first time.

'A silver ring for them.' Tanwen looked up into Offa's smiling face. As usual, Arild and another bodyguard were by his side. 'Just daydreaming,' she replied raising herself to her feet. He indicated that she should remain seated. 'I wish to speak with Tanwen,' he said to Arild. 'Have a servant bring us food and give us space to eat alone.' Arild's companion hurried off to order the food and Arild found a place to sit a discreet distance away from the king.

Offa stretched out on the warm grass and propped himself up on one arm. He picked a blade of grass to chew on. 'A nice spot,' he said. 'Yes,' Tanwen agreed, 'your mother and I often sat here.'

'Ah, hence the melancholy mood,' They sat in companionable silence for some time before he spoke again. 'The harbour is becoming busier by the day, trade is improving, and men are flocking to join my war-band.'

'Your victory has brought stability to the land, Angeln is thriving again, and its people have much to thank you for.'

'Tomorrow I am sending messengers to Hedeby, inviting Cedd, Lady Hebeke and Modpruth to join us.'

The smile swiftly disappeared from Tanwen's face. 'Really, lord king?'

'Arrangements need to be made for my marriage to Modpruth, it will be easier if her mother and brother are present.'

'Offa, you can't mean it. You're not going to marry Modpruth?'

'We are betrothed. It is my duty.'

'Oh, Offa, you can't - you can't marry that abomination.'

'I must.'

'No one will expect it of you. Please, Offa, you must reconsider.'

'My mind is made up and Thorndor agrees. The marriage will go ahead.'

'Thorndor - what does Thorndor know about it? Did he hear Modpruth insulting you, day after day? Did he see her bite you or spit at you? And was he there when she rejected you in favour of your father?'

'These things are unimportant. It's only natural that a beautiful young woman would choose a powerful king over a prince. But now that I am a king, Modpruth will have no reason to object to the marriage.'

'And Lady Hebeke certainly won't object. And Cedd - are you truly prepared to have him here, knowing the terrible things he has done?' Tanwen turned away, afraid Offa would see the fury in her face.

'It was my father's wish that Wigheard and Cedd be at my side in battle. I intend to honour all of my father's wishes. Wigheard is no longer with us, and Cedd is a chief with a war-band of his own. I will make him an earl in his father's place and name him my heir until I have sons of my own. When the need arises, we will fight side by side like brothers.

'Have you lost your wits? He would stick a dagger in your back at the first opportunity.'

Offa shrugged. 'Cedd is ambitious; there are greater opportunities for advancement when sworn to a king.'

Tanwen snorted. 'I daresay the rewards are greater, too.'

'A warrior earns his worth.'

'And what of Hilde and the children? Their lives will be in constant danger while Cedd is here.'

'They will be under my protection. No harm shall come to them.'

'Even you can't protect them every moment of the day.'

'I will provide men to guard your hall and to accompany Hilde and the children at all times.'

'So, they are to become prisoners?' Tanwen snapped contemptuously.'

'Am I a prisoner? Their lives will be no different from mine. I can go nowhere without a bodyguard, yet life is comfortable, and I have no complaints.'

'That is no recommendation. You have never complained about anything in your life, but I am made of different stuff. I'm afraid I cannot live here amicably with Modpruth, nor can I stand by and watch Hilde and the children being abused by Cedd.'

'You do not know that these things will happen, Tanwen, you only surmise it.'

'If Cedd is here, these things will happen.' Tanwen argued.

'You are being unreasonable.'

'There is no reasoning with a man who puts honour before good sense. The time has come for me to move on, and with your permission, lord king, I will leave Angeln at the earliest opportunity.'

'You are a free woman, Tanwen. You do not need my permission to leave.' Offa's eyes were filled with sadness, but his jaw was firmly set. He turned on his heels and departed.

***

'Tanwen, you are upset and don't know what you are saying. Where will you go?' Thorndor was shuffling around the room with his hands behind his back. There was more than a hint of irritation in his voice.

'To Bryneich, in search of my family.'

'So - you still harbour childish notions of being a shield-maiden?'

'It has always lurked in my mind, but I have not allowed myself to consider it seriously since Aelfrun died. Now that my obligations are fulfilled, I am free to do as I please.'

'And what of Hilde? Will you leave her to the mercy of Cedd?'

'I will speak with Hilde. She is welcome to join me if she wishes.'

Thorndor grunted derisively. 'Into war, as part of your army?'

'I haven't got an army, perhaps Hilde will help me raise one.'

Edyth and Hilde could not contain their excitement at the prospect of going Bryneich. Edyth had convinced herself that Tanwen was about to raise an army and go to war and spent most of her free time practising with her bow or singlestick. 'Let's make it an all-woman army - we can fight as well as the men.' She suggested.

'If you wish, I'll leave the recruitment to you,' Tanwen replied, with a smile.

'A fine army that would be,' Hilde retorted. She was fussing around making preparations for the long journey. 'We'll need extra clothes, at least two of everything - and shoes - and plenty of dried meat and fish,' she said as she tried to stuff woollen garments into a pouch that was much too small to accommodate them.

'Yes.' Tanwen agreed absent-mindedly. She had been cleaning the leather tunic and breeches Aelfrun had given her before Offa was born. It was well worn but she had looked after it, keeping it supple by feeding it regularly with warm sheep fat. There had been a few rips over the years, but Mae had repaired them with tiny stitches, and they were barely noticeable. She held it up to examine it in the light and was pleased with the results of her effort.

'I'm not packing that with our clothes, the grease will rub off.' Hilde warned her.

'There's no need.' Tanwen folded the garments and put them in a basket. 'I'm going out for a while.'

The harbour was heaving. Seven foreign merchant ships were being loaded or unloaded and two more were being pulled ashore. Fishermen were selling their morning catch from wooden boxes laid out on the timber walkway and the stench of fish filled the air. Traders were bickering over the prices of pelts, oils, and pottery piled up on the quayside, while bawdy women and rowdy seafarers were drinking in the alehouse.

Tanwen threaded her way through the crowd to where ships were being built or repaired or bobbing about on the water waiting for the tide to turn. She approached a group of weather-beaten men sitting around a table drinking ale.

'I'm looking for passage for five people to Bryneich.'

The bleary-eyed men looked her up and down. 'Never heard of it,' one said and returned to his ale.

'Where is this Bryneich?' Another asked.

'To the west. It's north of Tine and the first big river after Ynys Medcaut.'

'Ah, well, we'll have no trouble finding it then.' They all laughed and banged their wooden cups on the table.

'I can pay for our passage, and my father, King Cunedda of Bryneich will reward you well for your trouble if we arrive safely.'

'Well now, princess of Bryneich …?'

'Tanwen. My name is Tanwen, just Tanwen.'

'And mine is Ferin. Well, now Tanwen, what you offerin'? See that fine ship over there? That's my ship and we'll be sailing west within a se'en night. I daresay we'll have room for a few passengers; if the price is right.'

'Let's find a private table and I'll show you what I have to trade.'

The men roared with laughter again, Tanwen attempted to silence them with a frosty look, but they laughed even louder. Ferin helped himself to ale from the tray of a passing serving girl and heaved himself to his feet. 'That, Lady Tanwen, is an offer too good to refuse.' He winked at his companions, took her arm and with the characteristic rolling gate of a seafarer he escorted her to a free table out of earshot of his friends.

'Here we are. You won't get a table more private than this, so let's see what you have to trade.'

Tanwen spread the leather riding gear on the table. Ferin took a swig of ale and wiped his mouth on his sleeve. 'It'll never fit,' he said patting his belly.

'It's the finest doeskin and has a lifetime of wear left in it.' Tanwen told him.

'No good if it don't fit.'

'It's a woman's size, it would make a wonderful gift for your wife - or daughter.'

'Giftin's not my line - it's profit I'm after, lady, so show me what you've got that'll make me a profit.'

'It is valuable, it was a gift to me from Queen Aelfrun, any woman would be proud to wear it and happily pay you a good price for it.'

'The women I know, know their place and don't go cavorting about the land on horseback. Now, stop wastin' my time, what else have you got?'

She removed a gold brooch from her basket and placed it on the leathers. The man inspected it closely. 'Nice,' he said, 'but not enough.'

She grudgingly placed the box of carved rune sticks Thorndor had given her, on the table. Ferin curled his lips, shook his head and shoved the box aside without comment.

Tanwen's hands were shaking. She had only two items of any value left and did not want to part with either of them. 'This is only part payment. I've told you; my father will reward you generously when you get me home.'

'Lady Tanwen, I'm a fair man - you ask anybody in these parts, and they'll testify to my fairness - but if I'm to get you to Bryneich, wherever it is, I have to buy provisions for my men. It costs a lot to feed thirty oarsmen these days.'

'But you don't need thirty oarsmen - ten will do it comfortably.'

'I'll be the judge of how many men I need to row my ship.'

Reluctantly, Tanwen took her precious amulet from her neck and placed it next to the brooch. He did not even bother to inspect it. Tanwen lowered her eyes for several heartbeats to hide her tears, before slowly removing the dagger Hunlaf had given her, from her belt.

Ferin whistled, showing interest for the first time. He picked it up and examined it closely, slowly caressing its jewelled hilt before hacking off the corner of the table with its gleaming blade. Tanwen winced.

'Perfect,' he said,' nodding in admiration. 'As fine a piece of work as I've ever seen. Where did you get it?'

'It was a gift.'

'Five you say?' he said without taking his eyes off it. 'Well, lovely as it is there's barely enough here to cover the cost of half that many passengers.' He carefully placed the dagger on the table.

'Please, Ferin, this is all I have, and we've got to get to Bryneich.'

Ferin cocked his thumb in the direction of the alehouse, 'then better get yerself in there, Tanwen, and earn a bit more.'

Incensed at the insult, Tanwen rose, and with all the force she could muster, she slapped his face, gathered up her belongings and stormed off.

'You should have spoken to us first.' Hilde said when Tanwen related the afternoon's events.

'You could have taken the gold arm ring Cedd gave me when we wed - I've no further use for it.'

'And the buckle Queen Aelfrun gave me.' Edyth added, 'that should be more than enough to pay my way.'

'You are very kind, both of you, but I can't possibly …'

'Yes you can,' Hilde interrupted, 'how else are we going to get away before Cedd finds us here?'

'We'll all go to the harbour tomorrow and show Ferin we're a force to be reckoned with.' Edyth said, biting hard into an apple.

The following morning the women accosted Ferin while he was breaking-fast. Edyth swiped away his plate of mutton and bread and Tanwen replaced it with their basket of treasures.

'We've brought more gold. Now there's more enough to pay our passage - when do we leave?'

Offa strode into Tanwen's hall and ordered his guards, Edyth and Hilde to leave them.

'Lord King, to what do I owe this honour?' she asked.

'Solemn faced, Offa placed Tanwen's dagger on the table.

'Where did you find that?'

'Don't take me for a fool, Tanwen. Was it not enough to wound me with your threats of leaving? Was it necessary to humiliate me further by trading your possessions for passage to an unknown destination with an untrustworthy seafarer?'

'Offa. You know I would never deliberately hurt or humiliate you. When Modpruth arrives there will be no place here for me. You will have a family of your own and it will be time for me to go in search of mine.'

'You are my family. Lady Hebeke has no room in her heart for me and Cedd could barely disguise his contempt of me. But your love, Tanwen, was steadfast. In my mind, you were my mother and Mae and Edyth my doting aunts.'

'Oh, Offa, I never tried to take your mother's place. Everything I did, I did in memory of her and for my love of you. You are a fine man, Offa, and will be a great king. Your mother would be proud of you, and I would be proud to be your mother.'

'And yet you would leave me?'

'Don't you understand? I need to find my birth family. I need to know if my parents survived and what became of my brothers. I need to see if Bryneich truly exists or is a figment of my imagination.'

'You will never find Bryneich.'

'Your father once told me that Lords Hengest and Horsa visited a land called Britta and that Rowena was married to King Vortigern. It was then that I remembered that I was betrothed to Vortigern's son and that my brothers were supposed to be taking me to him. Don't you see, Offa? If Vortigern is in Britta, Bryneich must be near this same island.'

Offa sighed. 'So it is for personal reasons you leave, not because of my impending marriage to Modpruth.' He kissed her brow. 'Then I wish you well. May the Great Sky God protect you, but you will not leave these shores ill-prepared. I will arrange a ship and bodyguard for your voyage, ask Arild for anything else you will need.

Eighteen

Offa was right, she would never find Bryneich. Was it fair to take Edyth, Hilde and the twins into the unknown? Was it too late to change her mind? Offa promised that the ship would be ready to leave in a few days.

'Tanwen. Tanwen.' Edyth was running along the beach. 'Tanwen. It's Lord Hengest.' Tanwen sprang to her feet. Her ears must be playing tricks. 'What did you say?'

'Lord Hengest. The ship in the distance - it's Lord Hengest come back; he's waiting to come in on the tide.' Edyth shouted between wheezes.

'How do you know?'

'Everyone knows. Look, they're all making their way to the harbour to greet him, be quick or we won't get near - see, Hilde and the girls are already there.'

Tanwen's heart was pounding. 'Is Horsa with them?'

'I don't know, oh, do hurry Tanwen.'

They raced along the beach to the quayside and pushed their way through the gathering crowd. 'We could be in for a long wait, so I brought food,' the ever-practical Hilde said.

'Is Horsa with them?' Tanwen asked.

'I don't know.' Hilde replied with a hint of irritation in her voice.

Tanwen was too agitated to eat. *Is Horsa aboard? Surely someone must know? Will he remember her? Perhaps he is married - what if he's brought his wife? Will she recognise him after so many years? What will he say? What will she say?*

Finally, the waiting was over. The ship was safely in and the men were gleefully jumping ashore. Tanwen scanned their faces, there was no sign of Horsa, but despite the ravages of time folk still recognised their hero, Hengest, and cheered him ashore. His eyes darted through the throng, searching for someone. They alighted on Tanwen and as he strode through the crowd to meet her, Tanwen froze, knowing there could be only one reason for Horsa's absence.

Hengest took Tanwen's hands in his. 'Greetings, Tanwen, I am pleased to see you looking well.'

Her heart throbbed and her eyes burned, 'Horsa?' her voice was croaky and muffled. She wanted to say more but the words refused to come.

Hengest swallowed hard and slowly shook his head. 'I'm afraid …'

Not wanting to hear any more, Tanwen took to her heels and fled to the hall, where she locked herself in her bed-chamber and sobbed.

The women followed her and Edyth tapped on the door. 'Tanwen?'

'Go away, Edyth, please. I want to be alone.'

***

Offa ordered street fires to be lit and huge cauldrons of water heated so that Hengest and his crew could bathe before entering the mead hall for the feast that was being hastily prepared for them.

Tanwen emerged dry-eyed and ready to face the world. 'After all,' she said to Edyth and Hilde. 'It has been many years since we met. Horsa may have no longer loved me or forgotten me or even married. I shall carry on with my life as before.' But the hurt in her eyes could not be hidden from her companions; the ladies knew that Tanwen's heart was breaking.

As Offa was unmarried, and although he objected strongly, Tanwen insisted on serving ale and mead to his guests. It was a raucous affair and dodging the groping hands of the crew was tiring, but it took her mind off Horsa and that made the work sufferable.

She attracted the attention of an oarsman sitting at the end of a long table. He never spoke, but every time she refilled his goblet, he stroked her arm or squeezed her hand and her heart fluttered.

It was growing late, the odours of greasy food and ale combined with the stifling heat, was overpowering. She drank a goblet of thin ale and stepped out for a breath of air.

Wrapped in thought, she strolled to the pond and was alarmed when the quiet oarsman, approaching her from behind, placed a hand on her shoulder. 'Is the feast not to your liking?' she asked overcoming her fear.

'The feast was very much to my liking, but the noise and heat were not.' His voice had an unusual lilt.

'You are not from Angeln or Jutland?'

''fraid not.'

'Yet you speak English very well.'

'Thanks to my fellow crewmen.' He slipped his arm around Tanwen's waist and effortlessly steered her away from the pond. 'Shall we walk?'

She was shivering, not from the cold, but the closeness of the stranger. It was wrong to be here with him, what would Horsa say? *Imbecile. Horsa no longer has anything to say.* Nevertheless, she knew she should push him away, but something prevented her. It felt right to be with him, and excitement pulsed through her body as he steered her towards the riverbank. They walked in comfortable silence for about half a mile leaving the noise of the town behind them before Tanwen realised that the stranger had allowed his arm to slip and had closed his hand over hers.

'I'm sorry. I hope I have not tired you. Shall we sit?'

'I never tire. Why have you brought me here?' Tanwen's voice wavered, she was afraid of her response to the nearness of him.

He sat on the grass and gently pulled her down beside him. 'You are very beautiful,' he whispered, running his fingers through her hair. He leaned forward and released the clasp that held her tunic and its weight lifted the cloth away from her body, exposing her undertunic. He kissed her. She was shaking. She knew she should push him off and run away, but something was compelling her to stay. She wanted to be with him. He gently lifted her amulet and unexpectedly fell back as if he had been stung, his eyes widened in horror. Trembling, he stared at the amulet. 'Where did you get that?'

Tanwen held the amulet out to show him. 'My mother gave it to me when I was a child.' In an instant he was on his feet.

'Oh, what have we done?' Holding his head in his hands and tugging at his hair he dropped to his knees. 'I swear I meant you no harm.'

Feeling utterly humiliated Tanwen fastened her tunic and stood. 'Fortunately, only my pride is wounded. By putting an abrupt end to our brief dalliance and the possibility of calamitous consequences, you have preserved my honour, and for that I am thankful. However,' Tanwen's eyes narrowed, and her jaw tightened, 'I swear that if you ever come near me again you will incur the wrath of not only my father, Lord Thorndor but also my dearest companion, King Offa of Angeln.'

With all the dignity she could muster she walked slowly away. A few heartbeats later she turned her head. The stranger was staring after her, but several moments passed before he called, 'you don't understand, come back, please.'

Tanwen continued on her way until he shouted, 'Gwynedd, it's me, Rhufon.' She stopped - dead. She waited - had she misheard?

'Yes, Gwynedd, it's me. Your brother, Rhufon.' His voice was soft and filled with emotion. She turned.

'Rhufon?'

'Yes, Gwynedd.' He walked towards her. 'Oh, Gwynedd, I'm so sorry, I had no idea it was you. I just wanted to be with you. It felt so ... natural as if we were meant to be together. The moment I saw you I wanted to be with you. I wanted to touch you - hold you. Praise the gods you were wearing that amulet. As soon as I saw it I recognised it, and I ... oh, Gwynedd, I'm so sorry for what might have happened.'

Too stunned to speak, she stared into the face of her sworn enemy. She hated him. No, detested him, all her life she had wanted to kill him and yet she had been willing to ... She shuddered.

'Gwynedd, we need to talk, is there somewhere ...'

'What could we possibly have to talk about? You threw me out of the boat and left me to drown.'

'No. I wanted you to live. I tried to save you but Ysfael ...'

'You were a craven, afraid to stand up to him.'

'I was twelve years old.'

'And I was five.'

'We were children, Gwynedd. We didn't know what we should do.'

'Ysfael was fourteen. He knew what he was doing - he was saving his own skin at my expense and you did nothing to stop him.'

Tanwen put her hand to her belt to draw her dagger and glared at him for several heartbeats. Rhufon stepped forward, holding out his hand in peace. 'Oh, sweet sister, what have we done to each other?'

Swiftly bringing the dagger into action she lunged at his throat drawing blood, but Rhufon grabbed her wrist and wrestled the dagger from her hand. It shot through the air and dropped into the river. She rushed after it, but Rhufon grabbed her arm and pulled her back. 'No, Gwynedd, don't go there, it's a swamp.'

'Leave me alone.' She shouted, struggling to free herself. 'Get off me.' She managed to break away but slipped on the marshy ground and her feet sank into the mud. Rhufon grabbed her cloak and tried to pull her back. She wrenched it free. 'Stop it. Get off me, I don't need your help.' She was sinking further. Again, Rhufon tugged at her cloak, at the same time grabbing her arm and dragging her out of the mire. 'My dagger is in there …'

'It's only a knife, Gwynedd. Let it be.'

'It's Hunlaf's dagger, I must get it back.'

'I promise you, sweet sister, that I will be here at first light to retrieve your precious dagger.' He put his fur around her shoulders, 'now come along, let's get you to the fire to dry off.'

From a distance, they spotted torchbearers in the woods, around the pond and along the main street. As they approached the mead hall, the townspeople were milling about.

'Hurry, it looks as if they are searching for someone.' Rhufon urged.

'I wonder who is missing.' Tanwen replied.

Arild was mounted when he spotted them. He sprang down and rushed over, 'Why, you …' with one hand he grabbed Rhufon by the neck lifting him off the ground and with the other slapped him so hard across the face that blood spurted from his nose.

Tanwen attempted to pull Rhufon free. 'Why did you do that? He's done no wrong.'

Arild slapped Rhufon again. 'The swine was up to no good, the men saw him follow you out. If he's touched a hair of your head …'

'No, Arild, it's not what you think,' Tanwen cried, trying to separate them.

'If it is he'll soon be watching me feed his guts to the dogs.' He flung Rhufon to the ground. 'Get up and fight, you spineless …' He unsheathed his sword and held its tip to Rhufon's throat, poised for the kill, but Offa approached and Tanwen rushed to his side.

'Oh, stop him, Offa, please, before he kills Rhufon.'

'What's all this about?' Offa demanded as he relieved Arild of his sword. 'This man is unarmed.'

'He has dishonoured Tanwen and …'

'No Arild, that's not true …'

Offa intervened, 'he was seen following you away from the hall and your appearance suggests you found it necessary to put up a fight.'

'I have a right to take his life. This man has broken his oath to …'

'No, Arild,' Tanwen cried. 'He has broken no oath and has done me no harm. Rhufon is my brother.'

They all glared, speechless, at Rhufon until moments later, Offa broke the silence. 'Is this true?'

'Indeed, it is my lord. Gwynedd and I were separated twenty-three years ago, and I have been searching for her ever since.'

Arild's shock was obvious. 'This is one of the brothers you were going to raise an army against?'

Tanwen nodded and took Rhufon's hand. 'Yes, I am ashamed to say that had we met ten years ago I would have killed him without a second thought.'

***

Later, in the mead hall, Rhufon spoke. 'The Picts raided our settlement, and our people were overwhelmed. Father put us, with our older brother, Ysfael, into a boat and told us to sail south to Tine, where we would be met by Vortigern's men.'

'Vortigern.' Hengest exclaimed.

'You know him?' Rhufon asked.

Hengest and Offa exchanged glances. 'Vortigern is the high king of Britta,' Hengest lowered his voice 'he is also the husband of Rowena.'

Everyone gasped.

Rhufon looked bemused. 'You were aware of this?'

'Yes.' Tanwen replied. 'However, it was so long ago it slipped my mind. It is odd though, that when we left, Father told us that because I was betrothed to Vortigern's son, we would be given protection until he could send his men for us. Imagine, Hengest, Rowena may have been my step-mother.'

There was a ripple of laughter.

'And Mother gave me this amulet. She said I must wear it always to protect me from evil and identify me to father's men when they came to rescue me.'

Rhufon smiled and squeezed Tanwen's hand. 'And so it did. The moment I spotted it I knew that I had found my sister, Gwynedd, at long last.' He paused. 'We ran into a great storm and lost our bearing. Convinced that we were hopelessly lost at sea and would need to travel overland on foot, to find Vortigern, Ysfael and I decided that Gwynedd would be a hindrance to us and needed to be disposed of. So, hoping she would be discovered by a friendly tribe, we agreed to put her ashore.'

'That is not true. Ysfael wanted to throw me overboard and leave me to drown, you tried to stop him.'

'But I didn't succeed.'

'Ysfael threw me into the water, and they sailed away. I begged and begged him to come back, but he ignored me. I was picked up by warriors in a longboat, I couldn't understand their language, nor they, mine, but they were kind. They fed me and let me sleep. It is all a bit hazy now but I was with them for at least two nights before they put me ashore on a deserted beach. I was so scared of being captured by an evil sea monster that I climbed onto a tree for safety.'

'And that's where I found her.' Thorndor said.

Clearly moved, Offa, kissed her hand. 'Dear Tanwen, I had no idea you had suffered so much.'

Overcome with remorse, Arild gripped Rhufon's arm in the warrior's greeting. 'I don't know what to say, except I am truly sorry.'

'Me too.' Hengest added. 'For the many times I have shown impatience when you inquired about your sister.' He spoke to Tanwen. 'In every town and village we visited and on every ship we passed, Rhufon inquired about his sister, Guwyn … Giwyni …'

'Gwynedd,' Rhufon corrected Hengest, laughing for the first time.

'How is a person supposed to get his tongue around such an absurd name?' Hengest replied.

'That is why we changed it to Tanwen,' Thorndor said, 'Wynn thought it a more civilised name for a child.'

Everyone laughed.

'Sadly,' Rhufon began. 'When Ysfael and I came ashore, we discovered that we were no more than five miles from our land and Gwynedd would not have been a hindrance.'

Tanwen swayed and Offa was at her side in an instant. 'What is it, Tanwen? Are you ill?' She gasped, clutching her chest to ease the sudden pain. *It was all for nothing!* 'It's nothing; an elf-shot, that's all,' she whispered.

'The shock has been too much. It's all my fault. I didn't think before I spoke. I'm so sorry, Gwyn …Tanwen.' Rhufon said.

'What of Mother and Father?' she asked, anxiously.

'They were safe, but the settlement was destroyed. Mother died of the fever some years later. Father was, persuaded, by Vortigern, to take his men south-west to repel the Eriu incursions.'

'Cunedda.' Hengest exclaimed. 'Your father is Cunedda ap Edrin?'

'Yes.' Rhufon and Tanwen replied, together. 'Do you know him?' Rhufon asked.

'I know of him,' Hengest faced Offa. 'He is one of Vortigern's kinglets.'

Tanwen scowled at Hengest 'Then you do know Bryneich?'

'No, I swear, I do not. All I know is what your brother has told us. 'Except that after the Eriu had been repelled, Cunedda founded a settlement in the west, and named it Gwynedd, after his lost daughter.'

Tanwen laughed. 'You're making that up. It can't be true.'

'I swear I have heard Vortigern mention this place, and why else would Cunedda give it such a name?'

'It has indeed been a night of revelation,' Thorndor said. 'Who would have dreamed that the scraggly little urchin I found that night could have been the daughter-in-law of the high king of Britta and have a land named after her?'

'There is one more thing you should know, Tanwen.' Hengest's voice was low and grave. Tanwen's heart missed a beat. 'Vortigern promised my brother and me a large area of land in payment for work against the Picts. The job was done, but he would not honour his promise. He left us no option but to go into battle and we fought at Aegelsthrep. Sadly, Horsa was killed. By Vortigern. My brother was a fine warrior to the end and was buried with all honours.'

There was a moment's silence before everyone offered their condolences to Hengest and said what a privilege it had been to know his brother. Only Tanwen was silent.

'There is one minor item Hengest has been too modest to mention,' Rhufon said. 'Lord Hengest of Jutland, Fresia, Angeln or wherever, is now King Hengest of Britta.'

There was a loud cheer and a round of applause. When the noise subsided, Hengest spoke. 'A great honour, but at a great price.' Another brief silence, then Hengest clapped his hands and one of his men entered carrying a long box; he handed it to Hengest and left.

'The reason I am here today,' Hengest said, 'is because my brother asked me to deliver this to Tanwen in person.' "For the love of my life, and a worthy shield-maiden," were his words.'

Unable to speak, Tanwen opened the box. 'Felalaf,' she said, unable to prevent tears pouring in rivulets down her cheeks.'

'Horsa's sword,' Rhufon exclaimed.

'I can't believe it.' Tanwen said. 'It is beautiful, I swear I will treasure it and Horsa's memory forever.'

Offa ordered warm mead for all and they drank a toast to Horsa's memory.

'Now, Tanwen and I have an announcement to make.' Offa said. Everyone waited with bated breath.

'Will you speak, Tanwen, or shall I?' Without giving her time to reply Offa continued, 'Tanwen has decided that the time has come for her to leave us and go in search of her blood family. A ship will be ready for her and her companions to leave within seven days. If Hengest can spare him, Rhufon is welcome to join her, no doubt their father would appreciate a family reunion.'

A moments silence, then Offa continued, 'I have arranged a feast for the night before she leaves and invite, nay, command you all to attend.'

Nineteen

Tanwen was relaxing on the warm sand, supervising the twins at play. Lulled by the gentle lapping of the waves her mind slowly drifted back to Bryneich. She closed her eyes and saw Rhufon teaching her to swim, how gentle and kind he was then. She remembered a beard that tickled when she kissed her father's cheek, dark laughing eyes and a booming voice. She remembered the day the Picts came, and an image of her mother watching her children being taken away flashed before her; and she remembered being on a beach, with nothing but the rags she stood in and her mother's amulet around her neck, and a tree and Thorndor's comforting arms around her. But the memories were fading now and would soon be gone forever.

The twins were paddling at the water's edge and each time they were splashed by a wave they shrieked with glee and ran around in circles before going back for more.

Six horsemen led by Arild, came thundering towards her. 'Where are the twins?' Arild shouted without dismounting.

Tanwen pointed, 'over there, by the water.'

'Get them back to the hall as quick as you can. Where's Hilde?'

'At the market, but she …'

'Arild signalled to his men, 'two of you find her and don't stand any nonsense. Knock her out if you have to - and see if you can find the other one, Edyth, we don't want her disclosing their whereabouts.'

'What's all this about?' Tanwen demanded.

'Cedd's on his way. Offa wants them all taken to safety before he arrives. There's no time to waste.'

Tanwen called the girls and ran to meet them, shouting over her shoulder to Arild, 'how long have we got?'

'Not long. And for Woden's sake lock them in and keep them quiet.' Then he was gone.

Tanwen dragged the twins, protesting loudly, to the hall. Wulfrun brought them bread dough to make into toy animals, a selection of sweet fruit tarts and a jug of blackberry juice sweetened with honey. 'That should keep them quiet for a while,' she said with a smile, before departing.

Hilde sat by the fire. Expressionless and trembling. She would not speak and refused food and drink.

Offa sent a message inviting Tanwen to join him in the feasting hall to welcome his foster brother, Cedd. Her instinct was to send a curt refusal, the last person on earth she wanted to see was Cedd, but it was clearly a summons rather than a request, so she politely accepted the invitation.

Arild arrived to escort Tanwen to the hall. 'I'm quite capable of finding my way …'

'I'm not prepared to take chances with Cedd's war-band on the loose.' Arild said.

'I know these men. They won't harm me.'

'And I know warriors. When they have been on the road for seven days no woman is safe.'

'Does that include you?' she asked with a mischievous grin.

He smiled. 'I'm a bodyguard and I take my duties very seriously.'

***

Offa greeted Cedd warmly and said how pleased he was to see his brother again. Cedd gave him a curt nod and spoke to Tanwen. 'Where is my wife?'

Shocked by his brusque manner, Tanwen gave an equally abrupt reply. 'Resting.'

'Fetch her, and the brats. They should have been here to greet me.'

'I ordered Hilde and the children to remain in their chamber until I am convinced, they will be safe.' Offa said. Tanwen had never known him to assert his authority with such confidence.

'So, the imbecile really has found his voice.' Cedd said to his companions. 'But still hides behind his nursemaid's skirts it would seem. I demand to see my wife.'

Offa stood tall, shoulders back and head erect. 'Only I have the right to make demands in Angeln.'

'I said, I want to see Hilde and the brats.'

'And I said that Hilde and the children are to remain where they are until I am satisfied no harm will come to them.' Offa said.

'They are my property, and I will treat them as I see fit.'

'Then I will confiscate your property and treat them as *I* see fit.'

Cedd raised his hand to his belt. Arild leapt forward, grabbed his wrist and twisted his arm behind him.

'Your puppy is a little jumpy, lack-wit, you need someone to teach him manners.' Cedd said, attempting to thrust Arild aside, but Arild wrapped his foot around Cedd's ankle, and he fell with a thud.

Cedd's companions charged, snarling at Arild, with seaxes at the ready. Offa threw him a shield and he managed to fend off most of the blows. Offa grabbed two of the adversaries by the neck and while he rammed their heads together Tanwen drew a dagger from one of their scabbards and held it at the owner's neck, 'One move and you're dead.' She warned.

Cedd made a grab for Offa but Offa punched him hard under the chin hurling him across the room. Dragging himself to his feet and standing only a hair's breadth away from Offa he said, 'I have a right to see my wife.'

'You have no rights in Angeln.' Offa replied. 'Moreover, you have demonstrated that in your care your wife's safety would be compromised. Therefore, Hilde and the children will remain in Angeln under my protection.

'You have no right to keep my family here.'

Offa's guards filed into the hall, and roughly shoved Cedd's companions to the exit.

'I have every right. I am the king of Angeln, it is my duty to protect those unable to protect themselves. You are no longer welcome at my table. Food has been prepared for you to eat on your journey.'

Cedd and his men mounted, rejected the food offered to them, turned their horses and rode out at an easy pace.

Hilde ran out of the hall followed by Edyth, tugging on Hilde's tunic, struggling to pull her back and screeching, 'come back Hilde, you're not supposed to leave.'

Hilde called 'Cedd, Cedd, wait - don't go.'

Tanwen spotted them and yelled, 'Hilde - get back – it's not safe…

'I'm going to my husband.'

Cedd, aware of the commotion turned back.

'You don't have to go; you can stay here.' Edyth shouted.

Tanwen reached them and grabbed Hilde 'Why are you doing this?'

Hilde stopped abruptly and faced them with unexpected dignity. 'Cedd is my lord, my husband and the father of my children and I go to him because I love him.'

Cedd dismounted and Hilde ran to his arms, he cradled her lovingly in his left arm and then, too late, Tanwen glimpsed the glint of a blade in his right hand. Hilde fell, clutching the knife buried in her stomach. Cedd leapt onto his horse and rode off, followed by his men.

Within moments, Offa, Arild and the bodyguards were mounted and charging after them at full gallop.

Tanwen and Edyth dropped to their knees and frantically searched Hilde's body for signs of life. But there were none. Curious townsfolk were gathering. 'Go to the hall to look after the twins, we mustn't risk them running out here and seeing their mother like this,' Tanwen said to Edyth, 'and send one of the hall thanes to find Leofrun. We will need her help ...'

'There's no need,' Wulfrun was standing over them. 'I'll collect the twins and take them to the homestead. My children will keep them occupied until you are ready to collect them.'

'Oh, thank you, Wulfrun. That will be a great help.'

Six of Offa's men arrived, two of whom placed Hilde on a stretcher, covered her body with a blanket, and carried her to the healing chamber, while the others dispersed the crowd.

Edyth and Tanwen were heartbroken at the loss of their friend and shed many tears over the body while preparing it for the funeral. 'I tried to stop her,' Edyth cried. 'I kept telling her, but she wouldn't listen - and then she bolted - and I couldn't stop her.'

'You did all you could, Edyth. Hilde couldn't have had a better, more supportive, friend than you, but she loved Cedd.'

'What about the twins?'

'When we are finished here, we'll take them home and explain what happened …let's pray Nethrus will give us the strength to do so.'

To their relief, Wulfrun had already broken the news to the children and although subdued, they seemed more concerned about their future than the loss of their mother. 'Will we be sent away to live with father now?' Eawynn asked with a nervous quiver in her voice.

'Certainly not, sweetheart. You will stay here with Edyth and me.' Tanwen replied.

'And ronanary Uncle Offa will look after us all.' Cwenhild said with a confidence that brought a smile to Tanwen's face. 'Who or what is a ronanary uncle? She asked.

'The king.' The girls replied together.

'He told them, that as their mother was his honorary aunt, it was only fitting that he should be their honorary uncle.' Edyth said.

Tanwen smiled. 'And who are we to argue with a king?' She said embracing the twins and kissing them.

***

'Cedd and his men will leave for Britta with Hengest. He will not re-enter Engel Land without my consent.' Offa said.

'Where is he now?' Tanwen wanted to know.

'In chains on Hengest's ship, he will be heavily guarded until they reach Britta. Hengest will join us to break-fast and will leave on the noon-tide.'

'And Rhufon?'

'Rhufon must decide whether to travel with Hengest or wait a few days and leave with you and Edyth.'

'Oh.' Was all Tanwen could say.

***

Tanwen could not sleep. Her head was spinning, her heart racing and her stomach churning. It was no use; she would have to get up. Perhaps a warm drink would help her relax. The hall was in darkness and only a few embers burned in the remains of the fire. She ladled lukewarm water from a nearby pot and sipped it while collecting her thoughts. A shuffling sound came from across the room, she crossed her fingers hoping it was a mouse and not a rat. It was neither.

'Unable to sleep?' Edyth asked.

'I thought you were a mouse.'

'How much easier life would be if I were.' Edyth hesitated. 'Tanwen, what are we going to do with Eawyn and Cwenhild?'

'Love them, and care for them as we always have.'

'Will it be possible to keep them safe in Britta with Cedd there? He's certain to track them down.'

'And the outcome, without ronorary Uncle Offa's protection, is too terrible to contemplate.'

They chuckled, then sat in silence for several moments before Edyth spoke. 'Tanwen I know how important this journey is to you, and I feel dreadful about this, but I've given it a lot of thought and …'

'You no longer want to go to Britta?'

'I'm sorry, Tanwen, truly I am but …'

'Hush, Edyth. I understand, I've been expecting it.'

'But you can still go, Rhufon will be your travel companion and your father will be there waiting to greet you.'

'Yes.'

'And when the twins are old enough for the journey, I'll bring them to see you. I promise.'

Tanwen stood. 'No promises, please. They are easily made but difficult to keep. Wyrd often has other ideas. Now, let's try to get some sleep before dawn.'

But Tanwen did not sleep, she paced the hall until daybreak and then paid Thorndor a visit.

'What should I do, Thorndor? She asked after relating her tale of woe.

Thorndor patted her shoulder. 'Now, daughter, you know that my advice to others is to always follow your heart.'

'My heart is in turmoil. I believe Edyth is right, the twins will not be safe in Britta. But I can't imagine life without them all. I want to see my homeland and spend time with my birth father, but will there be room for me in his life after so many years? Will he even remember me?'

'Of course, he will remember you: and love you; and welcome you home, for that is the way of fathers.'

'You have been a father to me, Thorndor, a real father. I love you and I don't want to be parted from you again. Nor do I want to leave Offa to the mercy of that she-wolf, Modpruth.'

'Do you still dream of becoming a shield-maiden?'

'At my age.'

They laughed. 'Oh, Thorndor, why did Horsa have to die? And why Hilde, who had never spoken a harsh word in her life?'

'One life must be forfeit to make way for another, or soon the earth would not be able to support us all.'

'And we would all fall off,' she mused. 'What do the runes say, Thorndor?'

'The runes say that you should go home, wash your face and wear your prettiest dress for fast-breaking. After a hot meal and some good company, you will see things much more clearly.'

She kissed his cheek, 'thank you father, I'll heed your advice,' she said and left before the tears came.

She did not go straight home. Instead, she made a slight detour to Offa's shrine and asked The Great Sky God, His Son, The Spirit and the Lady Mother to help her make the right decision.

Twenty

'Something's going on,' Edyth said as she entered the hall. 'Offa has all his men in the hall.'

'All of them?'

'Yes, I watched them arriving while I was collecting the eggs.'

Tanwen went to the door to investigate. 'They can't be drinking, it's too quiet.'

'Perhaps they are planning a battle.' Edith grabbed Cwenhild's hands and twirled her around, singing, 'our dreaming days are past - we'll be shield-maidens at last - and be off to fight a war with Uncle Of - fa.'

'Can I come?' Eawyn cried, forcing her way into the dance. Tanwen lifted Eawynn onto Edyth's back, 'I'll strap Eawyn on your back, put your arrows in a sack and we'll be off a happy band togeth - er.' They frolicked around until the hall thane brought in the midday meal. 'Well done, Edyth, that's brought a smile to their faces at last,' he said.

***

There was a sudden uproar from the king's hall, stamping, banging of fists on the tables and the clash of steel on shields. Everyone rushed to the door to see Arild being carried out between two guards. They threw him twice into the air each time catching him and breaking his fall, on the third throw he landed on his feet and bowed to the applause and cheering of the hearth-troop.

'What's happened?' Edyth asked one of the men.

'The Wyrd sisters have looked kindly on Arild,' was the reply.

'How, what have they done? Why is everyone so excited?' Tanwen was bursting with curiosity.

Roaring with laughter, Offa approached Arild and patted his back. They had a brief conversation then sauntered over to Tanwen and Edyth. The twins charged forward to greet Uncle Offa and were rewarded with little bags of dried apple slices. They shrieked with delight and ran off to consume them in secret.

'Bring us thin ale,' Offa said to the thane, before leading Tanwen and Edyth into the hall.

'What have you been up to, Offa? I've never seen the men so excited.' Tanwen asked with a broad grin.

'As I will soon be setting off on my first visit to my territories, I have re-shuffled my war-band. Many new men have joined us, allowing the aged warriors who served my father to retire and some of those not so aged to be promoted. I am not expecting trouble with the Myrgings or the Swarbians, but with Freawine, Wigheard and Cedd all gone there is no one left in Hedeby to defend the southern marches, so today I have made Arild an Earl. He is to choose thirty of my men and be ready to move out in seven days. When he arrives in Hedeby, Hebeke and Modpruth, accompanied by what's left of Cedd's men, will leave for Angeln. Arild will take control of the town. and make it his home.' He raised his drinking horn. 'Well, what do you say? Shall we drink a toast to Earl Arild?'

They stood and raised their goblets, 'To Earl Arild of Hedeby.'

***

The town was abuzz. Some of Arild's men were taking their families with them: creating a frenzy of buying; selling, and exchanging household goods and animals between those staying, and those leaving. Fighting squares had been set up for weapon training and the unrelenting clamour of sword on sword, shield on shield, shouting and swearing filled the air.

Amid the pandemonium, Arild arrived at the hall. 'I'm sorry, Rhufon asked me to return this, but in the chaos, it slipped my mind.'

'Thank you, Arild. This dagger was a gift from Hunlaf and is precious to me, not only for its beauty but also

for the fond memories it holds. Has Rhufon decided yet?'

'I have invited him to join my war band. He is training hard.'

'He means to stay?'

'He must learn the warriors' ways and reach my standard of skill before that decision can be made.' Arild paused. 'Tanwen, I know it is your ambition to return to your homeland, but I wonder, would you consider joining my war band instead?'

'What!'

'I know it's a lot to ask, but I need good men to teach weapon-craft and you are one of the best. We would make a good team, Tanwen.'

Tanwen couldn't conceal her mirth. The idea was preposterous. 'I hate to disillusion you, Arild, but I am not a man. And contrary to the belief you held many years ago, I have never wanted, or tried, to become one.'

But you must admit you could be the most irksome individual.'

'And you the most exasperating.' Tanwen smiled. 'Thankfully even the most irksome, exasperating, children, eventually grow into acceptable human beings.'

'Will you join me, Tanwen? There will also be a place for Edyth.'

Tanwen laughed. 'I'm too old, Arild. I'd never keep up with the young blood.'

'I'm not asking you to go to war, just three or four mornings a week, training the young or inexperienced recruits. I saw you working with Offa, I know you can do it. I would also like Edyth to help train the archers.'

'You flatter me Arild, and I thank you for that, but I seem incapable of making sensible decisions at present.'

Arild grinned. 'Not the answer I had hoped for, but at least it's not a refusal. I'll leave you to give it some thought. You know where to find me.' He bowed his head and left.

***

Tanwen's mind was made up. 'I'm going to see Offa,' she called to Edyth.

Offa embraced her. 'Thank you, Tanwen. You have no idea how much it will mean to me to have you present at my marriage. I will have ships and men prepared and ready for you to leave on the first tide after the ceremony.

'Will there be room for Edyth and the twins if she can be persuaded?'

'Indeed, with room to spare.'

She kissed his cheek. 'I will speak to her when your honorary nieces are abed.'

Offa smiled. 'I thought they should have at least one man in their lives.'

'And they couldn't find a better one.' Tanwen replied.

***

'For one month, you say?' Edyth asked.

'Plus travelling time.'

'What if your father won't let us leave?'

'How can he stop us? We'll have guards to protect us and fast ships to get us back if needed.'

'And Cedd?'

'Cedd will be with Hengest, chained and confined until we are safely home. I have Offa's word on it.' Tanwen said.

'But what if he breaks free? We would be strangers and not too difficult to find.'

'He has no idea we are going and Thorndor says Hengest's camp is over two hundred miles away from Gwynedd, so he'd never find us.'

'Two hundred miles,' Edyth exclaimed. 'It would take him weeks to travel that far.'

'Well, Edyth?'

Edyth groaned. 'As you wish. But the twins and I return in a month, with or without you.'

When Lady Hebeke arrived in Angeln, Tanwen greeted her eagerly and affectionately, but she treated Modpruth with cool indifference and held only the briefest of conversations with her. It was difficult to judge the relationship between Offa and Modpruth. As expected, Offa treated his betrothed with kindness and respect which was repaid with obvious disdain.

True to his word, Offa allowed Tanwen, Edyth and the twins, escorted by Rhufon to leave immediately after the marriage ceremony and before the feast began.

Twenty-One

Tanwen gazed out over the endless sea; the watery road leading to Gwynedd. She turned and watched the muscles of the oarsmen flex as they heaved the oars in and out of the water in perfect harmony. It was a grand ship, long and broad with a curved bow and oars for thirty men. It brought to mind the little boat that took her away from her mother, and how she snuggled up to Rhufon because she was so afraid the flap, flap, flap of its leather sail was the sound of sea monsters lurking beneath them.

Not for the first time, she wondered if she had been wise to bring Edyth and the children with her into the unknown.

The twins were enjoying the journey, relishing the attention the crew lavished upon them. They had never been so spoiled. Whenever an oarsman took a break Rhufon ushered them onto the empty bench and set about teaching them how to row. They thought it a great game and shrieked with delight every time he raised the oar and deliberately soaked them.

Edyth seemed happy too, basking in the sunshine, laughing and chatting with the men; far different from the drudgery of Angeln and there was no doubt the men enjoyed her company.

The weather had been fair so far and the steersman was kind and considerate. Their first stop was at Cantwarebyrig where they spent a comfortable night in a draught free house made of stone. She remembered Horsa speaking highly of this land and no wonder, it truly did seem a perfect place to farm and raise a family. Cantwarebyrig proved an intriguing and fascinating diversion to the twins, who were much too excited to rest. Tanwen set them the task of counting how many stones there were in the walls and they dropped off to sleep in moments.

Last night they stayed in a timber alehouse on a piece of land called Ynys Weith, and it too was a place of great beauty surrounded by a deep blue sea.

The steersman brought her a drink of ale. She thanked him but declined the huge chunk of bread he offered. 'When will we reach Gwynedd?'

'If the weather remains fair, our next stop should be Ynys Tintagel and then if all goes to plan it's full ahead for Gwynedd.'

Tanwen beamed and the girls clapped and danced about. 'But no promises,' the steersman added with a stern frown. The seas can be rough around this land.'

They had never seen mountains in Angeln, and they were truly overawed by the splendour of Ynys Tintagel. The children were convinced that this mysterious land with its mist-covered hills, massive rocks, turbulent sea, and fast-flowing rivers, must surely be a land of giants, elves and wraiths, and were inconsolable when it was time to leave.

Rhufon sent messengers from Tintagel to advise his father that he had found his sister and they were on their way to Gwynedd with a small fleet of ships. Consequently, a curious, silent, crowd had gathered on the shore to watch them arrive.

For the first time, since the day she was found on the beach, Tanwen was trembling with fear. Her father was standing on the top of a hill looking down on her. Should she run to greet him, or wait for him to approach her? 'What shall say? How should I address him? Is my hair tidy? Oh, no, my hands are grubby. I need to go ...'

'Calm down,' Edyth whispered. 'He's probably just as scared as you are.'

'He's staring at me; he doesn't like me. I can tell. Why doesn't he say something?

'Because he's the king,' Rhufon replied. 'Are you ready?' He took her elbow and escorted her up the hill. 'Greetings Father,' he said. 'I bring you my sister, Gwynedd.'

The king: tall; broad, grey-haired and solemn-faced, stared at Tanwen for many moments before opening his arms to her. 'Welcome home, daughter,' he said.

About the Author

Elizabeth Bell was born in County Durham, married and lived in South Australia before returning to England and settling in Hampshire. She now lives in an 18th century farmhouse on the northern edge of the Lake District with her husband. She writes drama, pantomime and poetry.

I hope you have enjoyed reading this book as much as I have enjoyed researching and writing it.

If you have any questions or comments to make feel free to contact me at the email address below and I will reply as soon as possible.

Please remember to leave feedback, it is very important to me.

Best wishes,
Elizabeth

elizabethbell2@btinternet.com

Printed in Great Britain
by Amazon

60256794R00169